Robert Thorogood is the creator of the hit BBC One TV series *Death in Paradise*, and he has written a series of spin-off novels featuring detective DI Richard Poole.

He was born in Colchester, Essex. When he was ten years old, he read his first proper novel – Agatha Christie's *Peril at End House* – and he's been in love with the genre ever since.

He now lives in Marlow in Buckinghamshire with his wife, children and two whippets called Wally and Evie.

Follow him on Twitter @robthor

Also by
ROBERT THOROGOOD

A Meditation on Murder
The Killing of Polly Carter
Death Knocks Twice
Murder in the Caribbean

The
Marlow
Murder
Club

ROBERT THOROGOOD

ONE PLACE. MANY STORIES

HQ
An imprint of HarperCollins*Publishers* Ltd
1 London Bridge Street
London SE1 9GF

HarperCollins*Publishers*
1st Floor, Watermarque Building, Ringsend Road, Dublin 4, Ireland

This edition 2021

2
First published in Great Britain by
HQ, an imprint of HarperCollins*Publishers* Ltd 2021

Copyright © Robert Thorogood 2021

Robert Thorogood asserts the moral right to be identified as the author of this work.
A catalogue record for this book is available from the British Library.

ISBN:
HB: 9780008238247
TPB: 9780008435905

MIX
Paper from
responsible sources
FSC www.fsc.org **FSC™ C007454**

This book is produced from independently certified FSC™ paper
to ensure responsible forest management.

For more information visit: www.harpercollins.co.uk/green

This book is set in 11/15 pt. Bembo

Printed and bound in Great Britain by
CPI Group (UK) Ltd, Croydon, CR0 4YY

For Katie B

Chapter 1

Mrs Judith Potts was seventy-seven years old and entirely happy with her life. She lived in an Arts and Crafts mansion on the River Thames, she had a job she loved that took up just enough of her time and no more, and best of all, she didn't have to share her life with any man. This meant there was no one asking her what was for dinner that night, or wanting to know where she was going every time she left the house, or moaning that she was spending too much money on whisky, a small glass of which she'd have at about 6 p.m. each evening.

On the day Judith's life changed, it was the height of summer and England had been in the grip of a heatwave for weeks. She'd kept all of her windows open to capture whatever breezes blew down the valley, but it seemed to make no difference. The heat of the sun had got into the bricks and timbers of her home; into the oak staircase and minstrels' gallery.

After taking her evening meal in front of the television news, she put her empty plate to one side and got out the latest copy of *Puzzler* magazine. She turned to a logic grid and started to work on it. Usually, she enjoyed reducing the language of the clues down to mathematical ones and zeros, but tonight her heart just wasn't in it. It was too hot to concentrate.

Judith's hand idly went to the key she kept on a chain around her neck, and her thoughts began to drift into the past, into a much darker time. She shot up from her chair. This wouldn't do, she told herself. Wouldn't do at all. There was always something else she could do to keep herself busy. She needed a change of scene, that was all, and she had the perfect solution.

Judith began to take off her clothes. With each garment she removed, she felt more and more released from the stifling constraints of the day. By the time she was naked, she was buzzing with an impish delight. She crossed the hallway, past the Blüthner grand piano she only ever played when she was really very drunk, and took up a dark grey woollen cape she kept by the front door.

Judith's cape was her most treasured possession. She'd tell anyone who asked, and many did, that it kept her warm in winter, served as a picnic blanket in the summer, and she could pull it over her head if ever she was caught in a spring shower.

Best of all, Judith believed it was a cloak of invisibility. Every evening, come rain or shine, she'd take off her clothes, wrap the cape around herself and step out of her house feeling a delicious frisson of naughtiness. She would plunge her feet into a pair of ancient wellies and stride through the knee-high grass – swish, swish, swish! – to her boathouse. Like the rest of Judith's house, it was pink-bricked, timber-framed, and somewhat crumbling.

Judith entered the cobwebby darkness and kicked off her wellies. She hung her cape on an old hook, and, still hidden from the outside world by a pair of ancient boathouse doors, stepped down the stone slipway and into the Thames.

It was almost a religious experience for her, accepting the cold water onto her skin, and she exhaled with a whoosh as she leant forward into the embrace of the river. Suddenly she was weightless, supported by the soft water that felt like silk to her body.

She swam upstream, the evening sunshine flashing diamonds on the water all around. Judith smiled to herself. She always smiled to herself when she was out swimming. She couldn't help it. After all, there might be dog walkers on the Thames Path, and there were very definitely plenty of people in the near distance as she looked at the spire of Marlow church and the span of the Victorian suspension bridge that linked the town to the neighbouring village of Bisham. None of these people were aware that there was a seventy-seven-year-old woman swimming nearby entirely in the nude.

It was just as Judith was thinking, *This is the life*, that she heard a shout.

It came from the opposite riverbank, from somewhere near her neighbour Stefan Dunwoody's house. But from her position low in the water it was hard for Judith to see exactly what was going on. Only the roof of Stefan's house was visible above the thick bank of bulrushes at the edge of the river.

Judith strained her ears, but all was quiet. She decided it must have been an animal. A dog or a fox maybe.

And then she heard a man's voice call out, 'Hey, no!'

What on earth was that?

'Stefan, is that you?' Judith called from the river, but her words were cut short by the sharp retort of a gunshot.

'Stefan?' she shouted again, panic rising. 'Are you all right?'

All was silence. But Judith knew what she'd heard. Someone

had fired a gun, hadn't they? And Stefan's voice had called out immediately beforehand. What if he was now bleeding from a bullet wound and needed saving?

Judith swam towards Stefan's house as fast as she could, but as she reached his riverbank, she realised she had a problem. Beyond the bulrushes, Stefan had put corrugated metal across the span of his lawn to protect it from river erosion. Judith knew that swimming through the rushes would cut her body to shreds, and even if she made it to land, she wouldn't be able to pull herself out. She wouldn't have the strength.

Ahead of her she could see a blue canoe wedged in among the reeds. Could she somehow use it to help lever her body out of the water? She tried to grab hold of the end, but she couldn't get a proper grip, it kept bobbing around like a cork, and she realised she didn't have the balance to climb up onto the canoe anyway. But she gave it one last go, and this time just about managed to pull herself up onto the back of it. And then, oh so slowly, she and the canoe barrel-rolled over, she lost her hold and fell back into the water with an ungainly splash.

She came up for air and shook the water from her hair. The canoe was out of the question, so what else could she do?

Judith swam back to the centre of the river, desperately looking for someone who could help. Where were the dog walkers or canoodling couples when you needed them? She couldn't see anyone. There was only one thing for it. She turned and swam for home as fast as she could.

Reaching her boathouse, Judith climbed out of the water, wheezing, but there was no time to lose. She threw on her cape and strode out onto the lawn, turning back to look at what she could see of Stefan's house. Only half of his garden was visible behind the weeping willow that grew unchecked on her side of the riverbank.

She ran into her house, grabbed up her phone and dialled 999. As she waited for the call to connect, she moved over to the bay window to keep an eye on Stefan's property.

'I need the police!' Judith said as soon as the call was answered. 'There's been a shooting at my neighbour's house! Hurry! Someone's been shot!'

The operator took down the details of Stefan's address, recorded what Judith had seen, informed her that the emergency services would be on their way, and then ended the call. Judith felt deeply frustrated. Surely there was something else she could do, or someone else she could phone? What about the Coastguard? It was a waterside catastrophe after all. Or the RNLI?

Judith peered out of her window at Stefan's property. It was still sitting there, apparently innocently, in the evening sunshine.

If anyone had been out on the river at that precise moment, and had had occasion to look up at Judith's mansion, they'd have seen a very short and comfortably plump woman in her late seventies with wild grey hair standing entirely naked in her bay window, a cape over her shoulders as if she were some kind of a superhero. Which in many ways she was.

She just didn't know it yet.

Chapter 2

Half an hour later, Judith saw a police car arrive at Stefan's property and a uniformed police officer get out. Judith tried as best she could to keep her binoculars trained on him as he looked in through the windows of Stefan's house and took a wander through the garden. She wanted to bellow across the river that the man should jolly well look harder, but she bit her tongue. She had to believe that he knew what he was doing, and he'd find evidence of whatever it was that had happened.

However, after twenty minutes of what Judith could only describe as a cursory search, the police officer returned to his car, got in and drove away.

Was that it? The man had barely explored the garden, and he'd not even entered Stefan's house. Perhaps he'd gone to get reinforcements? So she kept on looking. And looking.

At midnight, Judith discovered that there was no more whisky in the decanter on the little table to her side. That was always a sign to go to bed. As she woozily ascended the heavy oak staircase, she found she had to hold onto the banister a bit more tightly than normal. She then turned left to go to her bedroom when her bedroom was really on her right, but once she'd corrected her course via a brief tangle with a recalcitrant aspidistra, she safely made her destination.

Judith adored her bedroom. The wood panels were painted light green, and there was a majestic four-poster bed with a tapestry of a medieval hunting scene as its canopy. That the room was covered in old clothes, half-finished meals, and piles of discarded newspapers and magazines didn't bother her one jot. Judith never noticed the mess. In fact, she let it encompass her in the same way that she let the river embrace her when she went swimming. The messier her bedroom, the more she felt cocooned and safe.

The following morning, Judith was woken by the sound of the phone ringing. She reached for it, blearily seeing it had just gone 10 a.m.

'Hello,' she croaked.

'Good morning,' an efficient female voice said. 'My name's Detective Sergeant Tanika Malik from the Maidenhead police station. I'm following up on the incident you reported at Mr Dunwoody's property last night.'

'Ah, thank you for calling,' Judith said, still somewhat groggily.

The detective sergeant explained that she'd sent a constable to inspect Mr Dunwoody's house and garden. He'd not found anything of note, so she was ringing to inform Judith that there was nothing to worry about.

'But I know what I heard!' Judith said.

'Yes, the report said you heard a gunshot.'

'Not just a gunshot. I heard someone call out something like "Hey, no!" and *then* I heard the gunshot.'

'But I understand you were swimming in the river at the time. Are you sure it was in fact a gunshot?'

Judith was now fully awake, and thoroughly irritated.

'I grew up on a farm. I know what a gun sounds like.'

'But what if it was something else?'

'Like what?'

'Well, for example, maybe it was a car backfiring?'

This hadn't occurred to Judith. She thought for a moment before answering.

'No. I'm sure I'd have known if it were a car. It was a gunshot. I take it this constable of yours reported that Stefan's car is still parked at his house?'

'Why do you mention that?'

'Because I presume Stefan didn't answer his phone when you called him, did he?'

'No, I'm sorry, I can't quite follow your line of thought there. What phone call?'

'You must have phoned him last night.'

'I'm afraid I'm not allowed to share specific details with you.'

'But a neighbour reports a shooting at a house, of course you phoned to check up on him. And the fact you haven't told me he answered suggests to me that he *didn't* answer. So, seeing as his car is still on his driveway, well, that tells me that something's up with him. After all, if you're at home, you answer your phone. If you're away, you take your car. At least someone who owned a car would. I don't.'

DS Malik didn't respond immediately.

'You've really thought this through,' she eventually said.

'It's all I could think about last night. I was so worried for Stefan. What if he's been shot, and the gunman's escaped? In fact, what if Stefan is right now lying bleeding in a ditch?'

'I don't think he's lying in a ditch. I'm sure there's some very innocent explanation for all of this. There wasn't any indication at his property that anything untoward had happened, and it's not that unusual for someone to ignore their phone. It's holiday season. People are away. I'm sure Mr Dunwoody will turn up in the next few days. And the moment he does, I'll let you know. Really, there's nothing to worry about.'

DS Malik ended the call by thanking Judith for being such a civic-minded neighbour and then rung off.

Afterwards, Judith lay in bed not knowing what to do. Was DS Malik right? Was there in fact a far more innocent explanation for what she'd heard the night before? After all, Judith knew one thing for sure: murders just didn't happen in Marlow.

She decided to put the matter from her mind, and get on with her work for the day.

When Judith had inherited her house from her great aunt Betty in 1976, she'd also received a portfolio of shares that provided her with a modest income, so she didn't have much need to work for a living, but nothing would have ever made Judith give up her job. She loved it too much.

Judith compiled crosswords for the national newspapers. She set two or three a week, and the hours she spent each day working on the puzzles were a cherished refuge for her mind. When she was setting a crossword, a calm descended on her and she could lose herself for whole stretches of time as she carefully worked through all the permutations of a particularly satisfying anagram, or considered an elegant phrase or word which could be interpreted in more than one way.

Judith crossed her drawing room to the card table by the bay window and smoothed down the green baize with her hand. Next she reached up onto a shelf and pulled down a sheet of squared mathematical paper. She then chose a 2B pencil from a mug of 2B pencils and, even though it didn't need sharpening, she pushed the pencil into her metal desk sharpener. It gripped the end, the old electric motor clattering as it spun, and the pencil Judith removed a few seconds later wasn't so much a writing implement as a lethal weapon.

Judith smiled to herself. A fresh pencil. The empty squares on the paper in front of her. The fight ahead.

Sitting down, she picked up her wooden ruler and began to mark out a fifteen-by-fifteen grid of squares. Next, she shaded in a pattern of darker squares around a single line of symmetry, so each darker square had a twin reflected on the right. There wasn't any particular pattern she followed, it was mostly her many decades of experience that guided her hand.

Once she had marked out her grid, all she had to do was fill in the blank spaces with words. This, she knew, would take her the next hour or so, and only once she was happy that she had an interesting collection of words intersecting with each other would she turn her mind finally to creating the clues.

As for the types of clues she liked to set, she eschewed the wilful opacity favoured by many setters, most famously represented by the near-impossible monthly puzzle that used to appear in the *Listener* magazine. She felt there was something a bit too 'male' about how they tried to show off how very clever they were. 'Look at me,' they seemed to be saying, 'you'll never guess how brilliant I am.' Instead, like many setters, she aligned herself with the principles of Ximenes, the legendary setter for the *Observer* newspaper from 1939 to 1972. Accordingly, her clues had to have two halves, the literal clue on one side, the riddle on the other. And the two halves had ultimately to 'play fair' with the solver, with the small caveat that if a clue was ingenious or witty enough, she was prepared on occasion to break the rules.

This morning, however, the muse wasn't with Judith. Having created her square of blocks and blanks, she couldn't settle on the correct words with which to fill the grid. She lacked all decisiveness. It was Stefan, she knew. She couldn't concentrate. She had to know that he was okay.

Judith reached for her tablet computer. She didn't much like the device, but it was useful for photographing and then emailing in her crosswords to the papers, so she'd come to terms with it some years ago.

She held it up to her face, but the stupid machine refused to unlock, claiming it didn't recognise her. Judith harrumphed, once again cursing at the indignities of being an older woman. The modern world treated her as though she were entirely invisible, and even her own bloody computer criticised her for not looking suitably like herself. But there was no point trying to fight with technology. Judith had learned that a long time ago in an incident that had involved a strawberry-coloured iMac, an electric cable that wasn't quite long enough, and a trip to Accident and Emergency.

Judith took a deep breath and composed herself.

She held the tablet up and looked at it again.

Nothing happened.

Bloody thing! Muttering to herself, Judith entered the passcode and then opened her web browser. Maybe there'd been some news about Stefan in the last twenty-four hours?

She typed 'Stefan Dunwoody' into the search bar, but all of the hits told her he owned an art gallery called Dunwoody Arts in Marlow, a fact she already knew. But she wanted to be thorough, so she clicked through the pages of results.

Although, what was this? One of the later results was a link to a webpage from a local newspaper, the *Bucks Free Press*. It was the headline that caught her attention: BUST-UP AT HENLEY REGATTA.

Clicking the link, she found herself reading a diary piece from a roundup of the Henley Royal Regatta, six weeks before.

Word reaches us that Stefan Dunwoody, local art gallery owner, got into a tipsy dispute in the Royal Enclosure with Elliot Howard, owner of the Marlow Auction House. According to our little birdie, when Mr Howard threatened to punch Mr Dunwoody, the stewards were called and both men were forcibly ejected.

Judith put her tablet down. So, Stefan had got into a drunken altercation at Henley with someone called Elliot Howard, and here he was, only a few short weeks later, and there'd been another set-to of some sort on his property.

A set-to where someone had fired a gun.

And then Stefan had subsequently vanished.

Sod this for a game of soldiers, Judith thought as she strode across the room, swept up her cloak from its peg and left the house.

She went down to her boathouse, approached an old punt that was half in and half out of the water and gave it a shove with her foot. She stepped up onto the back of it and grabbed the punting pole as the front of the boat bumped through the rotten boathouse doors and slipped out onto the river.

Despite her advanced years, Judith was an expert punter. With a flick of her wrists, she thrust the pole down into the riverbed, bent at the waist and pushed with all her might. As the punt shot forward, she twisted the pole up and out of the soft mud, and the boat had the momentum to cross the river.

Once she reached the further bank and the river was shallow again, it was no effort to punt upstream the fifty or so yards to Stefan's house, use the prow of the punt to penetrate the wall of reeds that protected his riverbank, and step up onto his land. She didn't need to secure the boat. Entirely surrounded by bulrushes, it wasn't going anywhere.

Checking her watch, Judith could see that just over eight minutes ago, she'd been sitting in her house, and now here she was, at the sharp end of her neighbour's mysterious disappearance.

Stefan's house was really rather splendid to Judith's mind. It was a converted watermill with a wooden wheel that still turned lazily, but differently sized rectangular glass windows had subsequently been cut into the building. It was both pleasingly old-fashioned and modern at the same time.

She went and looked at Stefan's car in the driveway. Judith knew nothing about cars, and cared even less, so all she could tell was that it was grey in colour, and it was gleaming, not a spot of dirt on it anywhere. She could see no other tyre tracks in the gravel, or any other clues that suggested that perhaps Stefan had left the house in a different vehicle.

She went for a walk around the garden, trying to work out where the sound of the gunshot might have come from, but it was hard to place herself accurately when her only reference point was from a position in the river below the height of the bulrushes.

In fact, it took only a few minutes of walking around and inspecting the reed bed by the riverbank for Judith to realise that she didn't even know what she was looking for. A drop of blood on a blade of grass? A muddy footprint?

Judith looked at the wooden wheel turning on the side of the house, and the millpond in front of it. Despite the heat of the day, the water here was dark and Judith shivered at the thought of it. There was something about still bodies of water that spooked her. Although, as she looked, she could see that the water wasn't quite still. There was a slight current tugging at the surface. Where was the water going?

Judith walked around the edge of the pond until she saw that it fed into a river that was about ten feet across. Where the millpond ended and the river began, there was a narrow brick causeway that crossed from one side of the garden to the other.

Judith considered the river beyond the dam. It had to feed back into the Thames somehow. But it was hard to see exactly how, as Stefan had allowed this section of the garden to grow wild, and the water soon slipped under dense shrubs and bushes that crowded in from both banks.

With a sigh, Judith realised she'd have to follow the course of the river. She had to be thorough. So she pushed her way through the bushes, branches whipping her body, cobwebs sticking to her face and hair as she struggled to the other side.

Once there, Judith was disappointed. It was even wilder in this corner of the garden, but she could see that the river passed through some iron bars onto a concrete weir that fed the water back into the Thames. There was nothing of interest to see.

Although, as she regathered her breath after her exertions, she became aware of something in the air, a fetid smell, like an old compost heap. Was it the river? She looked down at the water flowing through the grille. An old tree branch was half submerged, blocking the water, and leaves had backed up.

But then Judith realised something.

It wasn't a branch in the water.

· It was a human arm.

It was reaching out of the water, the skin of the hand as white as marble. And, deeper still, Judith could just make out the body.

It was Stefan Dunwoody.

And in the centre of his forehead was a small black hole. A bullet hole.

Judith staggered back, her hand going to her neck.

She'd been right all along.

Stefan Dunwoody, her friend, her neighbour, had been shot dead.

Chapter 3

An hour later, Judith was sitting on a bench in Stefan's garden being interviewed by Detective Sergeant Tanika Malik. The police officer was in her early forties, wore a smart trouser suit, and had an air of teacherly efficiency about her that Judith already found irritating.

'But I don't understand, Mrs Potts,' DS Malik said. 'You say you came *back* to Mr Dunwoody's property?'

'Yes,' Judith said, her chin raised in defiance. 'It's like I told you on the phone. I knew I heard a shout and a gunshot last night. And if your police officer wasn't going to investigate it properly, I thought that I should.'

'Was there any other reason you returned?'

'I don't understand.'

'Were you expecting to find a dead body?'

'No, of course not.'

'And yet, you did find one, didn't you?'

'Which is more than your officer managed, I can't help noticing. Now tell me, did you know Stefan had a bust-up with a man called Elliot Howard a few weeks ago?'

'I'm sorry?'

Judith told DS Malik about the local newspaper diary piece that described the argument at the Henley Royal Regatta between Stefan and the owner of the Marlow Auction House, Elliot Howard.

'This was six weeks ago?'

'That's right.'

'I see.'

DS Malik thought for a moment.

'What is it?' Judith asked.

'Can I ask you a question? As Mr Dunwoody's neighbour.'

'Of course.'

'Only, it's standard procedure to cross-reference named subjects in witness reports with the police database. So I looked up Mr Dunwoody. He doesn't have any kind of record. He owns the art gallery in Marlow, he lives on his own, it's all as expected. But five weeks ago, he reported a burglary to us.'

'He did? What was stolen?'

'That's the thing. He said he'd been out at a restaurant with friends, and when he got home he'd discovered someone had smashed a window and broken into his property. But by the time an officer arrived to take his statement, Mr Dunwoody had to admit that he couldn't find anything that had been stolen.'

'Nothing was stolen?'

'That's what he said. And yet it was very definitely a break-in. But his computer was still there. His collection of art. And I can tell you, Mr Dunwoody owns a number of oil paintings, and not one of them had been stolen.'

'This was five weeks ago? A week *after* the bust-up Mr Dunwoody had at Henley?'

'I suppose so. But did Mr Dunwoody mention the break-in to you?'

'I haven't spoken to Stefan in weeks, I'm afraid.'

'Or did you see anything suspicious at the time? Maybe someone lurking near his property? Or a car parked by his house that looked different?'

'I'm sorry, I didn't. More's the pity. The first I knew anything was wrong was when I heard him being murdered last night.'

'Ah, now I'm really going to have to stop you there, Mrs Potts. You see, we don't know for sure that someone shot Mr Dunwoody.'

'I'm sorry?'

'We don't know Mr Dunwoody was murdered.'

'Are you saying the bullet hole appeared in his forehead as if by magic?'

'Well, no, but we can't rule out that his death was a terrible accident. Or what if he did this to himself?'

'You think he committed suicide?'

'It's a possibility.'

'Poppycock!'

DS Malik blinked in surprise. Had the woman in front of her just used the word 'poppycock'?

'If he took his own life, the pistol would have dropped to the ground somewhere. Before he fell into the river. And I can tell you, when I was looking, I didn't see a gun on the ground anywhere.'

'Yes, I can see why you'd think that, but maybe the gun fell into the river after he'd shot himself. I've instructed divers to search the riverbed for it. In the meantime, you really mustn't jump to any conclusions, Mrs Potts. We must let the evidence lead us, not our assumptions.'

Judith appraised DS Malik. The woman might be efficient, capable even, but she clearly lacked imagination. She was a typical 'head girl' type, Judith decided, not entirely kindly. But then, Judith had been expelled from the very posh boarding school she'd been sent to as a teenager. She'd also been expelled from the really-very-much-less-posh boarding school she'd been sent to next. And the one after that. Suffice to say, she and the head girls of the schools she'd attended hadn't ever seen eye to eye.

Judith sighed to herself. Very well, if the police didn't believe that Stefan had been killed, then she'd just have to investigate his murder for herself, wouldn't she?

Once Judith had finished giving her formal statement, she stepped back onto her punt and, with a regal wave at the forensic officers in their paper suits as she passed, she allowed the river to carry her back to her house. She then got out her old bicycle and climbed onto it. After all, if she wanted to discover who'd killed her neighbour, there was an obvious place to start.

It was only a five-minute cycle along the Thames Path into the nearby town of Marlow, and for once Judith didn't acknowledge the little nods and waves she got from complete strangers as she whizzed along. But then, she never knew why so many people waved to her at the best of times. It never occurred to her that she was considered something of a minor celebrity in the town. To her mind, there was nothing interesting about her life, and every time she professed herself confounded by someone's interest in her, she only embellished her reputation for eccentricity even further.

Turning from the towpath into a little park with swings and

slides, Judith saw a flock of pigeons pecking idly at the ground. *Filthy creatures*, she thought to herself as she sped up her bike, a big grin spreading over her face as she bore down on them. And then, at full tilt, she cycled into the flock, calling out 'Pigeons BEGONE!', and scattered squawking birds into the air.

Judith loved Marlow with a passion. To her mind, it wasn't too large, it wasn't too small, it was just right. The perfect town for a Goldilocks like her. The High Street had an elegant Georgian suspension bridge and ancient riverside church at one end, an ornamental obelisk at the other, and, in between, there was every type of historic building from centuries of piecemeal development down each side. To tie it all together into an aesthetic whole, red-and-blue bunting criss-crossed the length of the High Street, creating the sort of 'chocolate box' image of an English Home Counties town that jigsaw puzzles were made of.

But what Judith loved most about Marlow was the way it was so much more than its picturesque High Street. There was the railway station, even if it was no more than a hut, from which it was possible to get trains into London. There was also a thriving business park on the edges of the town that employed thousands of people. And above all, Judith loved the two local schools that churned out a steady stream of well-educated teenagers who'd work the tills in the supermarkets or take your order in the coffee shops. Seeing all these youngsters, unfailingly polite and always pleasingly attractive to her eye, going about their day, or having picnics down by the river, or even hanging out in the skate park by the cricket pavilion, gave Judith a real glow of happiness. If this was the next generation coming through, then the world didn't have too much to worry about, she reckoned.

Judith was by nature an optimist, it was almost her defining trait, but she also tried to be as honest as she could, and she had to admit that as much as Marlow remained a jaunty place, like all towns in Britain it had taken a bit of a battering over the last decade or so. It was all right if you were a tourist visiting for the day. There were plenty of high-end restaurants and clothes shops, so maybe you wouldn't notice the dozen or so shops that were empty, their fronts tastefully postered to hide the absence of business going on inside. And the nice man who sold the *Big Issue* on one side of the High Street had recently been joined on the other side by a homeless man who sat cross-legged all day, a tin for coins in front of him.

The people remained good, that's what she reminded herself as she got off her bicycle at the top end of the High Street and leant it against a wall.

As for where she was going, Judith had made up her mind the moment DS Malik had told her that she was wrong to believe that someone had killed her neighbour. She was going to start her investigation at Stefan Dunwoody's art gallery.

Chapter 4

Judith had never set foot inside Dunwoody Arts before, but then she'd never had need to buy any artworks before. Why should she when she'd inherited her great aunt's collection of paintings at the same time as she'd inherited her house?

As Judith entered, a young female attendant looked up from her desk, tears in her eyes.

'Oh,' Judith said. 'You've heard.'

'The police just called,' the woman said. 'I'm still reeling.'

'Of course you are,' Judith said kindly as she crossed the gallery and sat down in the spare chair at the woman's desk. Next, Judith rootled in her handbag and pulled out a packet of pocket tissues. She handed one over.

'Thank you,' the woman said, before blowing her nose.

'I should introduce myself,' Judith said. 'I'm Judith Potts.'

'I know. You live in that big house on the river.'

'Oh. Have we met before?'

'Once, actually,' the woman said, smiling at the memory. 'I was being hassled by some boys outside the pub a couple of years ago. You stepped in and scared them off.'

'I did?' Judith had no recollection of the event, although it sounded very much like the sort of thing she'd do. She couldn't bear how men seemed to operate in packs at times, picking on young women on their own.

'I'm Antonia,' the woman said. 'Antonia Webster. And thanks for helping me that time. You were totally amazing.'

'I'm sure you didn't need any help, you look capable enough.'

Judith rootled in her bag again and pulled out an old-fashioned tin of travel sweets.

'Would you like a sweet?'

Antonia didn't quite know what to say to the question.

'No?' Judith asked. 'Then do you mind if I have one?'

Judith popped the lid of the tin, plucked a boiled sweet from within the icing sugar, put it in her mouth and sucked on it for a few seconds.

'Lime,' she pronounced with satisfaction. 'My favourite. Now, I hope you don't mind me coming here, but if I helped you in the past, then maybe you could help me this time. You see, I'm Stefan's neighbour and I'm trying to work out what happened to him. It's so terribly sad. I take it you work here?'

'I do,' Antonia said. 'And of course I'll help. I'm Mr Dunwoody's assistant. Just for the summer. Before I go to uni.'

'So you've not been here long?'

'No. But Mr Dunwoody was so kind, I can't believe he's gone.'

'I'd agree with you there. But how was he kind, would you say?'

'Well, he was interested in me. You know? About what I thought. About politics. Or the environment. Or what I was going to do at uni.'

'He was interested in you?'

'Not in that way,' Antonia said, picking up on Judith's tone. 'He wasn't a creep. He was just an old man. That's how he described himself. An old man. Who lived on his own with all of his art. I liked him.'

This description certainly chimed with Judith's limited wave-to-her-neighbour-once-a-fortnight relationship with Stefan. He always seemed happy enough to see her, and always had something to call across the river. 'Beautiful morning!' Or, 'Lovely day!' he'd shout. Judith smiled sadly at the memory.

'He was a good man I think,' she said.

'He was,' Antonia agreed.

The two women sat in companionable silence for a while, Judith contentedly sucking on her boiled sweet.

'And somebody killed him,' she said.

Antonia's eyes widened. 'What's that?'

'You didn't know?'

'No. The guy on the phone said he'd had an accident.'

Judith's handbag on her lap was still open and she closed the clasp with a snap.

'I'm sorry to say that's not what happened at all. He was shot dead.'

'No way?'

'Oh yes, I'm sure of it. So I suggest I help you shut up shop. You can't possibly be expected to do a day's work after a shock like this.'

'You think that's what I should do?'

'Of course.'

'You'd help me?'

'I've got nowhere else to be. Now how do we do it?'

Antonia got a set of keys, explained how the alarm system

worked, and together the two women locked up the gallery, turning over the sign at the front so it said it was closed. As Judith had suspected, the simple act of doing something physical seemed to give Antonia the space to process all that had happened.

Judith picked her moment with care.

'You know, he can't have been as perfect as all that,' she said, as though the thought had only just that moment occurred to her.

'What's that?'

'Mr Dunwoody. Logic suggests he was either not as blameless as he appeared, or he had at least one friend or acquaintance who was very much a wrong 'un. Seeing as someone did this to him.'

'Oh. I see what you mean. But that's not possible. He really was a nice guy. And there was no one bad in his life, either.'

Judith saw Antonia frown.

'What is it?' Judith asked.

Antonia didn't say anything.

'Go on,' Judith cajoled. And then she waited. She knew that sometimes the best way to get someone to talk was to stay silent yourself.

'Well, it's just,' Antonia eventually said, 'if you're going to suggest there was someone who was around here who was maybe a bit of a "wrong 'un", well, you put a person in my mind. That's all.'

'And who is this "someone"?'

'No idea. I don't know his name.'

'Then why don't you tell me about him, and let's see if we can work it out together?'

'He's an older gentleman. With grey hair. Or silver. It went down to his shoulders. He was very tall and grand.'

'And this was a friend of Mr Dunwoody's?'

'I don't think so. He came into the gallery last week.'

'What day last week?'

'Monday.'

'Okay, so this man came into the gallery last Monday.'

'That's right. And whoever he was, Mr Dunwoody took him straight to his office. It was like he was embarrassed that this guy had visited.'

'I see. How very interesting. Then what happened?'

'Well, I'm not sure. They were in Mr Dunwoody's office. But it wasn't long before I heard raised voices. I didn't know what to do. You see, it's my job to make coffees for Mr Dunwoody if he ever has any guests, and I was in such a panic. I didn't know if I should make them coffee or not.'

'Did you hear what they were arguing about?'

'Not while I was outside the office, but in the end I got up my courage, knocked on the door and asked if they'd like a coffee. It was like thunder in there. The tall man, the silver-haired man, he didn't want anything, and he was kind of rude about it. He dismissed me with a wave of his hand.'

Antonia lapsed into thoughtful silence.

'How interesting,' Judith said. 'But you say you didn't hear what they said while you were outside?'

Antonia wasn't able to follow the line of Judith's reasoning.

'What's that?'

'You said you didn't hear what was said while you were *outside*. That suggests to me that maybe there was something you heard while you were inside.'

'Oh yes, of course. Sorry. Anyway, after the silver-haired gentleman waved me off, I left, but as I was closing the door, I heard Mr Dunwoody say to him, "I could go to the police right now."'

'And what did the silver-haired man have to say about that?'

'I don't know. I left before I could hear his reply.'

'I see. But Mr Dunwoody definitely said that he could "go to the police right now"?'

'He did.'

'And you've really no idea what he was referring to?'

'None at all. I'm so sorry.'

'You didn't perhaps raise the matter with Mr Dunwoody later on?'

'No way. But he did, now you mention it. We were locking up for the night and Mr Dunwoody apologised that I'd had to witness the argument.'

'What did you say to that?'

'Well, I could see he was really uncomfortable about it all, so I just told him it was fine, I'd not really seen or heard anything. And then he said something weird. He said, "Desperation drives people to do stupid things."'

'What on earth was he referring to?'

'No idea. But it's what he said.'

Judith felt a buzz of excitement. Who was this silver-haired man who was in dispute with Stefan? Remembering how Stefan had got into an argument with Elliot Howard at the Henley Regatta, she had an idea.

'Is your computer connected to the internet?' she asked.

Antonia nodded.

'Then can you do a quick search for me?'

'Of course. What do you want to know?'

'Could you look up the name Elliot Howard?'

'You think he might be the man who was in here?'

'It's a possibility. But let's see if we can find a picture of him online.'

'Okay,' Antonia said, going over to her desk and firing up

the browser on her computer. She typed 'Elliot Howard' into the search field.

'That's the one,' Judith said, pointing at the top hit.

Antonia clicked the link that opened the website for the Marlow Auction House. Next she found a 'Who we are' tab on the home page, and they were soon looking at the names and photos of the key members of staff.

The very first image was of a handsome man in his late fifties with silver hair that swept down to his shoulders. The caption said that his name was Elliot Howard and that he was chairman of the Marlow Auction House.

'That's him!' Antonia said in surprise. 'That's the man who was here last Monday.'

Judith bent down to the screen so she could better see the photo.

'Got you!' she whispered to the man on the screen.

Chapter 5

A few minutes after her meeting with Antonia, Judith found herself leaning her bicycle against the wall of the Marlow Auction House, a creaking timber-framed building that always reminded her of the old barns she'd played in as a girl growing up on her parents' farm on the Isle of Wight: full of cobwebs, creaky floorboards, and damp hay bales that smelled of must.

As she straightened her cape on her shoulders, Judith realised that she didn't have any specific plan for what she should do next. All she knew was that she had to see Elliot Howard. She wanted to see the cut of his jib.

As for the wisdom of approaching a man she thought might be a murderer, she decided to ignore any such concerns. After all, she'd never met the man before, so what on earth was stopping her from visiting his place of work? She could pretend she was interested in selling a painting. Or some other ruse. Something would occur to her.

As Judith entered the building, she saw a woman sitting at a desk working at a computer. She was in her fifties, with dark wavy hair, bright red lipstick and smiley eyes.

'Good morning, and how can I help you?' the woman said in a friendly Irish accent.

'Good morning,' Judith asked brightly. 'Are you open?'

'I'm sorry but we don't have any viewings until tomorrow.'

'You don't?'

'I can give you a catalogue? This week it's coins and medals, which I can't imagine is what you're here for. It'll be mostly men who really should get out more,' she added with a conspiratorial smile. 'Although don't tell Elliot I said that. However, we've a fine art auction at the end of the month. That might be more your style.'

'Actually, it's Mr Howard I was hoping to see.'

'It is?'

'That's right.'

'May I ask why you would like to see him?'

'That's a very good question.'

Judith was about to think of her excuse when a man's voice spoke from directly behind her.

'Yes, why do you want to see me?'

Judith was so startled that her mind instantly went blank. To buy herself time, she turned and saw the man from the online photo leaning nonchalantly in a doorway behind her. He was in his late fifties with long-flowing grey hair that fell to his shoulders. He wore brogues, tan corduroy trousers, and an old checked-shirt under a tatty grey cardigan.

It was Elliot Howard.

There was an easeful, almost amused superiority to his manner, and Judith had a sudden insight that Elliot was inordinately proud of having a full head of hair at his age, which is why he kept it so long. And for all that Elliot was looking so relaxed, there was something about him that Judith found a touch unsettling.

'Well, wouldn't you like to know,' Judith said, in lieu of knowing what else to say.

'I do. Which is why I asked. Why do you want to see me?'

'Aha!'

Inside, Judith cringed. *Aha*? Was that really the best she could do?

The woman at the computer came to her rescue.

'I know, why don't you both go into Elliot's office? You can have a nice chat there.'

'Okay, darling,' Elliot said to the woman with a smile. 'You're the boss,' he added, although it was clear from his patrician tone that she wasn't.

Elliot led the way into his office and Judith had no choice but to follow. Her mind was scrabbling for something to say, *anything* to say.

'That's Daisy,' Elliot said as he went and sat behind a large office desk. 'A wonderful woman. My wife. Don't know why she puts up with me. Anyway, how can I help you?'

Judith's mind was still a whirling blank, but she could see a number of photos in frames on the walls, so she went over to look at them. They were faded with age and mostly showed teenage boys rowing on the river, or wearing blazers while holding various silver cups and medals. The shield above each photo was of one of the local school's, Sir William Borlase's Grammar School, and she could see the hand-written names of the boys underneath always included an 'A. Howard'.

'Oh, you're a rower?' Judith said, just to fill the dead air, but it was as she was looking at the photos that inspiration finally came to her.

'You owe me money!' she blurted.

'I'm sorry?'

'Yes, I should have said sooner. My name's Mrs Judith Potts, and you owe me money. From Henley Regatta. When you really didn't behave very well at all.'

This got Elliot's attention.

'What on earth are you talking about?' he said, but Judith got the impression that he'd maybe been rattled by her allegation.

'As far as I'm concerned, you were a disgrace. In the Royal Enclosure. The way you carried on in that argument with that man.'

'What man would this be?'

'Stefan whatever-his-name-is. He runs the art gallery in Marlow. I thought you were very rude to him. But then you pushed past me when you left and made me spill my red wine down my dress. It's cost over seventy pounds to dry clean, and I expect you to pay the bill.'

Elliot considered Judith for a long moment.

'I don't remember spilling anyone's drink,' he said.

'But you don't deny the argument, do you?'

'It's true Mr Dunwoody and I had a difference of opinion that day. But I don't remember you at all.'

'I'm not surprised. You were in such a state I can well imagine you don't remember anything from that day. That poor man you were shouting at, he'd done nothing wrong.'

'Oh he'd done wrong all right.'

'It can't have been anything worth losing your temper over like that.'

'You've no idea what you're talking about.'

'That's as well as may be, but even so—'

'He was a fraud,' Elliot said, interrupting Judith.

'I'm sorry?'

'In fact, I'd go further. Stefan Dunwoody was a fraud and a liar. And a cheat and a crook. Now, if you don't mind, I'm a busy man. I'd like you to leave.'

With a cold smile that said the meeting was over, Elliot picked up some papers on his desk and started reading.

'But what about my dress?' Judith spluttered.

'If you ask me,' Elliot said without looking up, 'you've invented the whole thing. God knows why. Because I have an excellent memory for faces and I'm sure we've not met before. What's more, I definitely didn't spill any wine on anyone's dress at Henley. And if I had, I'm sure that person wouldn't have waited nearly two months before approaching me. Now, I must ask you to leave my office.'

Judith opened her mouth a couple of times, rearranged her hold on her handbag, and then realised she still had nothing further to add.

She turned to leave, but stopped as she was about to open the door.

'What do you mean he "*was*" a fraud?' she asked.

'Are you still here?' Elliot said with a sigh as he looked up again.

'Yes, and I want to know why you're talking about Stefan in the past tense.'

Elliot shrugged as if it was of no concern to him.

'Isn't it obvious?' he said. 'He's dead, isn't he?'

'But how do you know that?'

'It's all over the office this morning. How the doyen of the art world Stefan Dunwoody has had a tragic accident and been gathered up to God. But let me ask you a question. How do you know?'

'How do *I* know?'

'Yes. This auction house knows Stefan well. But what's your connection to him?'

'That's rather an impertinent question.'

'Hardly, considering,' Elliot said and leant back in his chair, looking at Judith levelly. Once again, Judith couldn't quite place Elliot's manner. What was it he was reminding her of?

'So what's your connection?' he asked again.

'As it happens, I'm his neighbour,' Judith said, unable to keep up the subterfuge any longer. 'The police interviewed me this morning, and if you ask me, it wasn't an accident, someone killed him.'

'Oh I see!' Elliot said, delight lighting his face.

'I beg your pardon?'

'You seriously believe someone killed him?'

'Shot him dead. Yes.'

'How interesting. This was never about the dress, was it?'

Elliot's smile didn't waver, but the light seemed to die from his eyes and Judith felt as if the air had been sucked out of the room.

'Of course it was about the dress,' she said, knowing that Elliot could see through her lie.

'No, I don't think so. Because I think you're a nosy neighbour, aren't you? A nosy neighbour who's got it into her head that just because I argued with Stefan at Henley a few weeks ago, and now he's dead, you wanted to have a poke around here, thinking yourself the amateur sleuth. I'm right, aren't I?'

'Nothing of the sort.'

'Very well, then perhaps you can tell me precisely when Mr Dunwoody died?'

Judith was surprised by the question. How could Elliot talk so easily of times of death like this? But it was all part of his attitude that she couldn't place.

'About eight last night,' she said. 'Maybe ten past eight.'

'Well, wouldn't you know it, but I've an alibi for then.'

'You have?'

'At eight o'clock last night I was at All Saints' Church. You see, I sing in the church choir. Have done for years. And every Thursday night, between the hours of seven and nine, we have choir practice. So that's where I was. In front of the vicar, as it happens. Along with the verger, various sidesmen and women of the church. And the Mayor of Marlow.'

Elliot smiled, and Judith suddenly realised what was unsettling her about him. He seemed to be *enjoying* the conversation. Like a cat toying with a mouse.

'And don't worry,' he continued. 'I won't wait for that bill for your dress, we both know you were making that up, don't we? Now why don't you piss off before I call the police and have you forcibly removed?'

Judith didn't have an answer to that. For the first time in years, she was entirely lost for words.

Chapter 6

Judith cycled back into Marlow replaying the conversation with Elliot in her head. *What had she been thinking?* Despite herself, she couldn't help but feel a delicious thrill at her audacity. She'd just confronted a man in broad daylight who might have been a killer! And the encounter had gleaned important information, not least the fact that Elliot believed Stefan Dunwoody had been a liar, a cheat, a fraud and a crook. Those were a serious list of crimes, weren't they? Although, how could her lovely neighbour Stefan, who his assistant Antonia had agreed was a perfect gentleman, be in any way a criminal? It didn't seem possible.

Judith was deep in thought as she cycled down the High Street. She didn't see any of the elbow nudges and amused looks from the locals as she passed, her dark grey cape flying behind her, her legs pedalling as hard as they could. Before she reached the suspension bridge, she lifted her feet from the pedals and freewheeled down the path that led through the graveyard to the entrance of All Saints' Church.

Judith leant her bicycle against the wall and tried to put her thoughts in order. Her immediate concern was simple. She had a theory that Elliot was involved in Stefan's death. And if he were, then he could hardly have been at choir practice the night before, could he? She just had to prove it, which was why she was popping into All Saints'.

Judith wasn't a regular churchgoer. She was one of those people who'd happily tell anyone who asked that she only went to church on high feasts and holidays, whilst not quite noticing that she didn't go to church on those days either. But she was on nodding acquaintance with the vicar, a very nice young man called Colin Starling. Perhaps he'd be in the church and would be able to tell her if Elliot had attended choir practice?

Once inside, Judith took a moment to enjoy the feeling of peace that came over her. How a stone building many hundreds of years old could feel so light and airy was always a mystery to her, but she couldn't help but smile at the sight of the high, vaulted ceilings, the elegant stone pillars, and the ancient banners and standards of local regiments hanging from the walls. The Church of England was the perfect metaphor for the country as a whole, she felt: pleasing to the eye, staunchly old-fashioned, and waning very much in popularity.

There were notices on a corkboard by the entrance, and Judith started looking for any kind of reference to choir rehearsals. Or, better yet, a list of everyone who sang in the choir. She couldn't find anything that helped her, which she found briefly irritating. There must be choir notices somewhere. Where were they?

Judith decided to go and look in the vestry where the choir got changed.

Pushing open the oak door, Judith called out, 'Hello?'

There was no one about, so she entered. She could see that the choristers' surplices and ruffs hung from pegs, there was an old cupboard built into the wall that Judith guessed contained the vicar's vestments, and she also saw a desk with papers and a computer on it, but otherwise the room was empty.

Or was it? Judith felt a prickling sensation, as if someone was watching her. But how could that be possible? There was no one else in the room. Very well, she thought to herself, it was time to find out about the choir's rehearsals.

Judith searched the desk, but she still felt unsettled. Some sixth sense was telling her she wasn't alone. But the room was so tiny, there was nowhere to hide. Although, Judith supposed, there was the built-in cupboard. But why would anyone hide inside a cupboard?

Judith saw some choral music on a shelf, so went over to see if she could find a list of choristers there, but she had to stop herself again. She still felt as though someone was looking at her.

To settle her mind more than for any other reason, Judith went over to the cupboard, opened the door and saw that it contained nothing more than the vicar's robes on hangers. Just as she'd suspected.

Although it also seemed to contain a middle-aged woman who was looking straight at her.

'Oh,' Judith said, surprised. 'Hello.'

'Yes, sorry, about being in a cupboard,' the woman said, embarrassment pinking her cheeks. 'You must think me quite strange.'

Judith was baffled. The woman in the cupboard looked entirely respectable. In fact, more than that, she positively glowed with expensive good health. She was in her early forties, with sleek blonde hair, and was wearing a quilted black gilet over her top half, tight-fitting jeggings over her lower, and bright pink running shoes. What on earth was she doing hiding in a cupboard in an empty church?

'It does seem a bit unconventional,' Judith conceded.

'I can explain,' the woman said in a rush. 'You see, I only came in to tidy up the vicar's crockery.' The woman held up her hands, each of them brandishing a floral mug. 'Colin is so bad at tidying, and they've been in here gathering dust and mould for days. Anyway, I didn't think I'd meet anyone. And then I heard someone come into the church, and I panicked. I just didn't want to meet anyone today. Especially one of Colin's parishioners. Oh God, that sounds bad, doesn't it? You're not one of his parishioners, are you?'

'I wouldn't worry about that,' Judith said with a smile.

'Good! I mean, not that it's good that you don't come to church, oh I'm sorry, I'm making rather a hash of this, aren't I? But anyway, the point is, when I heard footsteps approaching the vestry I hid in the cupboard.'

'And closed the door behind you?'

'That's right. It sounds mad, doesn't it, now I'm saying it out loud. Do you think it's mad?'

'Not at all. But let me introduce myself. I'm Judith Potts.'

'Yes, I know.'

'You do?'

Now it was Judith's turn to be surprised. She was sure she'd not met the woman in front of her before.

'And I'm Becks Starling,' the other woman said, offering her hand. 'Becky, actually. Although most people call me Becks.'

'You're the vicar's wife?' Judith asked, delighted.

'I'm afraid so,' Becks said with a bashful smile. 'Someone has to be. Do you mind if I get out of the cupboard?'

'No, please do.'

'Thanks,' Becks said, and clambered out.

This left the two women at something of an impasse. There wasn't any kind of agreed etiquette for continuing a first meeting between two middle-class women when one of them has just been found hiding in a cupboard.

'I mean it's not ideal, is it?' Becks said. 'Hiding away like that. At my age.'

'Oh I don't know. I remember at university I had a ground-floor set of rooms and I hid under my desk when a friend came to visit who I didn't want to see.'

'You did?'

'Only for a few moments. Or so I thought. Turned out my friend really, really wanted to see me. She waited outside my window for nearly three hours, which meant I had to hide under the desk for nearly three hours. But I could never reveal I was hiding from her, it would have been too embarrassing. I ended up having to pee in a metal wastepaper bin, and you've no idea how hard it is peeing in a metal bin while hiding under a desk.'

'I don't normally hide in wardrobes,' Becks said in an attempt to distance herself from the woman in front of her who openly admitted to peeing in bins, and who, she now realised, could very well be mad.

'But how can I help you?' she continued. 'Are you looking for Reverend Colin?'

'Oh no, nothing so grand. I was just wondering if there was a list anywhere of the people who sing in the church choir.'

'Well, as it happens, there is,' Becks said, heading over to a piece of paper that was hanging on the back of the door to the vestry. 'It's here.'

Judith saw thirty or so names on the paper written out in different hands and different inks, with quite a few crossed out.

Before Judith could find Elliot Howard's name, Becks straightened the piece of paper as it wasn't hanging neatly from the drawing pin.

'Sorry, if you could let me read—'

But now it was skewiff in the other direction, so Becks rotated it back.

'Sorry, it's not straight.'

'If you don't mind—'

Becks yanked the paper from the wall and carried it over to the desk.

'I'd better write this out again, it's a mess,' she said, getting a sheet of A4 from a printer to the side of the desk.

'I only wanted to see if Elliot Howard was a member of the choir.'

Becks stopped what she was doing and looked at Judith, surprised.

'Elliot? Oh yes. He's been in the choir for years.'

'He has?'

'For as long as I can remember.'

'Then can you tell me, was there a choir practice last night?'

'There was.'

'And he was here, was he?'

'He was.'

'Are you sure?'

'Quite sure. You see, I sing in the choir as well. He's a baritone, I'm a soprano.'

'What time was choir rehearsal?'

'Well, we first have a full rehearsal with the boy trebles from seven to eight. And then at about eight we let the trebles go, and the adults stay on to rehearse until about nine.'

'So Elliot was here at eight o'clock?'

'He was here the whole time from seven until nine.'

'Are you sure?'

'Absolutely sure. But why are you asking?'

Judith hesitated, wondering what to say. Then, as was so often the case with her, she decided that honesty was the best policy.

'I think he's involved in a murder.'

Becks shot up from her chair.

'*What?*'

'In fact, I think there's a chance he killed my neighbour last night.'

Judith could see Becks' mind spinning, speech very much beyond her.

'I know,' Judith agreed. 'It's quite the statement.'

'He's a *murderer*?'

'Would that surprise you?'

'Of course, we're talking about Elliot Howard here.'

'You know him well?'

'Not really. Now you mention it. He's one of those men who prefer the company of the men in the choir, I think. Sorry, what murder? There's been a murder?'

Judith explained the chain of events that had led her to the church, and Becks hung on her every word.

'You think Elliot killed Mr Dunwoody and you went and *talked* to him?' she asked when Judith had finished her tale.

'Someone has to. The police are being useless. They think Stefan's death was an accident or suicide.'

'Well, I can tell you that Elliot was here last night between seven and nine.'

'And you're sure he didn't slip off at all?'

'Oh yes. Quite sure.'

'Not even for a few minutes?'

'There's always a short break at about eight o'clock, as the trebles leave, and people go for a loo break. So it's possible Elliot left then.'

'You think maybe he left the rehearsal at eight and didn't come back for the second half?'

'I'm not sure. I don't know. Although, now you mention it, I remember seeing Elliot arrive for seven, but I'm not sure I noticed him after that. It's possible he left during the loo break at eight and didn't come back. It's like I said, he and I don't really talk.'

Judith was thrilled. If Elliot left the rehearsal at eight, he'd maybe have had time to get in a car and drive over to Stefan's house to shoot him dead at ten past eight. It would have been tight, but just about possible, she thought.

'I don't suppose the church has any security cameras, does it? Any kind of video recording that might show the choir rehearsal last night. Or people coming or going.'

'As it happens, we do. There's a little camera in the gallery. In case of break-ins or any other sort of anti-social behaviour.'

'Do you think we could look at the footage from last night?'

Judith could see that the idea shocked Becks.

'I'm not sure about that. I don't think I should be showing you anything on Colin's computer.'

Judith considered Becks for a moment, and then she reached into her handbag and pulled out her tin of travel sweets. She popped the lid in a puff of icing sugar and held the tin up for Becks.

'Travel sweet?' Judith asked.

'No thanks,' Becks said, who was startled that someone would offer her a sweet. Did she look like someone who ate sweets?

Judith put a sweet into her mouth and sucked on it while she considered her options.

'Then I suppose we've no choice,' she said, snapping the lid closed and putting the tin back into her handbag. 'We'll have to get the police involved.'

'You think the police will need to look?'

'It's inevitable, I'm afraid. Once I tell them about Elliot, there'll be police with search warrants crawling all over this place. I imagine it will cause quite the scandal, and the press will follow, you know what they're like. There'll be paparazzi hiding in your shrubbery and publishing unflattering photos of you taking out the bins.'

Becks was waking up the computer before Judith had even finished speaking.

'No, you're right. We should have a look for ourselves so the police don't need to get involved.'

Judith smiled warmly.

'Now that's an *excellent* idea.'

Becks began clicking various icons on the monitor and opened up a window that showed a live black-and-white feed of the main body of the church, including the choir stalls.

Becks double-clicked a video file and another window opened, looking exactly the same as the live feed, but Judith could see it was dated the day before. She then watched as Becks dragged the slider on the window until the time stamp read 7 p.m. As she did so, the choir stalls started filling up with an assortment of boys in the front pews and twenty or so men and women in the others.

It was possible to see that Elliot Howard was standing in the back row.

'I don't believe it,' Becks said in horror.

'What is it?' Judith asked, excitement blooming as she wondered if this was the moment she was about to discover that Elliot Howard was the killer.

'Am I really that fat?' Becks said, pointing at the recording of herself as she chatted to friends.

'You're not fat.'

'I am if that's how I look.'

'Believe me, you've nothing to worry about,' Judith said.

'That's it, I'm going to cut *all* dairy out of my diet.'

Judith struggled to be sympathetic. Why couldn't people be happy with who they were? But there was no point arguing with a woman like Becks, she was too far gone. Instead, Judith peered at the monitor.

'That's Elliot there, isn't it?'

Becks refocused on the screen.

'That's him. And if I fast-forward, let's see if he leaves.'

Becks hit the button a few times until the time stamp in the bottom corner started whizzing forward, and Judith could see that the choirmaster and choir were in position the whole time. Then, as the clock rushed up to 8 p.m., the boys all suddenly left, and plenty of the adults left their positions, chatting to each other or heading off for a few minutes. But Elliot stayed where he was.

By 8.07 p.m., the adults were all back in the choir stalls, and the rehearsal carried on. And still Elliot hadn't moved. Not once. Nor did he pluck out his mobile to make a call or check it in any way. He just sat on his own in quiet contemplation.

'He didn't go anywhere,' Judith said, disappointed.

'Well, that's good news, isn't it?' Becks said.

Becks kept the footage whizzing forward, and the two women saw that Elliot didn't leave his position until shortly after 9 p.m., when the rehearsal began to break up for everyone.

Becks took her finger from the mouse, and the footage resumed playing at normal speed.

'So there we are,' Becks said. 'Elliot was there from seven to nine. He can't be your murderer. Thank heavens.'

'I suppose not.'

Judith felt cheated. This wasn't the answer she'd been looking for, and as she watched Elliot chatting easily with three other men as they left the rehearsal, she had to admit that he wasn't behaving like someone who'd been involved in a murder, either. He seemed relaxed and in good spirits.

'Hold on,' Judith said, indicating the monitor, 'what was that?'

On the screen, Elliot had just passed out of shot with his friends.

'What was what?'

'Can you rewind to show Elliot leaving?'

Becks rewound the footage, Elliot and his friends walking backwards into the frame.

'Can you replay it from there?' Judith asked.

Becks pressed play and Elliot and his friends started to walk down the aisle again.

This time, both Judith and Becks saw it.

Just before he disappeared from view, Elliot looked directly into the lens of the camera. But almost as soon as he'd looked, he turned and clapped one of his friends on the back, the men all leaving, chatting happily together.

'He looked at the camera,' Becks said.

'He did, didn't he? He knew it was there.'

'I suppose he's had years to notice it. Maybe it's a coincidence?'

'I don't think so. You saw it too, didn't you? That look on his face.'

Becks bit her lip. It was true. She'd seen it as well.

'It's like he knew someone would watch the footage. To check up on his alibi. And for a split second his ego took over and he couldn't help himself. He had to look at the camera.'

'But how would you describe that look on his face?'

'I know exactly how I'd describe it,' Judith said. 'It was a look of triumph.'

The women looked at each other. They both knew that Judith had hit the nail on the head. Elliot had looked at the camera *triumphantly*.

Becks shivered.

'Sorry, these old stone buildings. Even in the height of summer, they're cold.'

'Okay,' Judith said, 'so what's our next move?'

'I'm sorry?'

'That footage proves he can't be the killer, but he's definitely involved in Stefan's murder. Somehow he managed to be in two places at once. Or he hired someone else to do the killing. But that look he gave to the camera proves his guilt as far as I'm concerned. Don't you think?'

'Hang on, what do you mean "what's our next move"?'

'Well, we're the only two people in the world who currently believe Elliot's implicated in any way in Stefan's murder. So it's up to us to work out how he did it.'

'Oh no, I couldn't possibly get involved,' Becks said. 'This is a matter for the police. We have to let them do their job. That's what they do. Catch criminals and murderers. Whereas I make sandwiches, that's my job. I serve tea and biscuits, raise my kids, and help my husband. So I'm sorry, it's been lovely meeting you, Judith, but I couldn't possibly get involved.'

And with that, Becks left the room, all of a twitter.

Judith smiled to herself. She remembered being that young. Not neurotic like Becks, or desperately worried about what people thought of her. But, in her book, anyone who could pick up a couple of coffee cups, and a few short minutes later find herself hiding inside a cupboard, was okay by her. She looked forward to meeting Becks again.

In the meantime, though, how could she prove Elliot was involved?

Chapter 7

After her encounter with Judith, Becks hurried back to the vicarage, a gorgeous bow-fronted Georgian house to the side of the
church, but she found she couldn't settle. Her second-hand brush
with a possible murder had upset her more than she'd like to
admit. So, to calm her nerves, she did what she always did when
she felt anxious, and that was tidy up. She plumped cushions
that were already plump, straightened pictures on the walls that
weren't askew, and ran a hoover over a kitchen floor that was
entirely dirt-free.

Her fourteen-year-old son Sam was slumped over his phone
at the kitchen table.

'Where's your sister?' Becks asked.

'I don't know,' Sam said without looking up. 'Probably snort-
ing nitrous oxide somewhere.'

'Don't say that!' Becks yelped.

Although Sam was joking, both he and his mum knew that

while Sam was a high-achieving student who liked to follow the rules, his sixteen-year-old sister Chloe was very much the opposite. All she wanted was to hang out with her friends and party. But then, in her moments of honesty, Becks knew that Chloe wasn't doing anything that she hadn't done at the same age, it's just that her behaviour worried her sick.

Not that she really understood Sam, either. In the last year or so he'd become increasingly withdrawn, and as far as Becks could see, the only meaningful social interactions he had outside of school hours were with his hamster, who he doted on.

'You look lovely, darling,' the Reverend Colin Starling said as he entered the room wearing his black suit, bib and white collar.

'How can you say that?' Becks snapped. 'These are my yoga clothes.'

Exasperated with her husband's lack of sensitivity, Becks went upstairs to get changed. At some deep level she knew she'd behaved unreasonably, but she couldn't shake her feeling of unease.

In the bedroom, she grabbed up her mobile phone to see if Chloe had been in touch. She hadn't.

'Becks?' Colin called up from the bottom of the stairs. 'You remember we're having Major Tom Lewis and his wife over for dinner?'

Becks didn't even bother to respond. Of course she knew they had guests for dinner. She'd been up at six that morning rubbing fennel into a belly of pork so it could have the full ten hours in the slow cooker. Even though Major Tom would be drunk before he arrived, and Mrs Lewis would criticise her by a whole set of criteria she'd only reveal once Becks had failed to meet them.

Becks couldn't help thinking to herself, where had she gone wrong in her life? It wasn't that she was unhappy. Far from it. But she wasn't happy, either. Colin had been a banker when they'd first met, and although they'd both been regular churchgoers, he'd not expressed any interest in the ministry before they'd got married. It was only after Chloe was born that he began to have 'doubts' about all the lovely money he was making. And then, right after Sam's arrival, when their need for money had spiralled, he'd had his 'calling'. Being a good wife, Becks had supported her husband in his radical change of career from rich banker to country vicar.

And here she was, all these years later, a homemaker, a wife, and a mother. All wonderful roles, and she kept telling herself she was lucky her life was so blessed, but she couldn't help noticing that everything about her existence seemed to be defined by someone who wasn't her. She was the *kids'* mum, the *vicar's* wife, and the *house's* wife for that matter.

Becks opened a social media app on her phone. She was looking for a community group she'd joined not long after her husband had been made vicar of Marlow. The group was called Let's Talk Marlow. When Becks had joined, she'd not used her real name. She'd used the moniker 'Jezebel'. This anonymity had allowed her to be a bit more loose-lipped online than she'd ever be in real life. But she'd made herself give up on the site a few years ago. It had been altogether too intoxicating having an alter ego, and she knew it wasn't healthy, especially when she suspected she liked her alter ego more than she did her real self.

For the first time in a long while she went to the forum. A quick scan of the live threads told her it was still mostly preoccupied with the fear of travellers moving into Seymour Park, and the refusal of people to pick up dog poo. So, no change there.

Becks started a new thread.

I've got some old furniture I want to sell. I'd like to use the Marlow Auction House, but I've heard some bad things about the owner, Elliot Howard. Can he be trusted?

Her finger hovered over the 'Post' button. Could she really be so daring? By day, mild-mannered vicar's wife, but by teatime an anonymous cyber warrior?

Before she could stop herself, Becks pressed the button and the post went live.

A joyous thrill ran through her. She couldn't remember the last time she'd been so daring.

The following morning, Judith was sitting at her desk struggling to find a satisfying crossword clue for the word 'shoulder'. She'd recently noticed that it could be constructed from the conditional word 'should' and the hesitation of 'er'. The difference in pronunciation between the two 'shoulds' pleased her enormously, and her instincts told her there was a satisfying link to be made between being unsure – 'er' – after having an obligation – 'should'. But every time she tried to focus on how best to phrase a clue, the image of Elliot Howard popped into her head: how self-assured he'd been when he met her; how smug he'd looked as he'd glanced at the CCTV camera in the church.

And if Elliot wasn't ruining her concentration enough, Judith also couldn't stop thinking about poor old Stefan. She found herself remembering the only face-to-face conversation they'd ever had. It had been a few winters ago, when the country had been blanketed in snow and Stefan had appeared at Judith's door to check that she was okay. Stefan hadn't known that the whole drama of getting in supplies and making sure she had enough wood for her fire had been galvanising Judith for days. What's more, he'd not been nosy or judgemental about Judith's solitary life, the way most people seemed to be. And he'd not tried to get inside to see what her mansion looked like. Most casual callers were desperate to see if the interior of her house matched the grand exterior. But not Stefan. He'd been respectful, polite, and as soon as he'd seen that Judith was well-prepared for the coming snow, he had bidden her good day and left.

A good man, that's what he was, Judith thought to herself, and, for the hundredth time that morning, she found herself idly looking out of her window towards her neighbour's empty house.

There was a woman standing in Stefan's garden.

It took Judith a few moments to process what she was seeing.

There was a woman standing in Stefan's garden!

Judith jumped up, pencils clattering to the floor, strode over to her front door, threw her cape around her shoulders and dashed outside. *Who was she? What was she doing at Stefan's house?*

Marching through the thick grass of her garden, Judith stopped at the river's edge. The woman was standing on Stefan's lawn, turning slowly on the spot. It was as if she was trying to get a sense of where she was. She wore jeans and a dark T-shirt, and had a thick head of auburn hair. It was wild-looking and a bright copper colour. Like a pre-Raphaelite painting, Judith found herself thinking.

'Hello!' Judith called out from her garden.

The woman turned at the sound of Judith's voice.

'Hello!' Judith called out again. 'I'm Judith Potts, Stefan's neighbour. Can I help you?'

Judith's eyes weren't quite what they'd once been, so it was hard for her to make out the woman's features clearly, but she was pretty sure the woman looked panicked by her sudden appearance.

And then all doubt was removed as the auburn-haired woman turned and all but ran away.

'I only wanted to say hello!' Judith called after her, but it was too late. The woman had vanished around the side of Stefan's house.

Chapter 8

DS Tanika Malik was reading the ballistics report on Stefan Dunwoody's death when an officer rang through to tell her that a woman called Mrs Judith Potts was waiting in the reception area for her. DS Malik was briefly puzzled, but told the officer to take Mrs Potts to a meeting room and tell her she'd join her in a few minutes. There was a very pressing matter she needed to deal with first.

She picked up her phone and dialled the number at the top of the report.

'Are you saying the bullet that killed Mr Dunwoody was an antique?' she asked the forensic officer as soon as she was put through.

'That's right,' the woman on the other end of the line said.

'Are you sure?'

'The bullet we retrieved from Mr Dunwoody's skull was a 7.65 millimetres by 21 millimetre parabellum, and that's a very specific size that was only used up until the Second World War by the German armed forces.'

'Are you serious?'

'I'm afraid so. It was fired from a Second World War German Luger pistol.'

'And that would work, would it? A seventy-year-old bullet?'

'The Germans knew how to make pistols. Still do. Sure it would work.'

DS Malik thanked the officer for her help and hung up the call. One of the truisms of policing in the UK was how hard it was to lay your hands on a working handgun. It was just as hard to get hold of an antique gun that hadn't been decommissioned.

Unless you were an antique dealer, perhaps?

After her second conversation with Judith, DS Malik had rung Elliot Howard to follow up on her tip-off. Elliot had happily admitted that he had indeed had an argument with Stefan at the Henley Royal Regatta, but it had only been because Stefan was blocking his view. And although it had got rather heated, it had been six weeks ago, so it was all water under the bridge.

As for his movements on the night Stefan died, DS Malik knew that the pathologist's report had concluded that Stefan had been shot sometime between 7 p.m. and 10 p.m., so she'd asked Elliot where he'd been between those hours. He'd explained that he'd been at choir practice at All Saints' Church, then gone to the pub for a pint afterwards, and he hadn't left the pub until around 10 p.m.

DS Malik hadn't much liked Elliot's manner. He'd seemed too smooth, almost as if he'd been expecting her phone call and had prepared for it. In her experience, members of the public got flustered when they became part of an investigation, especially when it was to do with a possible murder. But a quick call to the vicar in Marlow confirmed Elliot's story. In fact, the vicar said that he'd gone to the pub with Elliot after choir practice as well, so he was able to say that he'd been in the same room as Elliot between the hours of seven and ten. And seeing as Elliot's alibi was the local vicar, DS Malik hadn't taken things any further.

But now she'd learned the murder weapon was an antique German pistol, was it perhaps worth revisiting him? Or was it just a coincidence? DS Malik tried to shake the thought. Stefan Dunwoody had taken his own life, it was the only thing that made sense. Even if he'd used an old pistol to do it.

Although, DS Malik thought to herself, there was still the mystery of the bronze medallion, wasn't there?

This was previously the only aspect of the case that had given DS Malik pause. When the divers had fished Stefan's body out of the river, they'd found a small medallion about the size of a two-pound coin attached by a silver chain to a buttonhole on Stefan's jacket. The medallion was clearly very old, a dull brown in colour, with a swirling pattern of leaves carved around the edge of it and the word 'Faith' carved across the middle. It was something of an anomaly, if only because none of her team had come across a medallion attached to a jacket like that before.

But an old religious symbol was hardly the sort of evidence they could use to build a murder case. Any more than they could use an antique German Luger.

On her way to see Judith, DS Malik stopped briefly at one of her constables' desks.

'Have we found the gun yet?'

'Not yet,' the officer replied. 'The divers completed their fingertip search of the riverbed this morning. They didn't find it.'

'Then what about in the pond?'

One of DS Malik's working theories was that Stefan had

perhaps stood on the brick dam that separated his pond from the river, shot himself in the head, and had then fallen backwards into the river while his gun had fallen forward into the pond.

'They've looked on the pond side of the wall as well. No gun.'

'They're sure about that?'

'They can't be one hundred per cent sure. Not unless we dredge the pond and river properly.'

'It may have to come to that.'

It was a very thoughtful DS Malik who finally met up with Judith.

'I'm sorry I kept you waiting,' DS Malik said as she sat down in the meeting room.

'Don't worry,' Judith said. 'I know you must be very busy. I won't take up any more of your time than I have to. But I've found a few things out and I think you should know. As a matter of some urgency.'

'Okay,' DS Malik said, getting out a notebook and pen. 'What do you want to tell me?'

Judith explained how she'd gone to Stefan's gallery and learned from his assistant Antonia Webster that Elliot Howard had visited Stefan at the beginning of the week before he'd died, that they'd had an argument, and that Antonia had heard Stefan tell Elliot that he had enough to go to the police.

DS Malik was surprised. Just as she'd ruled Elliot out from her enquiries, here he was popping up again.

'Mr Dunwoody said that, did he?' DS Malik asked.

'"I've got enough to go to the police." Those were his exact words to Elliot. According to Antonia. And later on, when Antonia spoke to Stefan about it, he said "desperation drives people to do stupid things".'

'He was suggesting that Elliot was desperate?'

'That's it exactly!'

'Although, what if he was referring to himself? Seeing as he possibly took his own life. His "desperation drives people to do stupid things" could have been a veiled reference that he was about to commit suicide.'

Judith threw her hands up in exasperation.

'You don't still believe it was suicide, do you?'

'It's a possible explanation.'

'I bet there wasn't a suicide note, was there?'

DS Malik frowned. The truth was, Judith was right. They'd found no suicide note on Stefan's body. Or in his house.

Thinking of Stefan's body reminded DS Malik of the bronze medallion they'd found, so she decided to do a bit of digging.

'Would you say Mr Dunwoody was a religious man?'

'I'm sorry?'

DS Malik explained how they'd found a medallion with the word 'Faith' carved into it attached to Stefan's jacket.

'You mean he wore it like a badge?'

'Yes. Something like that.'

'How was it attached to his jacket?'

'It was on a short chain looped through the middle buttonhole on his jacket.'

'Oh, like those badges they wear at rowing regattas.'

'That's right. Just like that.'

'I see. Well, I've no idea whether Stefan was particularly religious. I don't go to church that often, so I wouldn't know. But you've not answered my question. Did you find a suicide note?'

'I'm sorry, but I can't discuss operational details with a civilian.'

'Which is all I need to know that you *didn't* find a suicide note. Because he didn't take his own life. Elliot Howard killed him.'

'You really must stop saying that. Mr Howard can't have done it.'

'Oh, you mean because he was at choir practice?'

'How on earth do you know that?'

'After Antonia told me about the argument in his office, I went and talked to Elliot Howard.'

'You did *what*?!'

'I had to see him for myself.'

'Was that wise?'

'If we only did what was wise, nothing would ever get done, would it? Anyway, that's when he told me he'd been at choir practice when I heard the gunshot.'

'Yes, he said the same to me.'

'Oh, so you've spoken to him, have you?'

'I had to follow up on the lead after you'd told me about him.'

'I bet you didn't like him, did you?'

'What's that?'

'It's his tone, isn't it? Like he's playing with us.'

DS Malik was about to agree with Judith before she caught herself.

'Less of this "us" if you don't mind, Mrs Potts. I'm happy to talk to you as the witness who found the body, and because you knew the deceased. But you mustn't go around thinking you can do the work of the police.'

'Of course,' Judith said. 'That's your job, I completely understand. But tell me, have you found the gun yet?'

'What's that?'

'I imagine you've not, have you?'

DS Malik didn't immediately know what to say.

'You see! There's no suicide note and no gun! Because the murderer took it away with him afterwards. And even if Elliot

Howard was at choir practice when Stefan was killed, he's still involved. Somehow. I'm sure of it. Is it possible he hired a hitman?'

'I don't think that's likely.'

'But it's a possibility, isn't it?'

'Mrs Potts, Marlow's won the "Best in Bloom" prize every year for the last seven years. And the last time I was called to an incident there, it was because two swans were taking a walk down the High Street and had stopped the traffic. I can promise you, there are no hitmen in Marlow.'

The door banged open and an out-of-breath police officer stuck his head into the room.

'Sarge, a guy's just been shot dead in Marlow.'

Chapter 9

The murder had happened in a bungalow on the Wycombe Road, a perfectly ordinary street that linked Marlow to High Wycombe with suburban houses on both sides and smart hedges and cars on driveways.

Once she arrived, DS Malik got out and saw a squad car already at the scene, lights flashing. It was parked on the driveway next to a white van and an old Prius that she could see had a taxi's licence plates.

There was a male police constable guarding the front door.

DS Malik took a deep breath to steady herself. The truth was that she wouldn't normally head up a case this serious. After all, she was only a detective sergeant. But her boss, Detective Inspector Gareth Hoskins, had signed himself off work with a stress-related illness three weeks before, and DS Malik was therefore the Acting Senior Investigating Officer. Just as she was the Acting SIO in the Stefan Dunwoody case.

DS Malik had spent the previous three weeks reading and re-reading her copy of Blackstone's *Senior Investigating Officers' Handbook* on the off chance that a big case might land in her lap. But she knew that it was one thing to be 'book smart', it was quite another to put her knowledge into practice in the real world.

Just follow the rules and regulations, she said to herself as she approached the front door of the cottage. *Just follow the rules and regulations.*

'Good morning, Constable,' she said with a confidence she didn't feel. 'So what have we got?'

The constable explained how the dead man inside the house was called Iqbal Kassam. He lived on his own and was a taxi driver.

'Who discovered the body?'

The constable said that a young delivery driver had arrived with a package for Mr Kassam, but when he'd got to the door, he'd seen that it was already open. So he'd stepped into the hallway to put the package on the side table, which was when he'd seen into the bedroom where Mr Kassam was lying, blood all over the pillows, stone-cold dead.

'I see. Tell me about the delivery person who found the body.'

'He's pretty shaken up.'

'Could he be our shooter?'

'We've taken his clothes in for GSR analysis, but I think the body's been there a few hours.' He nodded at the van in the driveway. 'There's a tracking device in that. He was able to show me his route this morning. He'd been nowhere near Marlow until 12.37 p.m., which is when he found the body and called it in.'

'See if you can speak to the other people he made deliveries to this morning. Let's make sure his story stacks up.'

'Yes, Sarge.'

DS Malik pulled out a pair of crime scene gloves and put them on.

'What about the scene?' she asked.

'No signs of a break-in. No signs of a struggle, either. Or any kind of theft as far as we can tell. The body's in the bedroom with a bullet through its skull.'

'Okay,' she said, 'let's see Mr Kassam.'

Once inside, DS Malik took a moment to check her surroundings. The bungalow was modest, the mismatched furniture looked like it had all come from a second-hand shop, but it was tidy and clean. Far tidier, DS Malik knew, than her husband would keep a house if he lived on his own. She saw a little bookcase by the front door that was crammed with books on boats and sailing. There was also a bronze statue on the hall table that depicted an old-fashioned ship under full sail.

The constable coughed and nodded towards an open doorway to the side of the entrance lobby. She went over, entered, and saw a man she presumed was Mr Kassam lying in a double bed, blood all over his face and drenched into his pillows and sheets.

DS Malik approached the body and saw a blister pack of pills, a half-empty glass of water and a leather-bound copy of the Quran on the bedside table. She picked up the pills. They were a brand called Diphenazine.

'I looked them up,' the constable said from the doorway. 'They're prescription sleeping pills.'

'Thank you,' DS Malik said, putting them down and making a mental note to check Mr Kassam's medical history with his GP.

Looking at the body, she could see that Mr Kassam appeared to be in his thirties, had a thick black beard and curly black hair. He also had a bullet hole in the centre of his forehead, and the back of his head had been blown off, blood, bone and brain spread out in a shocking mess of gore on the pillow.

A shiver ran through DS Malik's body.

This was her second gunshot death in three days.

And the second bullet fired into the centre of a forehead.

But DS Malik knew that now was not the time for speculation. Initially her job as Acting SIO was to 'identify, secure and preserve' the scene. Theorising could come later. So she made herself focus on the physical evidence in front of her.

The constable had been right. There were no signs of a struggle. The duvet was tucked up neatly under the victim's chin, his arms still to his sides underneath. He'd not kicked out in any way.

This wasn't just a murder, it was an execution.

A high-pitched whine and scratching noise started up somewhere in the house. Like an animal in pain.

'What's that?' she asked.

'No idea,' the constable said, nonplussed.

DS Malik headed back into the sitting room. The strange keening sound was louder here. It seemed to be coming from behind a set of curtains. DS Malik pulled them back to reveal French doors that led onto a little walled garden.

There was a sleek-looking Dobermann pinscher dog outside on the grass, whining. The poor creature looked distressed, but DS Malik knew that Dobermanns could be vicious. How could she secure and process the scene with a dog like that in the garden?

'Sarge,' the constable said, entering the room from the main door. 'I think there's a woman outside spying on us.'

'What's that?'

'There's a woman in the garden hiding behind a bush.'

'Okay, keep the scene secure,' DS Malik said and left the house at speed.

Outside, it took her eyes a few seconds to adjust to the sunshine, but she could see that a laurel hedge separated Iqbal's front garden from the street, and there were a few bushes near a little gate that led onto the pavement. A bush snapped back and DS Malik saw a flash of clothing as someone went out of the gate and disappeared behind the hedge.

As DS Malik strode after the figure, she reached into her handbag and put her hand around a little extendable truncheon.

'Excuse me?' she called out as she stepped into the street.

The person slowed to a stop and turned to look at DS Malik.

DS Malik let go of the truncheon and took her hand out of her handbag as she saw that she was talking to a very solid-looking woman who was about fifty years old. She had ruddy, sunburnt cheeks and was wearing dirty walking boots, a tatty, wide-brimmed hat, and various little bags and frayed dog leads hung off a belt tied tight around her waist. A jolly farmer type, DS Malik thought to herself.

'Me?' the woman said, pointing at herself as though she was the last person in the world DS Malik would want to talk to.

'That's right. You've been spying on us.'

The woman put her hand to her chest in another show of mock surprise and this time mouthed the word 'Me?'

'Could you please tell me your name?'

'Sure. No problem. But why do you want to know?'

'Just tell me your name.'

The woman thought for a bit. Looked up at the sky. Wrinkled her nose. Basically, she had a good rummage around for an answer.

'Okay. My name's Denise.'

DS Malik could see that the woman was lying.

'It is?'

'That's right,' the woman said with a confident nod of her head.

'And your surname?'

'My surname?'

'Yes.'

'I'm Denise . . . Denison.'

'Your name is Denise Denison?'

'Yup,' the woman said and beamed, delighted with her cunning.

'You think I'm going to believe that?'

'Of course. It's like I said. I'm Denise Denison.'

'Then I'm going to make this very simple for you. My name's Detective Sergeant Tanika Malik, I'm at this property investigating a suspicious death, and you need to tell me your real name at once or I'll place you under arrest.'

This got through to the woman.

'You're not saying Iqbal's . . . dead? Are you?'

'So you know Mr Kassam?'

'Yes, yes I do. And I'm Suzie Harris,' she said, all attempts at subterfuge forgotten. 'I live at 14 Oakwood Drive.'

'Thank you, but why didn't you tell me your real name the first time around?'

'You never tell the Old Bill your real name,' Suzie said, as though it were a truth universally acknowledged.

DS Malik sighed.

'Can you tell me when you last saw Mr Kassam?' she asked.

Suzie took a moment to gather her thoughts.

'Yesterday, I think. When I came to walk Emma. That's his Dobermann. You see, Iqbal works nights. Sometimes. As a taxi driver. So I give Emma a once-around-the-block every morning.'

'Can you tell me why you were hiding behind a bush in his garden?'

'That was only because I saw the police car. I wanted to know

what was going on. But are you serious? You're telling me he's
dead? He can't be. What happened?'

DS Malik didn't want to share any details, but she knew that
in any murder there was a 'Golden Hour' immediately after the
investigation started when the chances of catching the killer were
at their highest. There was no one else who lived with Mr Kassam
to talk to, and she could see that there was only one neighbouring
property, and the garden was overgrown, the curtains drawn,
and there was a 'For Sale' board up by the pavement. There was
no one living there.

Suzie was currently the only witness they had who had even
remotely known the deceased. So DS Malik explained how it
looked as though an intruder had got into Mr Kassam's house
and shot him while he slept.

'But that's not possible,' Suzie said, once she'd absorbed the
news.

'Why not?'

'Iqbal was about the nicest person in the world. Ask anyone
who knew him. He was kind, he never lost his temper. All he
wanted to do was earn enough money to buy himself a nice boat
he could keep on the river.'

DS Malik remembered the sailing books and the little statue
of an old sailing ship in the house.

'Then what about family? Do you know who his next of kin
might be?'

'No idea. But he was from Bradford originally, that's what he
told me. And he spent some of his childhood in Marlow. That's
why he ended up back here.'

'Do you have any contact details for his family?'

'I think his parents died some time ago. And he was an only
child.'

'So he's got no immediate family?'

'I don't know. There'll be cousins, I suppose. Maybe. Somewhere.'

'One last thing. You say you walked Mr Kassam's dog every morning?'

'That's right.'

'So you have a key to Mr Kassam's property?'

'No way, you're not putting that on me. Iqbal was security conscious. Very. I could only access his garden, and I did it through there.'

Suzie pointed to a gate in between Mr Kassam's bungalow and the empty property that was for sale next door.

'You're sure he never gave you a key?'

'Quite sure, thank you.'

'Then can I ask, where have you been this morning?'

'Well, one of my clients picked up her black labs from me at about eight o'clock. I've been looking after them overnight. But since then, I've been at home.'

'Was anyone with you?'

'No. I live on my own. And if I was involved in any way in whatever happened here, do you think I'd turn up at Iqbal's house right after the police? You might think I'm stupid, but I'm not that stupid.'

A grey van with a satellite dish on the roof pulled up on the street outside the house and DS Malik's shoulders sagged. How did the press find out about a crime so quickly? She'd have to get the constable to see them off, but she was also aware that she had to get Mr Kassam's dog off the premises.

'Okay, then I've got two favours to ask. Firstly, would you take Mr Kassam's dog in for us? Just until we can find someone who's happy to look after her more permanently.'

'Sure. I'll look after Emma. What's the other favour?'

'That's the local press over there,' DS Malik said, indicating a reporter and camera operator getting their equipment from the back of the van. 'I'd appreciate it if you didn't speak to them.'

'Then you've nothing to worry about. My lips are sealed.'

'Thank you.'

DS Malik accompanied Suzie down the side of the house, and saw how happily Mr Kassam's dog welcomed her. Suzie also made a great play of fussing Emma; it was clear her connection with the dog was natural and authentic.

Once Suzie had left with Emma on a lead, DS Malik headed back inside and returned to the body. If it wasn't for the blood everywhere, Mr Kassam could well have been asleep. And the bullet hole in the centre of his head of course. It was clearly murder, but was Judith right? Was this the *second* murder? It didn't seem possible, but there was no denying the similarities between the two deaths.

DS Malik was about to turn away when the sunlight through the window flashed on something inside Iqbal's mouth. She'd not seen it the first time as his mouth was almost completely closed.

'Constable, have you got a light there?'

The constable came over with a torch.

'Could you shine it at the victim's mouth?'

The constable did so. There was a faint glow as it shone on a small object inside. What was it?

DS Malik reached in and carefully pulled out a short silver chain.

On the end of it was a small bronze medallion with flowery swirls carved into the edges. It looked identical to the medallion they'd found on Stefan's body. It even had a word carved across the front. But this time the word wasn't 'Faith', it was 'Hope'.

Understanding came to DS Malik in an ice-cold rush.

Judith Potts was right.

Stefan had been murdered. With a bullet to the centre of the forehead. The killer had then struck again by murdering Iqbal in exactly the same way. And then he'd left a bronze medallion behind at the second scene just as he'd done at the first.

But this wasn't the end of it, DS Malik knew. Because the old saying was 'Faith, Hope and Charity', wasn't it? With the first two killings they'd had 'Faith' and 'Hope', but they hadn't had 'Charity' yet, had they?

The message from the killer couldn't have been any clearer.

This wasn't going to be the end of it.

There was going to be a third murder.

Chapter 10

Judith was fizzing with excitement when she got home. Who was this second person who'd been shot in Marlow? She decided she'd only have a short wait until the local television bulletin came on after the six o'clock news. It was bound to be featured. But until then, what should she do?

Judith looked at all of the old newspapers, periodicals and magazines that lay littered around her drawing room. The mess was getting untenable, she knew. And as she looked at the piles of paper, her fingers went to the chain she wore around her neck day and night. As she pulled out the key that was on the end, her eyes slipped to the door to the side of her drinks table. She couldn't stop herself from looking. And thinking.

After a long moment, she shoved the key back down the neckline of her blouse. She had to keep herself busy, that was the answer. It was always the answer. So she went over to her dining table where she had an unfinished jigsaw puzzle. Yes, that would suit her much better, she decided. It was safe. Achievable. Just diverting enough but no more.

The puzzle she'd been working on depicted a West Highland terrier in a tartan waistcoat standing in front of Edinburgh Castle, not that Judith liked West Highland terriers, and she was *very* sure she didn't like West Highland terriers in tartan waistcoats. But she bought all of her jigsaw puzzles from the charity shops in Marlow and took them back once she'd completed them, so she'd just been grateful to find a puzzle she'd not done before.

The task absorbed Judith all afternoon, but by 6 p.m. she realised she was feeling peckish. She'd recently been trying to shift a bit of weight, so she decided she'd have a poached egg on a single slice of toast for her tea. Then again, there was no way that one egg would ever be enough, so she had two eggs and plenty of butter on two slices of toast. And a few oven chips 'to fill in the corners' of her hunger, seeing as the rest of the meal was so healthy. And a nice cup of sweet tea and one of those super-tiny bars of speciality chocolate for her pudding, although she'd not been able to find one of the tiny bars when she'd done her weekly shop, so she'd bought herself a family size fruit-and-nut bar. Not that she'd finish it in one sitting, of course. It would easily last her the rest of the week.

Judith was just finishing the last square of chocolate when the local news started on her TV, and she was thrilled to see that the murder in Marlow had top billing. Putting her lap tray to one side, she grabbed a sharpened pencil from her crossword table and a pad of graph paper. On it she was then able to record the basic details: the victim was a local taxi driver called Iqbal Kassam who had apparently been shot that morning, and the police were asking for witnesses to come forward. It wasn't much, Judith thought, but then she saw a brief interview with a woman who was filmed leaving the property with a Dobermann on a lead.

'I'm not allowed to talk to you,' the woman announced to the camera, but Judith could also see that she was delighted by the attention she was getting and desperately wanted to spill the beans.

'But are you a friend of Mr Kassam's?' the interviewer asked.

'My lips are sealed. You won't hear a peep from me. Although I'll tell you this much. Whoever did this to Iqbal deserves stringing up from the nearest lamppost. Come on, Emma.'

The woman walked off and Judith realised she recognised her. Not that she'd ever spoken to her before, but the woman often walked various dogs in the fields along the Thames Path that ran behind her house. She was a local dog walker, wasn't she? And if she'd been visiting Mr Kassam's house, then maybe she knew him well?

Judith went over to her sideboard and poured herself a dash of whisky. An evening glass of whisky was a ritual Judith had picked up from her great aunt Betty when she'd first moved into the house to nurse her through her ill health. That's how her great aunt would usher in every evening, with a splash of Scotch in a heavy cut-glass tumbler. It was medicinal, she'd say, going further and explaining that she'd never had a cold since she'd started taking a glass of whisky each evening. After Betty had died, Judith felt it only good manners to pour herself a small glass of Scotch each night. To honour her aunt. And anyway, what could be so bad about gently sipping barely an inch of something so organic and natural as Scotch?

As Judith took her first warming sip, she decided on a plan of action. She needed to talk to this woman who knew Mr Kassam.

Judith downed the rest of the whisky in one.

And poured herself another. It helped her think.

The following morning, Judith made herself a thermos of strong tea and some beetroot sandwiches that she wrapped in brown paper, then went for a walk along the Thames. The sun was already high in the sky, and she couldn't help but feel uplifted. On her side of the river, cows cropped idly at the grass, and on the other, the land swept upwards to Winter Hill, a thickly wooded ridge that ran all the way between Marlow and the pretty village of Cookham. What Judith loved most about this particular walk was how there was always activity on the river. Whether it was a local school's rowing eight scything at thrilling speed through the water; or a self-regarding older gent driving his motor launch like it was a Volvo estate; or maybe a feathery clutch of cygnets following their mummy in a line on the water.

The pathway was similarly busy, with teenagers splashing in little coves that had been created by the cows' nightly trips down to the river to drink; families on bicycle rides, everyone wearing sensible safety helmets; and every field always had its share of people letting their dogs off the lead so they could run wild.

Judith had a favourite spot in the shade of a weeping willow, so she swished off her cape, laid it down and sat on it to wait with her tea and sandwiches. She'd not brought a book, or indeed any of her crossword work to be getting on with, as she knew she'd be busy enough taking in the scene. Within a few minutes, her focus had drifted until all she was aware of was the ticking of a grasshopper nearby, and the sun warming her body, seemingly right down to her bones. It was bliss.

Judith's reverie was broken by the arrival of a pack of dogs who were barking, tumbling over each other and generally running riot. Judith was thrilled to see the woman who'd been interviewed on the news after Mr Kassam's death walking with the dogs. Just as she'd hoped.

Now all she had to do was get up, which was easier said than done at her age. With a grunt, Judith used a tree root for purchase and levered herself up off the ground, her knees finally unlocking and allowing her to stand. Bloody hell, she thought to herself. If she had one piece of advice she'd give her younger self, it would be: don't get old.

Judith picked up her cape, flapped it to get rid of the loose grass, put it on, and headed over. As she got closer, Judith could see that the woman seemed to have a very solid quality to her. It was the way she stood with her feet so firmly planted to the ground, Judith thought to herself. Like a general surveying her troops. Or a captain standing at the bridge of an old schooner. Yes, Judith decided, that was it. With her wide-brimmed hat, heavy walking boots and criss-crossed dog leads around her body that she wore like bandoliers, the woman had a faintly nautical look. Piratical, even.

'Good morning,' Judith called out as she approached.

'Good morning,' Suzie said with a friendly smile. 'I know you, you're that woman who lives in that mansion along the river from here, aren't you?'

'You know me?'

'I've been walking past your house for years. If I'm honest, I've always wanted to see inside.'

The woman chuckled at the thought, but Judith was baffled. What a strange thing to say to a complete stranger.

'I'm Judith Potts.'

'Suzie Harris.'

The women lapsed into companionable silence, both of them watching the dogs run in and out of the river.

'Lovely dogs,' Judith said.

'Aren't they? You know where you are with dogs.'

'I must confess I'm more of a cat person myself.'

'Cats?' Suzie said, in the same way that Captain Ahab might have said, 'Whales?' 'Can't say I agree with you there at all. They're always judging you, cats.'

'They are?'

'Dogs aren't like that. They're loyal. They don't let you down.'

'Yes. I suppose so. Look, I hope you don't mind me talking to you, but our meeting isn't entirely accidental.'

'It isn't?'

'I saw you on the TV last night. You knew that poor man who was shot, didn't you?'

'You mean Iqbal?'

'That's right.'

'I knew him very well,' Suzie said. 'I saw him most days. Did you know him?'

'Sadly not. But the thing is, I think my neighbour Stefan Dunwoody was murdered last week, and I'm trying to work out if Iqbal's murder is related.'

Suzie looked about herself to check they were on their own, which she already knew they were as they were the only two people in the field.

'Are you for real?' she whispered in delight.

'I'm sorry?'

'You're investigating your neighbour's *murder*?'

'That's right.'

'Well, I think you should go for it. Amazing. I love it.'

With a broad smile, Suzie went back to looking at the dogs. They were dashing in and out of the river, and she smiled at the sight.

Judith waited for Suzie to say more.

She didn't.

'So do you think they could be?' Judith asked again.

'What's that?'

'Could they be linked? The two murders?'

'Oh, of course!' Suzie said, remembering. 'Sorry, I got distracted.'

Suzie pulled out an old tin from a pouch on her belt, got out a pack of tobacco and some liquorice papers, and started rolling herself a cigarette.

'I know. Why don't you tell me *everything*? Go on.'

Judith launched into the story of how she'd heard Stefan being shot, later found his body, and then worked out that Elliot Howard was a possible suspect, even though he had an alibi for the time of the murder.

'That's amazing.'

'I know.'

'But you think Elliot Howard's the killer?'

'You know him?'

'I've lived here my whole life. I know everyone.'

'Then what can you tell me about him?'

'He's very tall, isn't he?'

Judith agreed with this statement and then waited for Suzie's next insight.

'And he's got all that lovely hair,' she added after a bit more thought.

This wasn't exactly the deep background Judith had been looking for.

'Do you remember the last time you spoke to him?'

'I don't think I've ever spoken to him, now you mention it. But he lives in that new house up at the end of Gypsy Lane, I know that much. That's something, isn't it?'

Judith tried not to let her frustration show.

'Well, that's very interesting. Can you tell me, do you have any idea why Iqbal might have been killed?'

'None at all.'

'Is it possible he was up to no good?'

Suzie picked a thread of tobacco from her teeth and flicked it away.

'No way. Iqbal was as honest as they come. You see that dog in the river?' Suzie nodded at Emma as she swam in the cooling waters. 'She's Iqbal's Dobermann.'

'He had a Dobermann?' Judith asked, knowing the reputation of the breed.

'I'm not having any of that. Dobermanns are the best. I mean, they're guard dogs. They can be dangerous if you don't introduce them to people properly. Or they think their owner is under threat. Or anyone they know for that matter. So yes, don't get on the wrong side of a Dobermann pinscher or they'll tear your arm off, and the females are more vicious than the males if you ask me, but Emma's the sweetest dog you'll ever meet.'

Judith waited for Suzie to continue. She didn't.

'And Emma is Iqbal's dog?' Judith prompted.

'Damned right she is,' Suzie said, her engines firing up again. 'But not originally. First of all she belonged to his neighbour, an old guy named Ezra. Ezra Harrington, I think. But Ezra got cancer last year, poor man. And he lived on his own. So if Ezra needed to go to the hospital, or pick up any medication, Iqbal took him in his taxi and never charged him. All out of the goodness of his heart. I mean, I wouldn't have done it for any of my neighbours, and I've known them for years!'

Judith smiled politely, not quite finding Suzie's joke as funny as she did.

'Anyway, things got bad for Ezra. He only had months left to live. Weeks. And he was in a panic because he didn't know who'd look after his dog when he died. So Iqbal, who I can tell you, didn't know the first thing about dogs, said he'd take Emma in. And that's what he did. He took Emma in when Ezra died. This was last year. And anyone else would have got rid of Emma as soon as they could. That's what I'd have done. But the way Iqbal put it to me, he'd made a promise to a dying man, he couldn't break it. So, Emma became Iqbal's dog. And seeing as Dobermanns needs a lot of exercise, he got me in every day to walk her. When Iqbal was asleep after working nights. And that's all you need to know about Iqbal. There's no way he could be mixed up in anything dodgy. He was nothing less than a saint.'

'Even so, someone had reason to shoot him dead.'

'Doesn't mean it had anything to do with Iqbal.'

'It must have had *something* to do with him.'

'That's not how I see it. What I'm thinking is, he's a taxi driver. He could have had some criminal in the back of his car and overheard something. Or seen something. And this criminal, whoever he was, realised Iqbal could put him in prison. Or whatever, I don't know the details. So he heads over to Iqbal's house and rubs him out.'

Judith realised that, for all her bluster, Suzie had a point.

'Yes, perhaps you're right. Maybe Iqbal saw something bad in his line of work. Although it rather begs the question, what on earth's going on in Marlow that's worth killing over?'

Suzie chortled huskily, took one last drag on her cigarette and then threw it away.

'Oh there's plenty of wrongdoing going on. Don't be fooled by the nice front gardens and smart cars.'

'You think so?'

'I've been a dog walker the best part of three decades, and I can tell you, people around here are wicked.'

There was a finality to Suzie's pronouncement that surprised Judith.

'Emma, no!' Suzie suddenly shouted, looking over as Emma the Dobermann started to chase down a Dachshund that was part of the group. Having caught the tiny dog, she grabbed it by the neck.

'Put Arnold down!' Suzie yelled, running towards the two dogs. 'Sorry, got to go,' Suzie called back to Judith as she ran after the Dobermann again. 'Emma, no! Put Arnold down!'

As soon as Suzie had left, Judith went over to the cigarette that she'd dropped and stepped on it to stop it from smouldering. With the sort of heatwave they'd been having, it could have started a grass fire.

She then took a moment to consider what she'd learned and realised that it hadn't been very much, although Suzie had been right about one thing. It was very possible that Iqbal had overheard or seen something in his taxi and that's why he'd later been killed.

Judith decided that she could do with a good think and a walk, so she carried on in the direction of Marlow. Passing through a couple of fields, she was soon in Higginson Park, where she briefly stopped to watch the children running around the playground like tiny hooligans. She loved their energy and joie de vivre.

She then carried on past the church and entered a field on the other side of town. In the distance she saw a woman walking towards her. She was a good way away, but Judith could see that she had red hair a bit like the auburn-haired woman she'd seen in Stefan's garden the day before. But then, as the woman got nearer, Judith realised something with a jolt.

It wasn't just someone who looked like the woman from Stefan's garden, it was the same woman!

Judith waved her arms and called, 'Hello!' across the field.

The red-haired woman stopped in her tracks.

'Hold on a second!' Judith called and started striding towards her.

The red-haired woman turned on her heels and ran out of the field.

Judith started to run as well, but the other woman was much younger, and although Judith's regime of swimming and cycling meant she was fit for her age, her legs weren't very long, and the grass was high, so she struggled to close the distance on the woman before she'd clanged back out through the metal gate again.

Judith reached the gate half a minute later, yanked it open and stepped into a little gravel car park. There were a dozen or so cars parked up, but where was the red-haired woman?

A maroon-coloured car pulled out of a parking space with a squeal of tyres, and Judith caught a flash of bronze hair as the driver drove away at speed, the old car briefly backfiring as it belched fumes from the exhaust.

Why had the woman run away from her a second time?

But it wasn't just that. There was something else as well. Now that she'd seen her at closer quarters, Judith knew that she recognised the woman. She'd spoken to her before. Or knew her from Marlow somehow. But she couldn't place the memory. Where had they met?

Judith racked her brain, but, to her frustration, the auburn-haired woman's identity remained tantalisingly out of reach.

Chapter 11

At work the next morning, DS Malik was feeling deeply frustrated. The local press were giving extensive coverage to Iqbal's murder, and she feared it would be only a matter of time before they found out that Stefan Dunwoody had also been murdered. As her Superintendent kept telling her, the clock was ticking.

But DS Malik and her team couldn't find a single person who might have had a motive to kill Iqbal Kassam. It was as the dog walker Suzie Harris had said. Iqbal was entirely blameless, or so it seemed. Their door-to-door enquiries also drew a blank. None of the people on his street remembered hearing a gunshot on the morning that Iqbal was killed, or saw anyone suspicious lurking nearby or entering or leaving Iqbal's property. And yet, someone had got into his bungalow and shot him dead.

DS Malik had briefly been excited when she'd discovered that Iqbal logged every taxi journey he'd made in an electronic diary. It was a complete list of customers, their contact details and times and dates. But as her team started contacting the people who'd used his services, all they heard was what a great guy Iqbal had been. He'd been upbeat, reliable and honest. What was more, there were a number of stories about how Iqbal was happy to go the extra mile, quite literally at times. And he didn't always charge for a journey if the passenger was in extremis or didn't have enough money.

Financial checks painted a similar picture of probity and hard work. Iqbal declared all his earnings, wasn't a big spender, had no credit card or store card debt, and he even gave 10 per cent of his income to charity. Despite this generosity, he lived so modestly that when he died he had nearly £23,000 in his bank account. Apparently Iqbal had been saving to buy a boat to keep on the Thames at Marlow. He'd been well on the way to that dream when he'd died.

As for the autopsy, the preliminary results showed he'd had no alcohol in his system when he'd died, although there'd been significant traces of Diphenazine, the brand of sleeping pills they'd found in Iqbal's bedroom. However, the dosage was well within safe limits. As far as the forensic toxicologist was concerned, it would have been enough to make Iqbal woozy but no more. Nonetheless, as it was a prescription drug, DS Malik rang Iqbal's GP, who confirmed that Mr Kassam had asked for help with sleeping the year before. He'd been working a lot of nights and he was struggling to sleep during the day.

This information gave DS Malik pause. After all, there'd been no break-in before the murder, or signs of a struggle for that matter. So, the fact that Iqbal was shot in bed while drugged on sleeping pills made it very unlikely that he'd got up to let the killer in.

This theory was given further credence by the pathologist's

assertion that Iqbal had died between 5 and 6 a.m. This fitted with Iqbal's diary, which showed that he'd been working until 3 a.m. on the night of his death. It seemed most likely that he'd come off shift at 3 a.m., got home, gone to bed, found he couldn't sleep and taken a dose of sleeping pills to help him on his way. Then the killer had let himself into Iqbal's house with a spare key and killed him sometime between 5 and 6 a.m.

But if the killer had a spare key, then that suggested that Iqbal had considered him a close and trusted friend. After all, Iqbal hadn't been prepared to give a spare key to his dog walker.

But no matter how hard DS Malik and her team hunted, there was nothing in Iqbal's diary, emails, phone and financial records or more general correspondence that suggested he had any regular friends. In fact, DS Malik and her team struggled to find anyone who knew him at all. As Suzie had told them, Iqbal was an only child and his parents had died many years ago.

There were only two meaningful leads.

Firstly there was the bronze medallion with the word 'Hope' written on it that they'd found in Iqbal's mouth. It had no fingerprints on it. Just as the medallion they'd found attached to Stefan's coat had had no fingerprints on it when they'd tested it.

But the medallions were clearly part of the same set. The bronze had burnished with age to the same patina, the leaves carved into the edges were similar, and the script used for the words 'Faith' and 'Hope' was identical.

Secondly, if the medallions suggested the two deaths were linked, the ballistics report removed all doubt. The bullet that killed Iqbal had been fired by the same gun that had been used to kill Stefan.

A Second World War German Luger pistol.

It made no sense to DS Malik. Why would someone want to kill an art dealer and then a taxi driver? And where could the killer have even got an antique German Luger from? It was as she asked herself this question that DS Malik once again noticed that there was a person involved in the case who might know the answer.

'You want to know how to get hold of an antique pistol?' Elliot Howard said once DS Malik had explained why she was phoning him. 'What a peculiar question.'

'Are they easy to get hold of?'

'It depends. There's certainly a trade in old weaponry, from halberds, maces and so on through to more recent memorabilia. But can I ask, do you mean a decommissioned pistol? One that's had its firing mechanism removed? After all, it's only legal to sell antique guns that have been decommissioned.'

DS Malik could hear an easeful glide in Elliot's voice, and she found herself wondering if Judith had been right. Was he *enjoying* himself?

'Do you sell such weapons?' she asked.

'We have a military memorabilia auction twice a year.'

'And all of your weapons have been decommissioned.'

'Of course. Or they wouldn't be legal.'

'Is it possible you've ever sold an antique pistol that hadn't been decommissioned? By mistake?'

'Impossible. We have a military expert who checks all the lots thoroughly before we put them up for auction. If we're ever offered a working pistol, we refuse to have anything to do with it and report it to the police. But why are you asking me about decommissioned pistols?'

'Because we've discovered evidence of one that hasn't been decommissioned.'

'Then I can tell you, it didn't pass through my auction house.'

'So where could it have come from?'

'Online, I'd imagine. There's a whole black market out there for historical weaponry. Mostly driven by re-enactors and fantasists, in my opinion. But you can buy functional antique pistols if you look hard enough, and there are plenty of people who offer advice on how to recommission old guns. So I imagine there's any number of ways of getting hold of a working antique pistol if you try hard enough.'

'I see. Then can I ask you something else?'

'Go ahead,' Elliot said. 'Always happy to help the police.'

'If I said "faith" and "hope" to you, what would say?'

'Well, "charity", as I'm sure anyone would.'

'And does that phrase mean anything to you?'

'"Faith, hope and charity"? It's a saying, isn't it? From the bible, I suppose. I can't say it has any special meaning for me.'

'It's from the first book of Corinthians, chapter thirteen, verse thirteen. But "Faith, hope and charity" is the old-fashioned translation of the text from the King James Bible. In modern versions, the phrase is "Faith, hope and love".'

'Is it indeed? You learn something new every day. Now is there anything else I can help you with?'

'One last question. Could you tell me where you were yesterday morning between five and six a.m.?'

'Where was I between five and six yesterday morning?'

'That's right.'

'Are you being serious?'

'If you could just answer the question.'

'I was in the same place I always am between those hours. I was in bed. Fast asleep.'

'Have you any way of proving that?'

'That I was asleep? You could ask my wife, Daisy, but I imagine she was asleep as well.'

'So you *can't* prove you were in bed?'

'Of course not, any more than I'm sure you can. I, like you, and pretty much everyone else in this country, was asleep in my bed between five and six yesterday morning. Now, are we done?'

DS Malik was pleased to hear an edge of irritation finally enter Elliot's voice, so she agreed that they were indeed done, thanked him for his time and hung up, and took a moment to replay the conversation in her head. Once again Elliot had seemed mostly unfazed by her line of questioning, but there was one thing she felt was significant. When she'd asked for his whereabouts between 5 and 6 a.m. on the morning that Iqbal had been murdered, he'd given his answer without asking why she wanted to know. In DS Malik's experience, nearly everyone when asked for their movements at certain times responded by asking why the police wanted to know. It was simple human nature. They were curious. But Elliot hadn't been.

And yet DS Malik knew it was all very well thinking that Elliot's manner was suspicious, but the truth was she and her team hadn't been able to find any reference to Elliot Howard anywhere in Iqbal's life. There were no phone calls. No emails. No texts. No taxi rides. And without any kind of evidence, she couldn't possibly spare the resources to investigate him further.

DS Malik checked her watch. Back home, she knew her husband would be sitting on the sofa, snuggling with their gorgeous daughter watching movies. The washing up from tea would still be in the sink, the piles of dirty clothes she'd separated out into piles of whites, darks and mixed would still be sitting on the upstairs landing, and no homework would have been done or packed lunches prepared for tomorrow. She'd have to do all that when she got back. She'd also agreed to pop in on her dad on the way home. He'd phoned earlier to remind her that his boiler was broken, and what sort of daughter would let an old man not have hot water to wash in?

With a start, DS Malik realised a constable had entered her office.

'Sorry,' she said. 'Drifted off there. What have you got?'

'I've had a call from the *Daily Mirror*. They're saying they know that Iqbal's the killer's second victim, the first was Stefan Dunwoody.'

DS Malik sighed. She'd hoped she'd have a few more days before the national press got involved.

'Did they mention anything about German Lugers or bronze medallions?'

'Not in their call to me.'

'Then we can be thankful for that. What did you tell them?'

'The usual. I wouldn't talk to anyone about an ongoing investigation, and if they had any questions they should direct them to the Press Office.'

Tanika's phone started ringing. It was the press officer for the Thames Valley police. She steeled herself as she answered the call.

It was going to be a long night.

Chapter 12

Judith was sitting in her favourite wingback chair nursing a small glass of whisky when the doorbell rang. She tutted to herself. The whole point of living on your own was that you didn't have to share your home with anyone.

Judith went to her front door, opened it and was surprised to see Becks Starling, the vicar's wife, standing there.

'I hope you don't mind me calling on you?' Becks said.

'No, of course not, but how did you know where I live?'

'Everyone knows where you live.'

Judith harrumphed. First, that Suzie woman had claimed to know where she lived, and now it turned out that another complete stranger knew as well. People in Marlow were so nosy!

'And I know I shouldn't have come around,' Becks continued. 'Particularly so late in the day, but I wanted to speak to you, and we had drinks after evensong tonight, and then I had to do dinner for the family. And the washing up. This is the first chance I've had to get away all day.'

'Is it to do with Elliot Howard?'

'It is.'

'Then you'd better come in,' Judith said, stepping to one side.

As Becks entered the house, Judith paused briefly on the threshold. She couldn't remember the last time she'd voluntarily invited someone into her house. What surprised her was how natural it felt. How easy it had been. Life was full of surprises, she thought to herself.

As for Becks, once she was inside, she couldn't help but be impressed by the faded grandeur of the house, from the grand piano in the oak-panelled hallway to the ancient oil paintings on the walls. But she also noticed that the air was thick with dust; piles of old newspapers and magazines covered just about every surface; crockery and empty glasses littered side tables and windowsills; and, most surprisingly of all, it appeared as though a grey bra was hanging from the shade of an old standard lamp.

Becks sneezed.

'Sorry,' she said, whipping out a fresh hankie from her sleeve. 'I've got a bit of an allergy to dust. Actually, I'm really quite allergic to it.'

'Then you wouldn't last a minute in this house,' Judith said with a complete lack of embarrassment. 'Would you like a whisky?'

'A whisky?'

'Yes. Whisky.'

'You don't have a cup of tea, do you? Herbal preferably?' Becks added hopefully. 'It is quite late.'

Judith pulled a face at the thought.

'Look, it doesn't matter,' Becks said. 'I only wanted to tell you what I'd found out about Elliot Howard.'

'Of course,' Judith said, happy finally to be getting down to the meat of the conversation. 'What have you got?'

'You see, I posted on a local online forum. Asking people if Elliot could be trusted.'

'That was rather courageous of you,' Judith said. 'Going public like that. As the vicar's wife.'

'Actually, I didn't use my real name. I used an alias. And I didn't check it for a few days. I forgot I'd even done it, if I'm honest. Then, today, I remembered the post and went to see what people had said.'

Becks handed her phone over and Judith tried to read the screen.

'I'm sorry, I can't read this without my reading glasses,' she said, handing it back.

'Well, there aren't that many comments, but they're mostly complimentary.'

'They are?'

'It turns out Elliot's well-liked and trusted. Although one person isn't very complimentary about his wife, Daisy. She's apparently the real power behind the throne. And ruthless when it comes to doing deals. She's tight-fisted where Elliot is generous.'

'I've met her,' Judith said, 'and that's not how she came across to me. But I suppose I wasn't trying to buy or sell anything.'

'However, the real reason why I wanted to see you isn't because of Elliot. You see, someone mentions Stefan here. Your neighbour. The one you told me had been murdered.'

'They do?' Judith asked eagerly.

'And it's not flattering. Let me get it up. It's a comment from someone called "John Wayne's Horse". No idea why anyone would call themselves that, but anyway.'

Becks scrolled through the replies until she found the one she was looking for.

'Here, let me read it to you. It says, "Elliot's a good guy. Which is more than his dad was. He was a real crook. Him and Stefan Dunwoody together."'

'It says Stefan was a crook?'

'It goes on. "Shouldn't speak ill of the dead, seeing as he's only just died, but I used to work at the auction house back in the day and Elliot's dad and Stefan had the place stitched up. It was scam after scam, I'm amazed they didn't end up prison. And I can tell you, things only changed when Elliot took over and started to clean the place up."'

Judith was stunned. Stefan was a crook? Just like Elliot had told her?

She began to consider an impossible thought: despite his off-putting manner, had she got everything the wrong way round about Elliot Howard?

Both at the same time, the women heard the sound of glass smashing in the distance.

Becks and Judith looked at the bay window, the direction the sound had come from.

'What was that?' Becks said.

'Shh!' Judith said as she went to look through the glass. All she could see were the dim shapes of shrubs and trees, and the river shining pewter in the gathering dusk. But then her eye caught a flicker of light upstream on the other side of the river.

'Do you see that?'

'What is it?'

'In the direction of Stefan's house.'

Judith pointed, and this time they both saw it, a stab of light behind a window. There was a torch moving inside Stefan's house.

'There's someone in there!' Becks said in surprise. 'You don't think it's a robber, do you?'

'There's only one way to find out,' Judith said, heading to the door. 'You call the police. Ask for DS Malik. And tell her there's a break-in at Stefan Dunwoody's house.'

'What? Who? Where are you going?'

'To his house, of course,' Judith said, throwing on her cape and swishing out of the door. 'We have to find out who that is!'

Chapter 13

Before Becks had even finished her phone call to the police, Judith had released her punt and once again thrust her way upstream to Stefan's house. Leaving the boat embedded in the reeds, she stepped up onto the grass. If she'd stopped to consider what she was doing for even one second, she'd have realised she was potentially putting herself in grave danger, but all she could think was that she'd allowed the killer to get away once, and she wasn't going to let it happen again.

As she strode through the darkness towards the old watermill, she kept to the grass verge so her feet didn't crunch on the gravel, and again she saw the torchlight swing in a downstairs room.

Approaching the back entrance, Judith barely paused as she saw that the lock had been jemmied off, the doorframe a mess of ripped wood, the door ajar. And nor did she break step as she pushed through into a stone-flagged hallway and turned in the direction of the room where she'd seen the torchlight.

'Hey!' she called out as soon as she entered.

She could just make out a figure at the other end of the dark room.

'I said "Hey"! Who goes there?'

The person was dressed in black, and their head was ominously covered in a black balaclava. Whoever it was turned on their torch again and swung the beam so it dazzled her eyes.

'Turn that thing off!' Judith said.

The intruder threw their torch at her, the beam of light spinning wildly as the heavy object flew straight for her head. Judith managed to drop to the floor before she was hit, a scream of pain shooting up her wrist as she broke her fall with her hands. Once the torch had thudded to the floor, she lumbered back to her feet, but it was too late. The dark figure rushed through the same door Judith had come in by.

'Stop right there!' she called out as she grabbed hold of her right wrist in agony.

But the person had gone, and Judith was awash with pain and adrenalin that made her feel sick. She leant against the wall to give herself a few moments to recover. Who had she just interrupted? Was it Elliot Howard? It was possible, but Judith knew she hadn't taken in any meaningful details of the intruder.

Once she'd got her breathing back under control, Judith found the light switch to the room and turned it on. Wall lights in sconces lit up and Judith whistled under her breath in quiet wonder. The burgundy walls were covered in dozens of paintings in golden frames, all hung with gallery precision. The pictures were mostly modern, but there was also a fair smattering of older oil paintings.

Judith shuddered involuntarily, her body continuing to expel tension as she tried to feel the bones in her right wrist. It didn't appear that anything was broken, and already some feeling was coming back to her hand. She'd be all right. But what should she do now?

She heard the sound of a car pulling up outside. A few seconds later, DS Malik ran into the room.

'Mrs Potts, are you okay?' she asked.

'I think so,' Judith said feeling bashful.

DS Malik could see that Judith was holding her right wrist with her left hand.

'Have you hurt yourself?' she asked as she went over to the older woman.

'Just took a bit of a tumble. That's all.'

'Are you sure? Let me look at that.'

DS Malik checked over Judith's wrist, asked her to wriggle her fingers, and even though she said there probably wasn't any major damage, Judith should still get it checked out at the Minor Injuries Unit in High Wycombe in the morning.

'Now, are you up to telling me what happened? Or do you want me to get you home, and we can do this in the morning?'

For once, Judith wasn't offended by DS Malik's concern.

'Don't worry about me,' Judith said. 'I'll be okay.'

There was the sound of another car arriving outside, and both women looked at the door as they heard a person approach.

Becks entered in a rush.

'Judith, are you okay? What happened?'

'I'm fine. Don't worry.'

'Are you sure?'

'Quite sure.'

'You're sure you're sure?'

'Honestly, I'm fine.'

'I've been worried sick. I called the police, but you were

punting across the river, that's the last I saw of you. Are you sure you're okay?'

'I'm fine.'

'Well, thank heavens for that. And you're sure you're okay?'

Recognising that Becks had got stuck in a loop of panic, DS Malik decided to cut in.

'It's Mrs Starling, isn't it?' DS Malik said.

Becks looked over and saw the policewoman for the first time.

'Oh hello!' she said, delight in her voice. 'You're Shanti's mum, aren't you?'

DS Malik smiled warmly.

'I am. You've got a trumpeter, haven't you?'

'I do,' Becks said proudly. 'Although Sam's threatening to give it up. He's reached that age.'

Judith looked from one woman to the other as though they were speaking a foreign language, which, in many respects, they were.

'What on earth are the pair of you talking about?'

'Oh sorry!' Becks said, realising she needed to explain. 'Our children both play musical instruments with the Chiltern Music Academy on Friday nights.'

'Mrs Starling's son is in the symphony orchestra,' DS Malik said, wanting to be fair. 'My Shanti's only a Strings Springer.'

'But the little ones make such a wonderful sound, don't they?' Becks said.

'They do,' DS Malik agreed. 'Nothing like the symphony orchestra, though.'

'Thank you,' Becks said with a modesty that nonetheless seemed to suggest that it was in fact her who played in the orchestra rather than her son. 'Anyway,' she said, turning back to Judith to explain. 'We've chatted a few times over the tea urn before. Haven't we?'

'We have,' DS Malik said. 'But what are you doing here?'

'Becks was with me when we saw the intruder,' Judith said, wanting to bring the conversation back to a reality she felt was a touch more pressing.

'That's right,' Becks said. 'It was me who phoned the police.'

'Then you'd better stay, if you're a witness, Mrs Starling. But Mrs Potts, I'd very much like to know how you ended up inside Mr Dunwoody's house. And why the door back there has been forced?'

'Of course,' Judith said. 'I'll tell you exactly what happened.'

Judith explained how she and Becks had been in her home, had seen someone moving in Stefan's house, how she'd punted over, and how the intruder had thrown his torch at her head before scarpering. DS Malik took notes as Judith spoke.

'I see,' she said once Judith had finished. 'Perhaps you could show me where this torch is.'

'It's over here,' Judith said, and led the two women to where the torch lay on the carpet.

'Do you think the intruder could have been the auburn-haired woman?' Becks asked.

'I don't know,' Judith said.

'What auburn-haired woman?' DS Malik asked.

Judith explained how she'd seen an auburn-haired woman in Stefan's garden, how she'd seen the same woman on the Thames Path the following day, and how the woman had run away from her both times.

'Do you know who she is?' DS Malik asked.

'No, infuriatingly. But I think I've seen her before. In fact, I'm sure I have. But I can't place her. I need to keep thinking. Hopefully it will come to me.'

'But you *don't* think it was her?' Becks asked.

'I don't know,' Judith said. 'It's possible, I suppose. Whoever it was had their hair hidden underneath a balaclava.'

'Can you tell me where the intruder was standing when you entered the room?' DS Malik asked.

'Over by that far wall,' Judith said, pointing.

The three women went over to look.

'Someone's left a terrible mess,' Becks said, indicating some wood shavings that were spread across a walnut writing table. There was also an old cloth and a hammer and a chisel.

'Yes, this was about where they were standing,' Judith said. 'By this desk.'

'There's no way the owner of this house left this mess here,' Becks said, suddenly animated. 'Because I'm telling you, there's not a spot of dust anywhere, and these paintings are all perfectly spaced. I mean, look at them.'

Becks indicated the walls, and the other women could see that she was right. The fifty or so paintings were all placed at perfect right angles to each other.

Becks was almost wistful as she spoke.

'Your neighbour was *very* tidy, I can tell you.'

'You're right about these tools,' DS Malik said. 'I checked over the house after Mr Dunwoody's death, and there were no wood shavings on this table, and no chisel or hammer, either.'

'Apart from that painting,' Becks said, puzzled.

'I'm sorry?'

Becks indicated a painting on the wall a few feet away.

'That painting's not quite straight.'

'It isn't?'

'Not quite.'

DS Malik and Judith shared a look.

'It is,' Judith said.

'It's *nearly* straight, but it's a bit off. Believe me.'

'You're at a crime scene,' Judith said. 'A scene where someone has been using a chisel, throwing a torch at me, and you notice that a painting is a bit skewiff?'

'I prefer it when things are nice and straight,' Becks said with a tight smile. 'Do you mind if I . . . ?'

Becks went over to straighten the picture.

'You mustn't straighten the picture,' DS Malik said kindly. 'This is a crime scene.'

Becks stopped, her hand hovering over the corner of the picture.

'But . . . it's not straight.'

'I'm sorry, you can't interfere with the scene.'

'I mean, who'd even know?'

'Me. And I'm the Acting Senior Investigating Officer here.'

'But I'll hardly touch it. Just a nudge.'

'Becks!' Judith barked. 'Step away from the painting right now.'

'I was only going to straighten it.'

'But I think you've uncovered what the intruder was doing in here.'

Becks was stunned.

'I have?'

But then, so was DS Malik.

'She has?'

'I think so,' Judith said as she went over to look at the painting.

'I don't understand,' Becks said.

'You'll see it when you see it,' Judith said.

DS Malik went over and joined the other two women looking at the painting. It was mid-twentieth century, she guessed. Just three thick bands of colour. A deep red across the bottom third, a light grey in the middle, and a warm yellow covering the top third of the picture. The effect was calming, she thought.

'I'm sorry,' DS Malik said, 'I don't see it.'

'Of course!' Becks said, stepping back and looking at the other paintings hanging on the wall. 'All the pictures in the room have frames, but this is the only one that doesn't.'

'Bingo!' Judith said.

Becks leant in closer to look at the edges of the frameless painting.

'And if you look closely,' she said, like a doctor describing a particularly fascinating X-ray, 'you can see how the wall is a darker colour around the painting. Where a frame has been stopping any sunlight from bleaching the paint on the wall.'

'Okay that's thorough,' DS Malik said.

'So this picture's lost its frame very recently,' Judith said, thinking the chain of events through for all of them. 'Which explains the chisel, hammer and wood shavings on the desk over there. Don't you think? The intruder broke in and was removing the frame from the painting when I interrupted him.'

'Was he holding anything like a picture frame in his hand when he attacked you?' DS Malik asked.

'I couldn't see,' Judith said, frustrated. 'It was too dark.'

'Or maybe you noticed something in his hands as he fled?'

'I'm sorry, I'd dropped to the floor by then. I didn't see anything in his hands.'

'But it makes no sense!' Becks blurted. 'The art in this room must be worth hundreds of thousands of pounds. Maybe millions. Who'd break in, ignore everything else and instead make off with a picture frame?'

Judith peered at the painting, and at the space where the frame had been. She then took a step back and looked at all of the paintings in the room.

'It's like a crossword clue,' she said.

'I'm sorry?' Becks said, frowning.

'A crossword clue never makes any sense when you read the surface meaning, but that's because you haven't decoded it yet.'

'I don't follow,' DS Malik said.

'Each cryptic crossword clue is made up of two parts. Generally. One half of the clue is the wordplay, and the other half is the basic definition. Unless it's the sort of clue where the whole thing is both the wordplay and the definition. But let's not get bogged down. The point being, when you know how to decode the clue, it makes perfect sense. But until that point, the clue appears nonsensical. Take "Two girls, one on each knee", seven letters.'

'Take what?' Becks asked, struggling to keep up with Judith's logic.

'"Two girls, one on each knee".'

'Why?'

'Not literally, just take the clue.'

'What clue?'

'"Two girls, one on each knee".'

'I have to be honest, I'm not really following this.'

'It couldn't be any simpler! "Two girls, one on each knee" is about the most famous crossword clue there's ever been. Compiled by a splendid setter called Roger Squires. It was his two millionth clue. Imagine that!'

'At the moment, I'm busy trying to imagine a famous clue,' DS Malik offered with a wry smile.

'Well, this one's a delight. Because if you look at the surface meaning of "Two girls, one on each knee", it maybe conjures up an image of a bawdy nightclub with lewd strippers on a business-man's lap. Or a loving parent with young daughters in a homely domestic setting. But the answer's got nothing to do with what it appears to be about.'

'Okay, so what's the answer?' DS Malik asked.

'In this instance, the first half of the clue is the wordplay. You're looking for the names of two girls, each short enough that when you put them together you get a seven-letter word for something that you have one of on each knee.'

'Just so you know,' Becks said, 'I'm still not following any of this.'

'Don't worry, I'm only saying there has to be a logical explanation for why the intruder broke into Stefan's house. We've got the surface meaning. He chiselled away a picture frame and then ran off with it. But let's not worry too much that it appears to make no sense, we simply need to break it down. Work out what the rules were that he was following, and I'm sure we can work out what the answer is. For example, maybe it connects with Stefan being a conman.'

'What's that?' DS Malik asked.

Judith explained how Becks had started a thread on an online forum and garnered a response that said that while people liked Elliot, his father had been in cahoots with Stefan, who'd apparently been something of a crook.

'How was Stefan a crook?' DS Malik asked.

'We don't know,' Becks said. 'The person online didn't say. They just said he ran scams with Elliot's father.'

'Okay, that's something I can get my team to check out.'

A silence descended on the women as they looked at the frameless painting. Why on earth had the intruder stolen the frame but not the picture?

DS Malik's face suddenly lit up.

'Patella!' she said.

'I'm sorry?' Becks said.

'I've got it. The names of two girls. Pat and Ella. And when you put them together, you get "patella". You have one of those on each knee. "Two girls, one each knee." Patella.'

'Bravo!' Judith exclaimed, delighted.

'I still don't get it,' Becks said.

'Don't worry, I'll explain later.'

'That's very clever,' DS Malik said as she got a pair of evidence gloves from her pocket and put them on. 'Anyway, I think it's time we looked at this painting more closely. Don't you?'

DS Malik lifted the frameless painting from the wall and angled it so they could see it better in the light.

'It's not signed by the artist,' Becks observed.

'Which maybe explains why the intruder didn't take it,' Judith offered. 'If it's not valuable.'

DS Malik turned the painting over and together they looked at the simple wooden backing and metal twine from which it had been hanging. It was dusty, but there still wasn't anything in particular of interest to see.

'I'm not saying you should dust the backs of pictures,' Becks said in a tone that suggested that she very much was, 'but they are such terrible dust collectors. Once a year, at the very least, you have to take them down for a thorough clean. What's that?' she added, indicating a smudge of something on the inside of the frame.

It was a small, faded sticker with spidery handwriting on it.

DS Malik bent down to look at it.

'It says "Sold by Marlow Auction House, fifteenth December 1988".'

'I was right!' Judith said. 'This proves Elliot Howard is involved, it's from his auction house. Elliot killed Stefan, and now he's broken into his house and stolen the frame from this painting he sold Stefan back in 1988. Don't you think, DS Malik?'

DS Malik looked at the short, passionate woman in front of her, and the tall, somewhat bewildered woman who was standing to her side, a woman she'd last seen trying to make a cup of herbal tea for herself while holding a trumpet case under one arm and a pile of sheet music under the other.

'You know what I think? I think you should call me Tanika.'

'Quite right,' Judith agreed. 'And none of this Mrs Potts nonsense. I'm Judith.'

'And I've never introduced myself properly to you, have I? I'm Becks Starling, I mean Becky Starling, Rebecca really. Most people call me Becks.'

Judith looked at Tanika with a feeling of real warmth. Tanika looked back at the two women with a similar understanding, although both she and Judith could see that Becks still wasn't sure if she should have introduced herself as 'Becky' or 'Becks'.

'So this is what I'm thinking,' Judith said. 'Elliot argued with Stefan at Henley. We know that. Not that we know what it was about.'

'He told me it was because Stefan was blocking his view of the races,' Tanika said.

'I find that very hard to believe.'

'I agree with you.'

'So they had their argument, and I bet it was about this picture. Then, a week later, there's a break-in at Stefan's house. But Stefan reported that nothing had been stolen. Which is interesting, don't you think? Because I think that was Elliot's first attempt to get hold of the picture frame. And it didn't work out for him on that occasion. But Stefan eventually worked out that Elliot had been behind the break-in. So he organised a meeting with Elliot at his gallery. Which is why it was such an angry encounter. And why, afterwards, Stefan told his assistant Antonia that he could "go to the police right now", and "desperation drives people to do stupid things".'

'You remember all that?' Becks asked.

'But it clearly suggests Stefan knew that Elliot was desperate. Desperate to argue with him at Henley. Desperate to break in a week later. But what Stefan didn't know was just how desperate Elliot was. Because Elliot decides to try one more time.'

'He must have really wanted the frame to this picture,' Becks said.

'It would seem he wanted it so much he was prepared to kill for it. But this time, God knows how, Stefan once again discovers what Elliot is up to. Or maybe Elliot always planned to kill Stefan. I don't see how we'll know for sure. But either way, Stefan was down by the little dam at the end of his millpond. Although that doesn't make sense, does it?'

'Why not?' Tanika asked.

'Well, what was Elliot doing down at that end of the garden? And why did Stefan agree to join him there? It seems odd when you think about it. Anyway, for whatever reason, Elliot and Stefan were down at that end of the garden when Elliot shot Stefan dead. He's finally free to steal the frame, but the absolute last thing he expects happens. He hears a woman's voice call out.'

'Really?' Becks asked, eyes wide, lost in the story.

'That's right. From the river.'

Becks was hanging on Judith's every word.

'And who was that?'

'It was me!'

It took a moment for the penny to drop.

'Of course it was you! You were out swimming! Sorry. I'm so thick sometimes.'

'You're not thick,' Judith said to Becks before getting back to her story. 'And I bet Elliot panicked when I called out. With a witness possibly about to haul herself out of the water to see what was going on, he no doubt shelved his plans to break into Stefan's house. For a second time. And instead he legged it. After all, you don't want to be found breaking into someone's house while the dead body of the man you just killed is in the garden, do you?

'But it left Elliot with the same problem he'd always had. The picture frame that had started all of this off, the very thing he'd originally broken into the house to get, that he'd been prepared to commit murder over, was still hanging on Stefan's wall. So he had to leave it a few days for the heat to die down, and then he made his third attempt to break into Stefan's house, stupid man. This evening. But this time, although I nearly managed to stop him, he finally got what he'd always wanted. The frame.'

'But how can a picture frame be that important?' Becks asked. 'Why would it be worth killing over?'

'I've no idea. But if we can find the frame, I'm sure we'll be able to work it out.'

'Well, I'll tell you this much,' Tanika said. 'It's an impressive theory.'

'Thank you.'

'Except for one small detail,' she added. 'When you say you heard Elliot Howard shoot Stefan dead, he was at choir practice in All Saints' Church in front of at least twenty other witnesses.'

'Including me,' Becks said apologetically. 'And there's also CCTV footage of him at the practice,' she offered to Tanika. 'He very definitely was at All Saints' the whole time.'

'But you've seen the look he gives the camera at the end!' Judith said in frustration. 'He's smug, he's superior.'

'All of which I'd say he is naturally,' Tanika said. 'And I can tell you, we've found no link between Elliot and Iqbal Kassam, none at all.'

'But Elliot has to be our killer. Because if he isn't, then who is?'

Neither Tanika nor Becks had an answer to that.

Chapter 14

Two police cars arrived and Tanika was soon leading her team in processing the scene of the break-in. Judith and Becks gave their formal statements and found themselves leaving Stefan's house at the same time.

'You can't possibly punt back home,' Becks said to Judith. 'Not with an injured wrist.'

'Don't worry about the wrist, it's feeling better already.'

'Even so, let me give you a lift home. You can return and pick up your punt tomorrow.'

'Actually, that would be very kind of you. Thank you.'

'Hop in,' Becks said, opening the passenger door to her gleamingly white 4x4. It was such a massive machine that Judith had to pull herself up to get into it. Why on earth did Home County housewives drive such monsters, Judith asked herself as Becks climbed in on her side.

A few minutes later, Becks was crossing the suspension bridge and turning down Ferry Lane, the single-track road on the Bisham side of the river that led to Judith's house.

'You must pop in for a quick drink when we get there,' Judith said.

'What a lovely idea,' Becks said with a sincerity that was entirely false, 'but I'll drop you off and head home if that's okay. It's late.'

'Nonsense! You've had a shock. We both have. You're coming in for a stiff drink.'

'Colin needs me at home.'

'Why?' Judith asked bluntly.

'Well, he works so hard during the day—'

'As I'm sure you do,' Judith said, interrupting. 'Has he rung you?'

'I don't know. I don't think so.'

'So we can assume he's fine.'

'Even so,' Becks said, trying to articulate why it was so important that she be at home for her husband. It was something to do with the fact that, since she didn't work outside the home, she felt a sense of duty to be there for Colin. And something to do with a sense of guilt that she didn't have a 'proper' career, so she had to be the best, most perfect, housewife, in order to feel a sense of worth. It was also, she knew, at a far more humdrum level, simply a habit she'd got into. But how could she even begin to put these half thoughts into words?

'. . . he needs me,' she eventually offered.

'You have needs as well,' Judith said as Becks drove up to Judith's house and parked by the front door.

There was a grey van outside the house that hadn't been there before.

As they got out of the vehicle, Judith saw the dog walker Suzie Harris looking in through a downstairs window.

'Excuse me?' Judith asked in her most matronly voice.

'Oh, there you are!' Suzie said, entirely unfazed at having been caught snooping. 'Just trying to see in through your windows.'

'What on earth are you doing here?'

'No, good question,' she agreed.

Judith waited and realised that Suzie had come to one of her halts.

'And the answer is . . . ?'

'Oh, right! Well, I've got a favour to ask. About Iqbal. And I was taking Emma for a late-night walk anyway, so I thought I'd knock on your door. See if you were in.'

'And when I wasn't?'

'I thought I'd look in through your window. It's like I told you, I've always wanted to see inside your house.'

Suzie was being so very matter-of-fact about her motives that Judith couldn't help herself and laughed, all offence forgotten.

'Who's Iqbal?' Becks asked.

'Sorry,' Judith said, turning to include Becks. 'I should introduce you both. Becks, this is Suzie Harris.'

'I'm actually Rebecca,' Becks said, offering her hand. 'Although no one calls me that apart from my mother.'

'Look, why don't you both come in?' Judith said. 'It's been a long day, and I could do with taking the weight off my feet.'

'I can have a look inside?' Suzie asked.

Judith smiled. 'Yes, you can come inside.'

Judith unlocked the front door, opened it and ushered Suzie in.

Becks still hovered on the doorstep.

'I don't think I can spare the time,' she said.

'Just one drink, and then I'll let you get on your way. Come on, think what we've been through tonight, we've earned it.'

Becks realised it would almost certainly take longer to convince

Judith that she had to leave than it would to have the quickest of quick drinks and then depart.

'Okay,' she said with her best vicar's wife's smile. 'If you insist. One small drink, then I'll be on my way.'

'Bravo!'

Following Becks inside, Judith found Suzie standing by the grand piano, agog.

'Bloody hell, you must be minted,' she said.

'I think you can guess from the state of the fabric that I'm not, as you say, "minted",' Judith said with a laugh as she went over to her drinks table and blew dust out of two extra cut-glass tumblers, lined them up with her regular glass, and poured three stiff measures of whisky.

'Even so, this house must be worth millions.'

Judith couldn't help but find Suzie's manner a breath of fresh air.

'I've no idea what it's worth,' she said, heading over with two drinks. 'I inherited it from my great aunt.'

'Didn't she have any children of her own?'

'Fortunately for me, no. She never married. So I was like the daughter she never had. Now, I strongly suggest you have these,' Judith said, holding up the two glasses.

'Is that whisky?' Becks asked, her forehead creasing.

'I think, when it's as cheap as this, it's better to call it "Scotch".'

'Oh well, thank you, but I'd rather have a glass of water. Or herbal tea if you have any. At this time of night.'

'I think we can agree we need something a bit stiffer than tea.'

'I'm with you there,' Suzie said, taking the glass and knocking it back in one, wincing as the drink burnt into her chest, and then she smiled.

'Now that hits the spot,' she said in appreciation.

While Suzie went over to the sideboard to return the glass, Becks finally took a tiny sip from her glass before rubbing at her lips with her fingers.

'It's better if you don't let it touch your lips,' Judith said. 'It stings less.'

'Sorry, is your toilet through here?' Suzie said, indicating the oak door to the side of the drinks table.

Before Judith could stop her, Suzie tried to push the door open, but it was locked.

'That door's locked,' Judith said with a polite smile.

'Why?' Suzie said, laughing. 'Is that where you keep the dead bodies?'

Judith's smile froze and Suzie's eyes widened in surprise. How come her joke had spooked Judith? As for Becks, being the vicar's wife, she was a past master at saving awkward situations.

'You were telling us about Iqbal,' she said to Suzie. 'Was he the poor man who was murdered?'

'He sure was,' Suzie said.

As Suzie filled Becks in on how she knew Iqbal, Judith went over to the sideboard, downed her drink and poured herself another. When the women weren't looking, she touched the silver chain around her neck with the key on the end. It was still there. Still safe. As Suzie finished telling her story, Judith put on a smile and went over to join the other two.

'And he was shot dead?' Becks asked, still trying to process what she'd heard.

'I know,' Suzie said. 'Crazy. But the thing is, Judith here came and found me because she thinks Iqbal's murder is connected to the death of her neighbour.'

'It must be,' Judith said. 'Murders don't happen in Marlow. If two happen in the space of three days, they have to be linked.'

'I reckon you're right,' Suzie said. 'It's the reason I wanted to speak to you. You see, Iqbal's imam rang me this afternoon. He said he was putting together the funeral arrangements, and the police gave him my number. Did I know how to contact Iqbal's family?'

'And do you?' Becks asked.

'No. Whenever I asked him about his family, he said he didn't have any, and then he'd change the subject. He was much happier talking about boats.'

'Boats?' Becks asked.

'God, yes, they were his passion. Once he got going on the subject, there was no stopping him. He was saving up to buy his own boat that he could keep on the river in Marlow. His dream was to do all of the waterways of the UK. But the point is, the imam said Iqbal didn't attend his mosque that much, so he didn't have any friends there. In fact, I was about the only person he could find who he could invite to the funeral. So would I come?'

'And what did you say to that?' Becks asked.

'I said I'd go, it's the least I can do. Iqbal was my friend. But it's not good that no one else will be there, so I was wondering,' Suzie said, turning to Judith, 'would you come as well?'

'To Iqbal's funeral?'

'Seeing as you think his death may be connected to your neighbour's. Maybe someone will turn up out of the woodwork like a long-lost sister or something. It'll give you a chance to have a poke around. And anyway, the more the merrier, I say, when it comes to funerals.'

'You do?' Judith asked, tickled by Suzie's turn of phrase.

'Of course! I've never been to a bad funeral, have you?'

'I don't suppose I have,' Judith said, after a moment's thought.

'And thank you very much for the invitation. You're right, no one should be buried on their own. I'd be *delighted* to come along.'

'Well, that's that sorted then, isn't it?' Suzie said. 'At least there'll be two people at his service.'

'I wouldn't worry too much about no one being there,' Becks said. 'Men from the mosque will be expected to attend the service, even if they didn't know him. Was this Imam Latif who called you?'

'It was,' Suzie said. 'You know him?'

'Only a bit. We do a food bank together on Thursday mornings. I have to say, he's lovely.'

Judith was impressed with how easily Becks talked about working in the local food bank with the imam of a local mosque. Maybe she'd been wrong when she judged her as solely being a gilet-and-jeggings Marlow clone.

In fact, as she looked at the two other women, Judith realised she was having more fun than she'd had in a long time and decided that she didn't want the evening to end yet.

'I'll come to the funeral on one condition,' she said to Suzie with a smile. 'I'd like you to help me for the next half an hour or so.'

'Doing what?' Suzie asked.

'Don't worry, it's nothing strenuous. But I want to see if we can work out the importance of a painting Stefan Dunwoody bought from Elliot Howard's gallery back in 1988.'

'And how can we do that?'

'Well, I suggest we pour ourselves a small glass of whisky and see what we can dig up on the internet. What do you say?'

Suzie didn't want to seem like too much of a pushover.

'I can't leave Emma on her own in the van.'

'Then bring her in.'

'All right. You've got a deal.'

Judith and Suzie looked at Becks, but she was just smiling soupily, no doubt from the whisky, Judith guessed. Good for her, she thought to herself. She deserved to let her hair down.

'So that's a yes from all of us,' Judith said, grinning. 'Then I suggest, ladies, we get to work.'

Chapter 15

The women were looking at their devices, Judith in her favourite
wingback, Becks sitting upright at the card table, and Suzie lolling
like the Queen of Sheba on some cushions in the bay window,
Emma lying at her feet, her head on her paws, eyes closed in
sleep. Every now and then one of the women would take a sip of
whisky, or make a passing comment about their research, or ask
a question of the others. It was companionable, collegiate, and,
in truth, all of them were having a terrific time.

'So do you have any kids?' Becks asked Suzie.

'I've got the two best kids in the world,' Suzie said, smiling.

'Tell me about them.'

'Well, they're in their twenties now. Rachel is twenty-two,
lives in Newcastle with her girlfriend. And Amy is twenty-five,
married, has a kid of her own.'

'You're a grandmother!'

'I am,' Suzie said proudly.

'How wonderful. Do you have a partner?'

'Ha!' Suzie said. 'There used to be. But he left me after Rachel was born.'

'After your second was born?'

'The same month. He said it was too much for him.'

'You raised your two on your own?'

'I did.'

'That must have been tough. What about other family? Does your mum live nearby?'

'My parents died when I was small. Like Iqbal. We had that in common.'

'I'm so sorry to hear that. What about cousins or aunts or uncles?'

Suzie took a sip of Scotch before replying.

'No. No family to speak of. This really is a horrible drink,' she said to Judith with a smile that Becks could see was a touch forced.

'It's the nectar of the gods,' Judith said before returning her attention to her tablet.

'Haven't you got any wine?'

'Sorry, I can't have wine in the house.'

'Why's that?'

'If I do, I drink it.'

Suzie and Becks shared a glance as they looked over at the all but empty decanter of whisky. If this was how Judith downed whisky, what on earth did she do to wine?

'Then what about you, Judith?' Becks asked, her cheeks radiating a warm glow from the Scotch. 'Do you have any kids?'

'Oh no, I wasn't so blessed.'

'But you're married?'

'I'm sorry?'

'If it's not rude to ask. I see you've got a wedding ring.'

Becks indicated the gold band on the ring finger of Judith's left hand.

'You're very observant.'

'Sorry. Occupational hazard. When you're the vicar's wife, you notice things like wedding rings.'

'If you must know, my husband died,' Judith said.

'He did?'

'My lovely Philippos. He was Greek. Philippos Demetriou. I fell in love with his name before I'd even met him. But he died in a boating accident. In Corfu.'

'I'm so sorry. When did this happen?'

'I was twenty-seven. Now, I think I've found something rather interesting,' Judith said, wanting to move the conversation on.

'Hold on,' Suzie said. 'You were widowed when you were twenty-seven? Has there been anyone else since then?'

'Why would there be? Most men you meet don't really pass muster, do they?'

'I can drink to that,' Suzie said quietly, or at least Judith presumed it had been Suzie who'd spoken, but she realised that Suzie's lips hadn't moved. She and Suzie looked over and they saw that Becks was raising her whisky glass in a quiet toast before she downed the remainder of her drink.

'This Scotch is very moreish,' Becks proclaimed, slurring slightly.

'It is, isn't it?' Judith agreed, going to refill Becks' glass.

'But what have you found?' Suzie asked.

'Well, it may be something, it may be nothing. But I've been looking at the website for the Marlow Auction House, since that's where Stefan's painting came from. There's a page that explains the history of the business. It was founded by Elliot's father. His name was Dudley. When he retired in 1985, Elliot took over as chairman. But this is what I've noticed, Elliot was initially only chairman for three years. Look,' Judith said, handing her tablet to Suzie.

Suzie looked at the website and saw that Elliot Howard was listed as the chairman from '1985–1988'.

'And then in 1988 a man called Fred Smith took over,' Judith said.

'Fred Smith?' Suzie asked, her interest piqued.

'That's right. And he stayed chairman for the next thirteen years. Until 2001. Which is when Elliot Howard became chairman again. For a second time.'

'So why did Elliot leave for a number of years and then come back?'

'Good question, but that's not what caught my eye. You see, Elliot stopped being chairman in 1988. But that was also the date on the painting we found at Stefan's house, wasn't it? Stefan bought it in 1988.'

'Maybe it's a coincidence.'

The women considered the evidence in their various states of alcoholic glow.

'It's strange, isn't it?' Judith said. 'Let's say it was Elliot who I surprised in Stefan's house tonight. It seems the most likely explanation. But if it were, then that would mean he just stole the frame from a painting he sold to Stefan in 1988. The same year that he resigned from the auction house.'

'You're right,' Becks said, enthused. 'When you put it like that, it's fishy, isn't it?'

'If you ask me, we need to find out why Elliot left his business in 1988.'

'Good idea,' Becks agreed.

'Which is lucky for us,' Suzie said. 'Because I know exactly how we can do that.'

'You do?'

'All we need to do is speak to the guy who took over from Elliot in 1988. Fred Smith.'

'Of course! He'll know what happened. But how do we find him?'

'Shouldn't be too hard,' Suzie said, smiling. 'I speak to him at about eleven o'clock every morning.'

'You do? How come?'

'Because if I'm not mistaken, Fred's my postman.'

Suzie's house was on the eastern side of town, in between the functional red-brick office blocks of the trading estate and the hammering racket of the A404, a dual carriageway that carried a constant roar of traffic. But despite the unprepossessing location, Suzie's street was rather sweet, Judith thought to herself as she cycled onto it just before eleven o'clock the following morning. There were pretty two-storey semis on both sides of the road, cars on driveways, and geraniums in hanging baskets. Yes, it was all very nice. And then Judith arrived at the address Suzie had given her.

The front of the house was missing.

Judith blinked, trying to make sense of what she was seeing.

No, her eyes weren't deceiving her. The front of the house didn't have any kind of wall to it and was instead a jumble of scaffolding, bits of blue plastic sheeting and exposed jacks and roof-supporting joists.

Judith couldn't help but be impressed. She knew that she was someone who was happy to let things slide when it came to keeping up appearances, but even she would draw the line at not having a front to her house.

However, as she looked closer, Judith realised that maybe the building work was actually an as-yet-to-be-finished extension, and the original house was still lurking behind the unfinished brickwork.

Suzie emerged from the front door as Judith was leaning her bike against an old cement mixer.

'Sorry about the building work,' she said.

'Nothing to apologise for. What are you having done?'

'Oh, just an extension,' she said airily.

'I imagine it will be splendid when it's done.'

'Sure will. That's the plan anyway.'

'How long will it take to finish?'

'Another two months, the builder says. Maybe a bit less if the weather remains good.'

'Well, there we are, then. It will soon be over.'

'Or that's what he told me three years ago when he took all my money and scarpered. I've not seen him since.'

'I'm sorry?'

'The house has been like this for the last three years.'

Judith was lost for words.

'Oh,' she eventually managed.

'But that's life, isn't it?' Suzie said breezily, as though it barely bothered her at all. 'People leave you. Your husband, your kids, and if you're me, your builder as well. Come on in, it's much nicer inside. And don't worry. I've got no dogs staying with me. It's only me and Emma.'

The inside of Suzie's house smelled of dogs and stale cigarette smoke. There was scuffed, heavy-duty linoleum on the floor, the door to the sitting room had been removed, and Judith could see that there was no furniture anywhere. Not in the hallway. Not in the sitting room. There were only old dog beds and blankets scattered about.

Emma padded in from the kitchen and nudged Judith's hand with her head for a stroke.

'She likes you,' Suzie said.

'And I like her,' Judith said, bending down to give Emma a quick fuss. 'Such silky ears,' she said to the dog.

'We should go upstairs. That's where I live. The dogs have down here. I have upstairs. Come on.'

Suzie unclipped the baby gate at the bottom of the stairs, told Emma to wait and headed upstairs.

Judith followed and was pleased to see that the first floor had deep-pile carpets, side tables with silk flowers in vases and lots of artwork in clip frames on the walls. In fact, it was very pretty, Judith thought to herself, even if the air was heavy with the punch of wall socket air fresheners and stale cigarette smoke.

'Well, this is lovely,' Judith said as Suzie led her into a sitting room that was covered in dozens of family photos through the years.

'Thank you,' Suzie said with obvious pride. 'So where's Becks?'

'She said she had a parish meeting she had to attend. If I'm honest, I think she was making an excuse. So what happens now?'

'I reckon we just have to wait until Fred delivers the post,' Suzie said as she picked up her metal tin from a side table. 'Mind if I smoke?'

'Of course not. You go ahead.'

While Suzie got out the materials required to make a cigarette, Judith went over to a large poster on the wall that had photos tucked into the frame. She pointed to a photo of a boy in a baby bouncer.

'Is this one of yours?'

'That's my grandson.'

'He's gorgeous. How old is he?'

'In that photo? About two years old.'

'Lovely,' Judith said. 'How old is he now?'

'Six, I think,' Suzie said as she lit her cigarette. 'Yes, that's right. Six.'

Judith realised there weren't any photos of the child older than about two or three years old. In fact, now she was looking more closely, all of the photos in the room looked quite old and faded.

'Do you see much of your grandson?'

'Oh yes, I see Toby all the time,' Suzie said, although Judith detected a brittleness to her answer. 'But this is my refuge. Where I have everything I need. My family,' she said, indicating the photos on the walls, and then she turned to the television. 'My entertainment. And even a chef if I need it,' she added as a final flourish, nodding her head in the direction of an old microwave on a hostess trolley.

'Yes, it's very nice,' Judith said, but she was aware that maybe Suzie wasn't telling the whole story, so she decided to change the subject and turned back to the poster that the photos were tucked into.

'I like this poster,' she said.

The picture in question was a reprint of the famous painting by John William Waterhouse, *The Lady of Shalott*. It depicted a pale woman sitting in a wooden boat who was wearing a flowing white dress, her copper-coloured hair falling down to her waist. Judith had always disliked the painting. Not that it wasn't beautiful – she loved the hippy-ish aesthetic with red and gold tapestries hanging over the side of the little rowboat – but she was 'done' with legends of passive women who pined away from unrequited love for a man. In her experience, the only women who pined at all did so because they were trapped with a man, not because they were liberated from one.

'It's beautiful, isn't it?' Suzie agreed.

There was the clatter of post being delivered through the letterbox downstairs.

'That'll be Fred!' Suzie said, stubbing out her cigarette at speed. 'We need to stop him before he gets away.'

Suzie dashed to the door and Judith followed.

Chapter 16

Fred Smith was an impish man with short white hair and a trim beard who'd had many jobs in his life, but he'd never enjoyed any of them as much as he did being a postie. As a Marlow boy, born and bred, he knew where everyone lived before he'd even taken up the job, so delivering letters around the town never felt like a chore. Not when you could stop and have a good natter on the doorstep with everyone as you went. It turned out that the one thing Fred liked above all else was gossiping. Not that he'd ever be indiscreet. That would be unprofessional.

When Suzie and Judith bombed out of Suzie's house after him, he was nonetheless surprised. It wasn't usual for women to chase him down the street.

'Suzie, are you okay?' he asked, startled.

'Can we have a quick word, Fred?'

'Always got time for quick word,' Fred said with a broad grin. 'And it's great to meet you finally, Mrs Potts.'

As Judith lived on the outskirts of Marlow, she had a completely different postman and had never met Fred before.

'You know who I am?'

'I'm a postie,' he said with a friendly wink. 'I know who *everyone* is. So, how can I help you, ladies?'

'It's about Elliot Howard,' Suzie said.

'It is?'

'Do you know him?' Judith asked.

'Of course. I used to be his boss. Back in the day, mind. A long time ago now.'

'So what's the gossip?' Suzie asked.

'About Elliot?' Fred said with a conspiratorial smile. 'Where do you want me to start?'

'Is he trustworthy?' Judith said eagerly.

'What a weird question. He could be difficult, I'll grant you that. A bit patronising in his manner sometimes. But he was totally trustworthy.'

This wasn't what Judith wanted to hear. First there were the online comments that Elliot was a good person and now Fred was saying the same thing.

'Was this when you were chairman of the auction house?' Suzie asked.

'That's right. You know about that?'

'We saw it on the website.'

'I'm on their website? That's something, isn't it?'

'It sure is,' Suzie agreed, and she could sense that Fred wanted to settle down to a good chinwag. 'Bet it's an interesting story. How you ended up working in an auction house.'

'You can say that again. I was sixteen when I joined. About a hundred years ago now, but that was under Elliot's dad, Dudley.'

'Yes, what was he like?' Judith asked.

Fred looked guarded.

'Why do you ask?'

'Only we've done some digging and we've heard he was something of a crook. Was he?'

'You're not wrong there. He was a piece of work, I can tell you. Always doing deals on the side or using stooges to push prices up in the auctions. If there was a sharp practice, he'd do it. And he didn't like his son, not one bit.'

'He didn't?'

'No way. Elliot's big thing was rowing when he was a teenager.'

Judith remembered the photos in Elliot's study of him in various rowing teams.

'And he was good. But his dad wouldn't have any of it. The way Elliot told it, Dudley spoke to his rowing coach to find out if Elliot could go professional, and as soon as he said he couldn't, that was it for him as far as he was concerned. He wouldn't pay for any more coaching. Wouldn't take his son to any of the training sessions or regattas. It was over.'

'That's harsh,' Suzie said.

'Dudley was a harsh man.'

'Where was Elliot's mother in all of this?' Judith asked.

'I think she left Dudley when Elliot was young. I don't know the story, but Elliot was raised by his dad on his own. That's why it was so bad for Elliot when Dudley said it was over for his rowing. He was his only parent, so his word was gospel.'

'Hang on a moment!' Judith interjected, an idea flashing in her mind. But what was it? There was a connection that her brain had just tried to make. Something to do with rowing.

But what could it be? What was the thought that she'd nearly had, but couldn't quite chase down?

'Rowing,' she said out loud, as though tasting the word, trying to let the sound of it help her thoughts coalesce.

'What about rowing?' Suzie asked.

Judith tried to recapture the moment, but the gossamer-thin idea had already dissipated.

'No, it's gone,' she said, frustrated, but she also knew that there was nothing she could do about it. At her age, if something slipped her mind, it tended to stay slipped.

'Sorry, ladies, but I have to get on,' Fred said, turning to go. 'I can't stand here gassing all day.'

'We aren't done though,' Suzie said.

'You aren't?'

'It could be important.'

'I'll get in trouble if I don't complete my round on time.'

'Then how about we come with you?' Judith asked.

'What's that?'

'We won't get in the way, but we do have a few more questions to ask.'

'You want to accompany me on my round?' Fred said, amused. 'Well, if you put it like that, I can't think of anything nicer than having an attractive lady on each arm as I deliver the post. Come on, then.'

Judith and Suzie spent the next hour accompanying Fred as he delivered the post to the neighbouring streets. It was a somewhat frustrating process because they only got to speak to Fred in between houses, and he kept stopping for a chat on the doorstep with his regulars. At one point, he disappeared inside for a few minutes, and when he came out he apologised and explained that the old woman lived on her own and the ballcock on her cistern had stopped working, but it was a quick fix, so it hadn't taken him too long.

But between the chatting, plumbing and the actual delivery of letters and parcels from his bright red trolley, Judith and Suzie were able to piece together some of Fred and Elliot's background.

Fred had left school at sixteen and had joined the auction house, first as their porter, and then, a few years later, working front desk, checking in the auction items. As he was only a few years younger than Elliot, they'd go for a beer together after work every now and again. It was in these sessions at the pub that Elliot revealed to Fred how much he felt trapped having to work for his dad. What made it all the worse was how Elliot was falling in love with the art they were selling.

'He started painting,' Fred told them. 'Apparently, there'd been a granddad who'd been a good artist. It's how the family had ended up owning an auction house. But Elliot threw himself into it. You know, reading books, educating himself so he could get better as an artist. And he was good. Even I could see that. I mean, Elliot's paintings were mostly abstract stuff. Very mid-twentieth century. You put two blocks of colour next to each other and call it art.'

Judith looked at Suzie, knowing that the 'two blocks of colour next to each other' was a very good description of the work of art that the intruder into Stefan's house had stolen the frame from. But Judith could see that Suzie didn't pick up on the connection. Of course she didn't, Judith realised, Suzie hadn't been with her, Becks and Tanika. But was this an important link? The sort of art that was the cause of the break-in was also the sort of art that Elliot liked to paint? Or was it a coincidence? After all, anyone learning to paint in the late twentieth century, as Elliot had, would no doubt paint like a painter from the late twentieth century.

'Anyway,' Fred said, 'there came a point, after a couple of years, where Elliot realised he wanted to give up the business and have a go at being a professional artist. So he applied to the Slade School of Art, and guess what? He got in. It's like the best art school in the country, and Elliot had got a place. An amazing achievement. But get this, his dad said no. Again. Elliot's painting was like his rowing, he told him. Just a hobby. No one made any money as an artist, the only money to be made was in selling the stuff. So he wouldn't give him the money to go to art school. It set Elliot back.'

'I bet it did,' Judith said.

'And it made him resentful. Because his dad swore that if Elliot walked away from the business, he wouldn't be allowed back. It was stay and help him run the auction house, or leave.'

'Wow,' Judith said.

'I know,' Fred agreed. 'So Elliot let his place at the art school go and stayed at the auction house. And then, when his dad got ill, he became chairman. I was managing director by then. But Elliot's heart wasn't in his work if I'm honest. He just didn't want to be there. And then his dad died. A heart attack on the golf course, of all things. Elliot couldn't wait to get out of the business. He reapplied to art school. He didn't get into the Slade this time, but he got into a good enough school in Reading. And he left the business.'

'Was this in 1988?'

'That's right.'

'When you became chairman?'

'Got it in one. Elliot wanted a safe pair of hands to run the shop while he trained. But it never worked out for him. He said he was so much older than everyone else on the course, and I know he resented the fact it wasn't as prestigious a course as the Slade. When he graduated, he tried to make it as an artist, but he was too old to be a Young Turk, and this was in the nineties when the art world was all about pickling sharks in formaldehyde. There wasn't much interest in the mid-century stuff any more.

'And you know what the kicker was? Turns out I wasn't all that good at running an auction house on my own,' Fred admitted without any apparent rancour. 'I could do it when I was just in charge of admin, but I never understood the art side of things. And the auction house took a dive. To be honest, Elliot should never have left me in charge. After a few years, he realised he'd never make it as an artist. That boat, if it was ever going to sail, had left harbour years ago. And if he didn't come back to run the auction house, he'd lose that as well. So he relieved me of my duties. And relief is the right word, from my point of view. The one thing I'd learned from running a business was, I never wanted to run a business. All that pressure. All those people working for you. This suits me much more,' Fred said, indicating his postman's uniform. 'I'm out in the fresh air, and when I finish my day's shift, I don't take work home with me. I get a good night's sleep, every night. And that's priceless.'

Fred smiled.

'But how was Elliot when he came back to the business?' Judith asked.

'The same. A bit superior, a bit full of himself at times, but a good person. Honest. Reliable. A good boss.'

'You really don't have a bad word to say about the man who sacked you?'

'Why should I? I hadn't run the business well, and he didn't

sack me. We agreed it would be better if I left, so that's what
I did.'

Suzie couldn't quite believe that Fred could be so laid-back,
but Judith smiled, finding that Fred's lack of regret for paths not
taken chimed with her.

'Now, if you don't mind, ladies, I need to get back to the
depot,' Fred said with a smile, 'or they'll think I've bunked off.'

'Thanks for your help,' Suzie said.

'Although, can I ask, why are you so interested in Elliot?'

'Oh no reason,' Judith said with a fake smile.

Fred considered Judith's answer, and then decided he'd let it
go.

'Very well. It's none of my business. Have a nice day, ladies.'

Fred touched his forehead in salute, turned and left.

'Oh, one last thing!' Judith said, catching up with him.

'What is it?' Fred said.

'Can you tell us about Stefan Dunwoody?'

'You want to know about Stefan?' Fred said, surprised.

He then looked up and down the street, saw that no one was
in sight, and stepped behind a buddleia bush in a front garden.

The women followed him into the garden.

'Now why do you want to know about Stefan?' he whispered.

'We've heard he was a bit of a crook. Working with Dudley.
Apparently they had a number of scams going.'

'I don't know if you heard, but Stefan died last week. I don't
want to speak ill of the dead.'

'But it could be important. We think someone killed him.'

'What?'

'I know. So anything you can tell us would be gold-dust.'

Fred wrestled with his conscience, but not for very long.

'Okay, so Stefan was always charming. Always well turned out. Always interested in you. Polite to a fault. The perfect gent. But it was all an act. Because you're right. He was a crook. Every bit as bad as Dudley.'

'He worked for the auction house?'

'As our art expert, back in the day. His trick was to misidentify art.'

'And how did he do that?'

'Well, someone who knew nothing about art would take a painting to Dudley's auction house, he'd bring Stefan in as the expert to value it, and Stefan would say it was a second-rate copy, or some such. Dudley would then convince the owner to sell it to him privately for a knocked-down rate. Then, wonder of wonders, the artwork would magically reappear at the Marlow Auction House a few months later, this time properly identified as being the work of a well-known artist. Mind you, the sort of art we're talking about was never worth tens of thousands, it was only a few thousand pounds here and there. But it was still illegal, and I know for a fact the pair of them were making a fair bit on the side each year. It was despicable.'

'Did anything happen in 1988?' Judith asked.

'Like what?'

'We think Stefan bought a painting from the Marlow Auction House the same year that Elliot left for art college.'

Fred thought for a few seconds before the memory came to him.

'He did! You're right. It was a massive scandal at the time. Or at least, it was to us in the industry. You see, when Dudley died, Elliot inherited all of his art. And Elliot got Stefan to value his dad's artwork to get it ready to be auctioned off. At that point he didn't know what a crook Stefan was. None of us did. And the collection was worth a few hundred thousand pounds, it was a serious windfall for Elliot. Even though, in among the good stuff, there was quite a bit of tat.'

'Including,' Judith said, 'an abstract painting that was three plain bands of colour. The top one yellow, the middle one grey, and the bottom a sort of dark red.'

'You know it?' Fred said.

'So, following your logic, I take it that Stefan said it wasn't worth much.'

'That's it. You see, it wasn't signed, and it was found in a box with a couple of other unsigned paintings. And the other two paintings were amateur hour, they weren't worth a penny. So Elliot was happy to let Stefan buy the box for a few quid. But it was another one of his scams, wasn't it? Because, as soon as he owned it, Stefan said he wasn't sure if it was what he thought it was. So he took it up to London for a second opinion. And it only turned out to be by Mark Rothko, about the most famous American painter of the twentieth century!'

'How much was it worth?' Suzie asked.

'The thing is, it was only a sketch, not the finished article. That's why Rothko didn't sign it. But there's a photo of him painting it, so the provenance is proven and that made it worth a few hundred thousand pounds.'

'You're kidding me!' Judith said, amazed.

'And Stefan refused to give it back to Elliot, or pay the correct market price for it. He told Elliot he was sorry he'd misidentified it, but there was nothing he could do. It was an honest mistake. And you're right,' Fred said in realisation. 'It was only a few months later that Elliot applied to art school. I'd not made the connection before. Stefan betrayed him, and Elliot had left the business by the end of the year.'

'Now that is *very* interesting,' Judith said. 'Thank you very much for your time, Fred.'

'No worries,' Fred said. 'And if you don't mind, I really must get back.'

'Of course, and thank you again!'

As Fred pushed his cart off, Judith and Suzie watched him go.

'So why,' Judith said, 'would Elliot break into Stefan's house, finally get his hands on the Rothko painting worth hundreds of thousands that he should have inherited from his dad, and then leave it on the wall while he steals the frame that was around it?'

'It makes no sense!' Suzie said as she and Judith returned to Suzie's upstairs sitting room a few minutes later.

'I'd agree with you there. But it explains why Elliot hated Stefan, doesn't it? And you know what else? Fred told us that Elliot's painting style was mid-century, didn't he?'

'Whatever that means.'

'It means he would have known all about Rothko. A mid-century painter. So, he'd have known his techniques. His palette of colours and how he made his paintings.'

'What are you saying?'

'Imagine you're Elliot, and you want to reclaim the Rothko that Stefan stole from you. What can you do? You can't very well walk in there and take it back. Stefan would notice the gap on his wall and know who'd stolen it. But Elliot is a painter who's trained in the techniques of Rothko, isn't he?'

'Oh! You think he painted a fake?' Suzie asked, her eyes alight at the idea.

'It's a possibility, isn't it? And I reckon Elliot is exactly the sort of person who'd think he could paint a forgery of Stefan's

Rothko. So let's say that's what he did. He painted a copy, then the plan was to break into Stefan's house, leave the forgery on the wall and make off with the real painting.'

'You think that's what he did?'

'It's worth hundreds of thousands of pounds. And from Elliot's point of view, Stefan stole it from him back in 1988. That would fester with anyone. But you know what? This could explain why there's no longer a frame on the Rothko in Stefan's house.'

'How come?'

'Let's walk this through. Elliot makes his forgery, but the one thing he can't do is fake the frame. So he breaks into Stefan's house with his forgery, but as he's in the process of taking the frame off Stefan's real Rothko, I interrupt him. And this is the third time he's either broken in or tried to break in to get the Rothko. Elliot isn't going to be thwarted. So he grabs the real Rothko from the wall, frame and all, and puts his forgery up in its place, hoping that no one will notice it doesn't have a frame on it.'

'I still don't follow,' Suzie said.

'I think the Rothko that's currently hanging on Stefan's wall is a fake painted by Elliot. And Elliot legged it with the real Rothko, frame and all.'

'Oh I see! Then we need to tell the police.'

'I'll ring Tanika the moment I get home. Tell her they need to have the Rothko in Stefan's house inspected by an art expert. But now we have a proper motive for why Elliot might have wanted to kill Stefan. Stefan found out that Elliot was the person behind the first break-in. And we know from his assistant Antonia that Stefan threatened Elliot, telling him he "could go to the police right now". Elliot must have feared he'd end up in prison. So he killed Stefan to silence him.'

'Brilliant! So Elliot's the killer, he has to be! Even though he can't be,' Suzie added.

'I know, it's so frustrating! How did he do it, that's the question. We should be following him when he's out and about, staking out his business, putting spy cameras in his house, but we're not allowed to, are we? We're only civilians.'

'Maybe I can help there.'

'You can?'

'Let me do some digging. I'm sure I know someone, or know someone who knows someone, who lives on Gypsy Lane where Elliot's house is. Maybe I can get him under a bit of surveillance.'

'Now that sounds like an *excellent* idea,' Judith said.

As she said this, Judith found herself glancing at the poster on the wall that showed the Lady of Shalott. She idly wondered why her eye was once again drawn to it, and then it hit her.

'Liz Curtis!' she suddenly blurted.

This by no means was what Suzie had expected Judith to say next.

'What?'

'That's who the woman is!'

'Come again?'

'The auburn-haired woman I told you about. The one who was in the garden of Stefan's house after he died, and who ran away from me in the field the first time I spoke to you. I knew I recognised her from somewhere. Her name's Liz Curtis.'

'How on earth did you work that out?'

'Well, she's got auburn hair, like your Lady of Shalott in the poster here. And just like your Lady of Shalott, the last time I saw her she was in a rowboat. You see, Liz Curtis runs the Marlow Rowing Centre.'

Now it was Suzie's turn to be excited.

'And you're sure the woman you saw those two times was Liz Curtis?'

'I am. Do you know her?'

'Damned right I do, and if you're looking for someone capable of murder, then I'd put Liz Curtis at the top of your list.'

'You think so?'

'I don't think so, I know so,' Suzie said darkly. 'You see, she's killed before.'

Chapter 17

The seats in Suzie's van were ripped, there were old bits of fast-food packaging strewn on the floor, and where the ignition key should have been there was an old screwdriver jammed into the wheel's steering column. Judith tried to pretend the van wasn't a death trap as Suzie lit herself a liquorice rollie, coaxed the engine into coughing life, and drove them both to the Marlow Rowing Centre.

'Told you I know everyone in Marlow,' Suzie said, very pleased with herself. 'Although me and Liz Curtis haven't spoken in about ten years. She had a Welsh Springer Spaniel called Crumble. The nicest dog you'd ever meet. All soft ears, energy and bounce, you know? And the most soulful eyes. Anyway, he wasn't Liz's dog originally, he was her dad's. That's how she told it to me. But her dad died. Which was when Liz inherited the rowing centre. And she also inherited Crumble.'

'Let me guess. She wasn't a dog person?'

'You can say that again. She brought him to me for walking, and for looking after overnight. But she didn't care about him. And she complained about how much I was charging her. Couldn't I leave Crumble in my garden and charge less? Or take in some other dogs at the same time to bring down the costs. Even though I don't like having more than one dog at a time. I can give better care if it's one-to-one. And then one day, she stopped bringing Crumble around.'

'Why? What happened?'

'I bumped into her on the High Street a few months later and asked her how Crumble was. And she said she didn't know. He'd gone out one day and not come back. Just vanished. And there was something about the way she said it. I could tell she was lying. Or trying to hide her guilt. Well, the next time I was at the vet's, I got talking to the receptionist. She and I go way back. We were at Great Marlow School together. So I asked her if Liz's Crumble had ever been found. She was shocked I knew about it, which I didn't, but I pretended I did. Anyway, she told me she'd heard that Liz had taken her dog up to the vet in Bovingdon Green and had him put down.'

'I'm sorry, she did what?'

'Even though Crumble was perfectly healthy.'

'She killed her own dog?'

'That's what the receptionist told me.'

'Is that even legal?'

'It may be legal, but there's no vet I'd use who'd kill a healthy animal.'

'I'd agree with you there.'

'Well, I don't think anything was proven, but I can tell you now the Bovingdon surgery closed soon afterwards when word got around it was run by a vet who was prepared to kill on demand. If I'm honest, I may have had something to do with that. But the point is, Liz got her dog put down when it was as healthy as you or me.'

'And you're sure that's what she did?'

'As sure as I am of anything. It's wicked. Crumble had such a lovely soul. Anyone would have taken him in if Liz didn't want the responsibility. I'd have taken him. But that's Liz. She's a dog killer.'

Judith and Suzie lapsed into silence as they pulled into the little gravel parking area of the Marlow Rowing Centre. It was made up of a clutch of Portakabins and huts that had been built on the edge of town on a bend of the Thames. The setting was gorgeous, but the buildings were weather-beaten, and the red, white and blue canoes and kayaks that were stored in metal stacks had all seen better days.

'You're right,' Judith said to Suzie as they got out of the van. 'We could be about to speak to the killer. Are you sure you want to do this?'

'Bring it on,' Suzie said, and there was something about her blind enthusiasm that gave Judith pause.

She pulled her phone out and dialled Tanika's mobile number.

'Judith, are you okay?' Tanika said as she answered the call.

'I'm fine, thank you for asking. I just wanted to let you know I've worked out who the auburn-haired woman is. You know, the one I saw in Stefan's garden. And in the field the day after.'

'You do? Who is she?'

'Her name's Liz Curtis, and she runs the Marlow Rowing Centre.'

'Are you sure?'

As Tanika asked the question, Judith saw the auburn-haired woman step out of a Portakabin with a paintbrush, shake the water out of it and then head back inside. She didn't look over and so didn't see Judith or Suzie.

'Oh yes, I'm sure,' Judith said.

'Then you have to promise me something.'

'What?'

'You won't try and investigate her.'

'What's that?'

'Because you've already put yourself at risk once, when you chased that intruder in Stefan Dunwoody's house. And I'm not having you do that again.'

'I wouldn't worry about that, it was very much a one-off.'

'Because I don't think the killer's done yet.'

'How do you mean?'

'I can't be sure, but I think there might be another murder. A third murder.'

Judith's hand tightened on her phone. How could Tanika possibly know this?

'So you have to promise me you won't do anything to put yourself in danger? I want to hear you say the words.'

'Of course,' Judith said. 'I promise. No more amateur sleuthing. You have my word.'

'Thank you.' Tanika sounded relieved. 'And thanks for the information about Liz Curtis. I'll see what I can find out about her.'

Tanika rang off, and Suzie, who'd only heard Judith's end of the conversation, asked her friend what it was that she had just promised.

'Oh, nothing important,' Judith said with a bright smile. 'Now come on, we need to talk to Liz Curtis.'

They went over to the Portakabin they'd seen Liz come out of. They found her inside, halfway up a ladder painting the walls white.

'Hello,' she said as she climbed down from the ladder.

Liz was tall, thin and angular, her limbs almost longer than seemed entirely natural, Judith thought to herself. Like a praying mantis. Most importantly, she also had a shock of flame-red hair and was very definitely the person who'd run away from her twice.

Liz's face fell as soon as she saw Judith.

'Oh it's you,' she said.

'Hello, Liz,' Suzie said.

Liz was even more dismayed to see Suzie standing next to Judith.

'Hello, Suzie,' Liz said, turning her back on the women and heading over to a metal samovar that was on a trestle table next to some tea things. 'Are you looking to make a booking?'

'Not on this occasion,' Judith said, glancing at Suzie. Both women could see how guiltily Liz was acting.

'You see,' Suzie said, 'my friend here wants to know why you keep running away from her.'

'What's that?' Liz said as she poured herself a cup of tea, still keeping her back to the women.

'Are you saying you didn't run away from me in the field?' Judith asked.

Liz didn't reply immediately. But once she'd stirred her tea and put her teaspoon down, she finally turned around.

'What's that?' she said, as if she'd not heard.

'I saw you in Stefan's garden two days after he died,' Judith said. 'And in a field the day after that. Both times you ran away from me. I want to know why.'

Liz took a gulp of her tea and then headed over to the reception desk. It was obvious she was trying to buy herself time.

'No, I'm sorry but I don't know what you're talking about,' she said.

'But we saw each other—'

'I said I don't know what you're talking about,' Liz said again, and Judith and Suzie could see that she was trying to hide her panic.

'Oh,' Judith said. 'Are you saying you *didn't* go to Stefan Dunwoody's house after he died?'

'That's right. I don't even know who Stefan Dunwoody is,' Liz said. 'I've never heard that name before. Now do you want to make a booking, or do I have to ask you to leave?'

'What about Iqbal Kassam?' Suzie asked.

Liz took a moment before answering the question.

'Who?'

'Iqbal Kassam. The taxi driver who was murdered the other day.'

'Yes, I read about that in the papers. It's horrible. But why are you asking me?'

'We want to know if you know him.'

Liz's eyes widened in surprise as she guessed why Suzie had asked the question.

'What on earth are you suggesting?'

'We're not suggesting anything, we're just asking if you know him.'

'Of course I don't. Why would I take a taxi when I've got a perfectly good car of my own? I have to say that I resent you coming in here and making insinuations.'

'I'm sorry?' Suzie said.

'I don't know why you're asking me all these questions about those dead men.'

'I think you know well enough.'

'I don't.'

'Then let me say one word to you. Crumble.'

Liz looked like she'd been slapped in the face.

'Because we both know what you did to that poor dog,' Suzie added.

'I didn't do anything to him.'

'You killed him.'

'You can't say that!' Liz yelped, tears forming in her eyes as a combination of fear, guilt and confusion seemed to overwhelm her all at once.

'You killed him because you never wanted him. Because he was too expensive!'

'You've got to believe me, you're right I never wanted him when Dad died. I knew a dog wouldn't fit with our lives. And he was expensive, it's true. But that's because we've got no money. I loved Crumble. Surely you know that? I was distraught when he went missing. We made posters, stuck them to lampposts, it was about the worst time of my life. How on earth can you say I killed him? I'm sorry, you're not doing this to me. Not today. Not now.'

Before Judith or Suzie could say anything more, Liz turned and scurried out of the Portakabin.

'Guilty as charged,' Suzie said to her friend.

'You know what,' Judith said, 'I think I agree with you.'

The two women emerged into the sunshine just in time to see Liz getting into a battered vehicle. It was the same maroon-coloured car that Judith had seen Liz driving when they'd met in the field, once again confirming that it had indeed been Liz she'd encountered. They watched as she drove out onto the main road, and, with a squeal of wheels and a loud bang as her exhaust backfired, the car turned right and disappeared in the direction of Marlow town.

'Now that's what I call an exit,' Suzie said.

'Where do you think she's going?'

'She's in a hurry, wherever it is.'

'And why would she deny meeting me? That's the car I saw her driving.'

'Because she's the killer.'

'Yes, it's how it looks, isn't it? Although, if she were the killer, you'd have thought she'd have prepared her answers a bit better. I mean, I saw her twice. She and I both know I did. So why didn't she come up with a story to explain her running away? Something like how she mistook me for someone else. Or how she was lost the first time I saw her at Stefan's, and she was embarrassed and ran away the second time.'

Judith looked around for further inspiration and saw a man in dark green overalls doing some work to a canoe down by the river's edge.

'You know who that is?' she asked.

'An employee?'

'Then I suggest we have a quick word with him, don't you? I think we should find out a bit more about our recently departed hostess.'

As Judith approached the man, she could see that he was tall and rather plump, his midriff in particular seemed to strain against the cotton of his overalls. Something of a beer drinker, she thought to herself as she called out a hello.

The man had been attending to a rack of old canoes, and he stood up from his work, a spanner in his hand.

'Hi,' he said.

'Sorry to interrupt, but could we ask a few questions?'

'Sure. What about?'

'Do you work for Liz Curtis?'

The man smiled.

'You could say that. I'm her husband. Danny Curtis.'

Danny offered his hand, and the women introduced themselves.

'So how can I help you?' he asked.

'I wonder if you can. You see, I'm Stefan Dunwoody's neighbour. I live on the other side of the river to him. And a bit downstream.'

'Sure, I know you. You've got that pile just before Hurley Lock. I see you from time to time in your garden when I'm out on the river. He died recently, didn't he? But the papers are now saying he was murdered, aren't they? Which is kind of hard to believe. Here in Marlow.'

'That's right. Can I ask, did you or your wife know Stefan Dunwoody?'

'Can't say I did. But Liz knew him.'

Judith and Suzie caught each other's eyes.

'She did?'

'He ran the art gallery, didn't he? Liz is always hanging out there.'

'She knew him well?'

'I don't know I'd go that far. But she'd pop in for a chat with him when we were shopping in town.'

'That's interesting. Do you know if she ever visited his house?'

'His home? No. I don't suppose she knows where he lives.'

'Was it possible she visited his house last Saturday?'

'I've no idea. You'll have to ask her. But I wouldn't want you to get the wrong idea. Even if Liz was friendly with Stefan, it's not like she ever bought anything from him. I mean, look at this place. We don't have the cash for fine art.'

As he said this, Danny nodded at the tired buildings of the rowing centre.

'Yes, I was wondering about that,' Judith said. 'Where is everyone? With it being the summer holidays, I'd have thought you'd have kids galore out on the river in your canoes.'

Danny sighed. 'We're still trying to get this place back on track after the floods.'

Judith knew the Thames had broken its banks a number of times through the winter. As her garden was sloped, her house hadn't been threatened, but there'd been plenty of days when her boathouse and garden had flooded.

'All of this was underwater,' Danny said, indicating the buildings of the rowing centre. 'And then the place was a mudbath once the waters receded. It was the toughest winter we've had in decades. We put out a call to the local community to help clear up. And people came, but there was only so much they could do. It's been about as tough a time as we've ever had. And we've had tough times.'

'You frequently get flooded?'

'Liz's dad used to say, when he first built this place, they weren't flooded one year in ten. Now it seems to happen every year.'

'I'm sorry to hear that.'

'Our facilities still aren't back up to what they should be, so we're limited to the number of people we can have on site on any given day. And there's only Liz and me here. The plan was to fix things over the summer, hope we survive another winter, and then hit the ground running next spring.'

'That sounds tough,' Suzie said, and Judith could see that there was something of a bond between her and Danny. They both knew what it was like to have to work hard.

'Liz is a good Christian. Goes to church every Sunday. Which is more than I do. But what we've had to put up with here has tested even her. Now, if you don't mind, I've got to get these canoes to Nottingham tonight for training.'

'Training?' Judith said, unable to stop herself from glancing at Danny's portly frame.

Danny laughed.

'Not me. The Youth GB squad. I coach them. They're based in Nottingham.'

'You train the GB team?' Suzie said, impressed.

'It's the youth team, and there are a few coaches, but yes, I'm involved.'

'Then we'll take up no more of your time,' Judith said. 'Thank you so much for talking to us.'

Judith and Suzie turned to leave, but Judith stopped after a few paces as it occurred to her that if Liz had lied to them about knowing Stefan, then maybe there was something else she'd lied about as well.

'One last thing,' she said, turning back to Danny. 'Did you or your wife know that taxi driver who was shot?'

'What's that?' Danny asked.

'Iqbal Kassam.'

Danny was puzzled by the question, but he nodded his head.

'I suppose so. I mean, I never met him, but we used him a couple of weeks ago. Our car was at the garage and we had to do our shopping, so we booked Iqbal to take us to the supermarket and back. He seemed like a nice guy when I spoke to him on the phone.'

'He was, wasn't he,' Suzie agreed.

'Oh, you knew him?'

'I was his dog walker.'

'And is it true what the papers are saying? That someone shot him as well?'

'That's what they're saying,' Judith said, not wishing to reveal how close to the case she and Suzie were.

'Christ,' Danny said. 'It's hard to believe, isn't it?'

'You don't by any chance have any idea who might have wanted him dead?'

'Me? No, I never met him. But you should ask Liz. She was the one who took the taxi.'

'It was your wife who used Iqbal?'

'It's Liz who does the shopping.'

'How many times has she used him?'

'I don't know, just that once I think. Why are you asking?'

'And how long was she with him?'

'A couple of hours. It's like I said. He took her up to the Handy Cross Asda. Waited while she went shopping. Drove her back. But I don't understand. Why are you so interested?'

'We're trying to work out what happened,' Judith said, deciding, as ever, that honesty was the best policy.

Danny frowned as he considered this. 'Isn't that a job that's better left to the police?'

'Oh, don't worry,' Judith said with a smile, 'the police know full well what we're doing.'

'They do?' Danny looked sceptical, and then shrugged. 'If you want to know more about your taxi driver or your neighbour, go and have a word with my wife. She'll be somewhere around here.'

'Thank you,' Judith said. 'If we see her, we will.'

Judith thanked Danny again for his help, wished him all the best with his coaching in Nottingham that night, and she and Suzie left.

Once they were out of earshot, Suzie said to Judith, 'Liz lied to us.'

'She did, didn't she?' Judith agreed.

'She knew both Stefan and Iqbal.'

'And yet she told us she knew neither man. Just like she

denied being in Stefan's garden. Or running away from me. She's involved in this up to her neck, isn't she?'

'What made you think of asking Danny about Iqbal?'

Judith paused, trying to work it out for herself.

'I don't know. I think it's all my years of setting crosswords. You get used to making connections. And once Danny had confirmed that she'd lied to us about knowing Stefan . . . Now, I think we need to find out a bit more about Liz Curtis, don't you?'

'And how can we do that?'

'Well, I couldn't help noticing that Danny told us that Liz was a regular churchgoer, in which case, there's one person I can think of . . .'

'Of course!' Suzie said, realising. 'Becks.'

Chapter 18

'What are you doing here?' Becks blurted as soon as she opened her front door and found Judith and Suzie outside.

'Pleased to see you as well,' Suzie said.

'You can't come here,' Becks tried again, desperation in her eyes.

'You don't know why we're here!'

'I've got a very good idea, and you can't bring your murders to the vicarage, what would Colin say?'

'Firstly,' Judith said, drawing herself up to her full but diminutive height, 'these aren't "our" murders. And secondly, if we can't bring them to the vicarage, where can we bring them?'

'Well, I'm sorry, but I can't be seen talking about murder.'

'Why not?'

Becks was affronted, but for reasons she couldn't quite specify.

'Why not?' Judith asked again.

'Who is it, darling?' a male voice called out from inside the house.

'No one,' Becks called. 'They're just going.'

'We want to know about Liz Curtis,' Suzie said.

This caught Becks by surprise.

'What do you want to know about Liz?'

'Do you know her?'

'Enough to say hello to after church on a Sunday. Why are you asking?'

'Because as far as I can see, she could be our killer.'

Becks' eyes widened in amazement.

'That's not possible, she does yoga!'

Judith wasn't sure she'd heard correctly.

'Are you saying people who do yoga can't commit murder?' she asked.

'Yes!'

'Then maybe,' Judith said, deciding to go in for the kill, 'you could tell us all about Liz Curtis over a nice cup of tea?'

Becks' smile froze. As a true-born Englishwoman, she knew there were no circumstances under which she could ever refuse the request of a cup of tea.

'What a lovely idea,' she lied, and then invited the women in.

'Bloody hell,' Suzie said as she stepped into the house, 'it's like an advert!'

Suzie was referring to the tasteful wallpaper, pictures and furniture in the hallway.

'An advert?' Becks asked, confused.

'You know, like you get in magazines. But it's not real. No one actually lives like this.'

Becks smiled at what she mistook to be a compliment.

'Thank you, that's very kind of you. Why don't you come through? Sorry about the mess,' she said as she led the two women into a kitchen that didn't contain a single mote of dust.

'Wow,' Suzie said in wonder.

'It really is very clean,' Judith agreed.

'Do you clean your sink?' Suzie said, going over to look at the sparkling metal sink.

'Only when I've finished washing, I'm not obsessive.'

Suzie turned to Judith and said, 'She washes her sink.'

Becks took up a bottle of spray cleaner, squirted it at an imaginary smear on the countertop and then wiped it away with a clean J-cloth.

'Now who'd like tea? I've got caffeinated or decaffeinated?'

'Normal tea's good for me,' Suzie said.

'Black, green or Oolong?'

'Oolong? What's Oolong when it's at home? Normal will do fine, thanks.'

'Or how about herbal? We've got Rooibos or Chai?'

'Just a cup of normal tea, milk, one sugar.'

Becks dithered, knowing she still didn't have enough information to proceed.

'What is it?' Suzie asked.

'Cow's milk?'

'What?'

'Would you like cow's milk in your tea or would you rather have soya? Or almond? Oat or coconut?'

'Cow's milk! Just an ordinary cup of tea with ordinary milk.'

'Oh,' Becks said, almost affronted, but also intrigued by the novelty of Suzie's wishes. Ordinary tea with normal milk? It clearly hadn't been heard of in the vicarage for a long time.

As Becks got down the polka dot Emma Bridgewater teapot which matched the polka dot Emma Bridgewater cups, polka dot Emma Bridgewater saucers and polka dot Emma Bridgewater milk jug, Judith explained how they'd discovered that it had been

Liz Curtis who'd visited Stefan's property after he died, and who ran away from Judith after Iqbal was killed.

'And the thing is,' Suzie said, 'when we asked her, she said she didn't know Stefan or Iqbal, even though her husband Danny said that Liz knew Stefan to say hello to at least, and she'd also travelled in Iqbal's taxi a couple of weeks ago.'

'She lied to you?' Becks said, not quite believing the other women.

'To our faces.'

'Why would she do that?'

'That's where you come in,' Judith said. 'What can you tell us about her?'

'Well, for starters, you know she's got an Olympic silver medal, don't you?'

'She has?' Judith said, knowing that the achievements of a person weren't how she'd have started an explanation, but also guessing that it was exactly these external badges of merit that defined people for someone like Becks.

'She's got that winner's attitude. So focused. So determined.'

'What's her medal for?' Suzie asked.

'She's a rower. Or she was. It's how she and Danny met. He was a rower as well. But only at a junior level, I think. Liz told me Danny had all the talent in the world, but he didn't have the necessary drive. I'll be honest, she could be a bit scary when she talked about what you needed to be a top-level athlete. It was all about the tiniest margins, she'd say. Being committed to your goal and not letting anything get in the way. Which is how you end up with an Olympic silver medal, I suppose.'

'What was her class?' Judith asked.

'Class?'

'What sort of rowing did she do? Was she in an eight?'

'No, I think she was a solo rower. It was her on her own.'

'Which is interesting,' Judith said. 'So she's a bit of a loner, would you say?'

'I don't know I'd say that. I don't really know her.'

'But she comes to church every week,' Suzie said.

'I know, but you have to understand, when I'm at church, I'm always representing Colin, so I have to talk to everyone who wants to talk to me. And Liz keeps herself to herself a bit. I get the impression her faith is a very private thing to her.'

'But you'd say she was a Christian?'

'Oh yes.'

'And had Christian values?'

'Of course.'

'Even though she killed her dog,' Suzie said.

'What?'

Suzie explained how she believed Liz had paid a vet to kill her dog.

'That's not possible.'

'It's not just possible, it happened.'

'Look, I'd agree with you she can be a bit grand at times. She's something like Marlow royalty with her Olympic medal. You can see it in the way she holds herself when she comes to church. She very much thinks she's Queen Bee. But then, everyone flutters around her and makes a fuss, so it's no surprise I suppose. Now, I've answered your questions, I'm afraid I have to ask you both to leave.'

'We're only having a cup of tea in your kitchen,' Judith said.

'I can't be seen gossiping about locals.'

'Locals who might have committed murder.'

'You have to stop saying that!'

'But it's true! *Someone* murdered Stefan. And then murdered Iqbal. We have to find out who it was.'

'Well, it won't have been Liz,' Becks said with finality. 'I can tell you that much. There's no way she'd commit murder.'

'That's what you think,' Suzie said. 'But not everyone's quite what we thought they were, are they? Judith here thought her neighbour Stefan was clean as a whistle, but we now know he stole a painting worth hundreds of thousands from under the nose of Elliot Howard. So there's no knowing what dark secrets lurk in the past of anyone. Isn't that right, Judith?'

Suzie was surprised that her question seemed to catch Judith off guard and the older woman spilled her tea down her chin as she was taking a sip.

'Look what I've done!' she exclaimed.

'No worries,' Becks said, yanking yards of the thickest kitchen towel from a dispenser and handing them over to Judith.

Becks attended to Judith, and Judith was so busy scolding herself for her slip that neither of them noticed that Suzie was looking at Judith somewhat askance. If she wasn't mistaken, and she knew she wasn't, Judith was behaving as though she had something to hide. Suzie had a hunch it was linked to the time Judith had blushed when they'd talked about her husband. And, now she was thinking about it, the memory of the locked door in Judith's house also popped into her head. Why did Judith, who was so open and upfront about so much, have a locked door in her house?

Everyone was startled by the sound of a mobile phone ringing. Suzie eventually realised it was hers and fished it out of her back pocket.

'I don't recognise the number,' she said as she looked at the cracked screen.

'Hello, this is Suzie Harris,' she said, answering the call.

Suzie listened for a few moments, and then lowered the phone from her ear.

'It's Iqbal's imam,' she said in a theatrical whisper that was some degrees louder than her normal speaking voice. 'He says the police have released his body, so the funeral's going to be tomorrow. He wants to know how many people I'm bringing.'

'You can count me in,' Judith said without a moment's hesitation.

Suzie turned to Becks, who tussled with her conscience only briefly.

'Look, I can't help you with your investigation,' she said. 'I just can't. But of course I'll come. It's the least I can do.'

Suzie put the phone back to her ear.

'Thanks for the invite. There'll be three of us at Iqbal's funeral.'

Chapter 19

Iqbal's mosque was situated on the edge of High Wycombe, surrounded on all sides by terraced houses. It was a 1980s red-brick building, but it had a grand white dome and minaret on top.

As for the funeral service, a ceremony that Becks explained to the others was called a 'Janazah', it was both nothing like a funeral the women had been to before, but also a lot like all of them.

The main difference was that they had to remove their shoes and put on head coverings before they entered the mosque. Judith had brought a rather splendid 1940s Hermès silk headscarf that had belonged to her great aunt. Becks had a pretty dupatta in red and gold, and in her handbag were two spares in case anyone hadn't come prepared, which turned out to be the case with Suzie.

Once inside, they were directed to a large prayer room that had a dark red carpet with thick golden lines woven into it that ran the full length of the room. There was also a midnight blue curtain strung down the middle, dividing the space in two. Apart from a few plastic chairs by the walls, there was no other furniture.

At the front, an elderly man in a salwar kameez was reading tonelessly from the Quran into a microphone as half a dozen men mingled. To the man's side, Iqbal's coffin lay under a clean white cloth on a trestle table.

One of the men saw the women enter and headed over, anger furrowing his brow.

'You can't come this side,' he hissed at them, indicating the curtain. 'Women are on that side.'

'I'm so sorry,' Becks said, defusing the situation with the well-practised smile of a vicar's wife. 'We're going straight there. Thank you.'

Becks led her friends to the other side of the curtain and saw a solitary woman waiting at the front. The woman noticed them and nodded a smile of welcome. The three friends smiled back.

'We'd better sit here,' Becks said, indicating some plastic chairs lined up against the wall.

As they sat down, the imam appeared at the front of the room and started the service. While the various prayers and chants were in Arabic, a language they didn't understand, the shape of the ceremony felt reassuringly familiar. It was also pleasantly brisk in comparison to a Church of England funeral, Becks found herself thinking, seeing as it came in at only twenty minutes long.

At the end, they saw the men from the other side of the curtain step forward, gather around the coffin, lift it up onto their shoulders and start to carry it out of the room. As they did so, Imam Latif crossed to their side of the curtain and approached.

'I take it one of you is Suzie Harris,' he said.

'That's right,' Suzie said, offering her hand. 'That's me.'

'I am so very sorry for your loss.'

'Thank you,' Suzie said, touched by the imam's words.

'And it's good to see you, Mrs Starling.'

'*Salaam*, Imam.'

'How are your flock?'

'My husband's flock. They're well. And yours?'

'Oh, the same. But I want to apologise to you. I saw how one of my congregation spoke to you when you came in. His tone was unacceptable, and he was wrong to make you move.'

'There's nothing to apologise for,' Becks said. 'And it's not so different in our church. You should see the looks Major Lewis gives if someone he doesn't know dares to sit in his family's pew.'

Imam Latif smiled.

'You always know what to say, Mrs Starling. The sad truth is, one tries to be progressive, but some people feel they have to cling to the old traditions, don't they? Now, why don't we walk together?'

Imam Latif indicated the door through which the men had carried the coffin.

The four of them started to follow.

'Now you I don't know,' Imam Latif said to Judith.

'I'm Judith Potts,' Judith said. 'Thank you for inviting us to your mosque.'

'The pleasure is all mine.'

'But could I ask you a few questions?'

'Of course. How can I be of service?'

'Well, it's just the awful way he died.'

'Indeed. A tragedy.'

'Would you say you were surprised, though?'

'Do you mean, did I think Iqbal was perhaps mixed up in malfeasance?'

'I suppose I do.'

Becks and Suzie looked at Judith to translate, which she was happy to do.

'Malfeasance. Wrongdoing.'

'Oh,' Becks said, impressed. Suzie shrugged as if to say, 'what use is that to me?'

'To be honest,' Imam Latif said, 'I can't say I knew Iqbal well. We rarely saw him here. Which is fine by me. Better to welcome someone infrequently than pressure them into not coming at all. But he always struck me as a sincere and thoughtful man. Maybe a little too inward. Too private. And there was a bit of anger there as well.'

'You thought so?'

'Perhaps I mean frustration. The one proper conversation I had with him, I remember him telling me it was his dream to travel by boat all around the UK.'

'He said the same to me,' Suzie said.

'But he said he'd had that future taken from him.'

'When was this?' Judith asked.

'About a year ago. Sometime last year anyway.'

'And did he say why his future had been taken away from him?'

'It was something to do with an inheritance, I think.'

The women exchanged glances. This sounded promising.

'From his neighbour,' Imam Latif continued.

'That'll be Ezra, I imagine,' Suzie said.

'That's right. He said his neighbour was called Ezra, and he'd died and left him all of his money and his house. But when it came down to it, someone else had made his neighbour change his will at the last minute. So this other person inherited from his neighbour and not Iqbal.'

'Oh,' Becks said. 'Poor Iqbal.'

'Indeed.'

'Was this other man called Elliot Howard?' Judith asked eagerly.

'I don't know. Iqbal didn't tell me the person's name. But I once saw him,' the imam said, brightening at the memory. 'Yes, it was the last time I saw Iqbal. Earlier this year, I bumped into Iqbal leaving the shopping centre, and when I went to speak to him, he was looking across the road at the car park. I asked him if he was all right, and he got very angry, pointed to a man who was getting out of his car and said that I was looking at the man who'd stolen his inheritance from him.'

'Was this man very tall?' Judith asked. 'In his late fifties? With long grey hair down to his shoulders?'

Imam Latif thought carefully before answering.

'No, I wouldn't say he was tall, although he might have been in his late fifties. In fact, now I think about it, he was short. And very podgy. Like a big ball of dough,' he said, pleased with his simile. 'He was a very short and very fat man.'

The women were nonplussed. They'd not met any man involved in either Stefan or Iqbal's case who was very short or very fat.

'Do you remember what car he was driving?' Suzie asked.

'Oh no,' the imam said, chuckling. 'I don't know anything about cars. But I can picture it now. This very short and fat man, wearing a suit and a tie, and carrying a briefcase, got out of his car and left the car park. Iqbal was insistent that this was the man who'd stolen his inheritance from him by making his neighbour change his will. I didn't know what to say. Iqbal was so agitated. But that was the last time I saw him.'

As they'd been speaking, Imam Latif had led the women out onto the steps of the mosque, and together they'd watched the men help some undertakers load the coffin into a black hearse.

'Thanks so much for talking to us,' Becks said, 'but don't let us keep you.'

'Thank you. I need to accompany the coffin up to the cemetery. And thank you again for offering your support today. You are welcome here any time.'

With a warm smile, Imam Latif went over to talk to the undertakers by the hearse.

'That's something of a bombshell,' Judith said.

'There's a short, fat man out there,' Suzie said, 'who stole Iqbal's inheritance.'

'But he wasn't just short and fat. He was wearing a suit and had a briefcase, so that suggests he's a businessman of some sort. But before we get too excited, how much money are we talking about?'

'Well,' Suzie said. 'I can tell you, Ezra's house is in a right old state. I don't reckon it can be worth that much.'

'But it's currently for sale?' Becks asked.

'There's a board outside the house.'

'And where exactly is it?'

'Halfway up the Wycombe Road, on the way out of Marlow.'

'Oh I know the one. Three-bed bungalow, plenty of potential for development, on for six hundred and fifty thousand pounds.'

The other two women looked at Becks, surprised.

'You know that?'

'Or nearest offer, but it will make the asking price. A local builder will snap it up, I imagine, knock it down and build something more substantial.'

'How do you know that?' Suzie asked.

Becks had the good grace to look a touch embarrassed.

'I'm interested in the local property market.'

'But you knew the exact amount it's selling for!'

'Yes, well it's like I say, I'm interested.'

'Do you know all of the house prices in Marlow?'

'Of course not. That would be stupid.'

'But you know the price of a bungalow on the Wycombe Road.'

'A lucky coincidence,' Becks said modestly.

'What about the house that's for sale on the High Street?' Suzie asked. 'Next door to the pet shop?'

'Oh I don't know,' Becks said, but the other two women could see she was lying.

'Go on,' Judith said, grinning. 'I bet you know *exactly* what it's on for.'

'Well, since you're asking, eight hundred thousand, but I wouldn't touch it with a bargepole. It's not got off-street parking, and none of the bedrooms are en suite, not even the master bedroom. And these days, that's the least you'd expect for a family home.'

Judith clapped her hands together in delight.

'It's like having Google right here, isn't it? What about that glass monstrosity that's for sale further down the river from me? I've always wanted to know how much that's on sale for.'

'You mean the "architect-built family home", five bedrooms, each with en suite, over two hundred feet of river frontage? It's on for three point one million.'

'That's a lot of money,' Judith said. 'But it explains why Iqbal was so angry, doesn't it? If he missed out on inheriting a house worth six hundred and fifty thousand pounds. It would make anyone angry.'

'Especially someone who was saving up to buy a nice boat. That sort of money would have paid for a real beauty.'

'So who was this doughy, short, fat man?' Suzie asked.

'Oh that shouldn't be hard to uncover,' Judith said.

'You think so?'

'It should be quite straightforward. The fact that Ezra's house is on the market suggests that his will has cleared probate. And once a will does that it goes into the public domain.'

'How do you know that?'

'I learned all this when I inherited from my great aunt Betty. But the thing is, once the will is in the public domain, anyone can order a copy of it. So all we have to do is log onto the relevant government website, order a copy of Ezra's will, and then we'll discover who inherited his money instead of Iqbal.'

'And hopefully he'll be the short, fat, doughy man,' Suzie said.

'Agreed. The short, fat, doughy man,' Judith said. 'Whoever he is.'

Chapter 20

Over the next few days, life returned to a semblance of normality for Judith. She managed to compile and submit a crossword to her editor at the *Observer*, she completed her jigsaw of the West Highland terrier before returning it to the charity shop she'd bought it from, and she swam every evening in the Thames. She felt she had no choice. The weather continued to be swelteringly hot all day, every day.

As for her new friends, Suzie was able to throw herself back into her work, but she couldn't shift a nagging feeling that she was missing out. It wasn't so much that she wanted to solve Iqbal's murder, it was more that she'd enjoyed the sense of camaraderie that working with Judith and Becks had given her. The sad truth was, despite being surrounded by dogs, getting out every day for long walks, and even having people constantly coming and going in her house, Suzie was lonely. She had Emma, of course. Suzie had grown to like her new

Dobermann a lot. But the truth was, she'd spent so many years as a single mother raising her two children to the best of her ability while also holding down a job that she'd lost touch with whatever friends she'd once had. And now that her children had left home, she felt stranded. Like an old boat that had been marooned on a beach as the tide went out.

As for Becks, she spent her time in an increasing tizzy of rising irritation. This was because, as far as she was concerned, she'd just had an amazing adventure, and yet no one in her house seemed at all interested in hearing about it. Colin had listened carefully as she'd explained about seeing Imam Latif, and how he'd told her the story of Iqbal Kassam possibly being cheated out of an inheritance from his neighbour. Once she'd finished, Colin told Becks she shouldn't gossip when she was out and about in a way that made Becks realise that he hadn't really been listening at all. As for her son Sam, he was so wrapped up in his own fourteen-year-old life that Becks didn't even bother telling him. And while she knew her daughter Chloe would have loved to hear about her escapades, they were currently refusing to talk to each other. This was because, the night before the funeral, Becks had caught Chloe slipping out of the house to visit her boyfriend, a nice boy called Jack, but what put Becks on the warpath was the discovery that her daughter had a bottle of gin in her bag. Becks had shouted at Chloe at the time, what sort of sixteen-year-old girl goes to see her boyfriend late at night with a bottle of gin?

The answer, of course, was: Becks. After all, Chloe got her transgressive side from someone, and it certainly wasn't Colin. In fact, Becks had a memory of stealing an old bottle of Cointreau from her mother when she was eleven years old, drinking it in a field with her best friend while smoking her mum's cigarettes.

But that was the childhood version of Becks. The one who was daring, who didn't give a stuff about rules.

What perhaps spiked Becks' irritation the most was the realisation that she was as culpable as anyone else for her lack of status within her family. When she married, she couldn't wait to put on her wedding ring and take her husband's name. But all these years later, without even her own name to cling to, she felt rudderless, cast adrift.

When Becks' phone rang, she was in the process of making mayonnaise with a hand whisk. She had a perfectly good food mixer that could have done the job in seconds. In fact, she lived next to any number of shops that would have sold her organic artisanal mayonnaise over the counter. But, in the absence of knowing quite what she was doing with her life, Becks clung to the only truth she knew: she was a housewife, and as such, her only sanity was to be the best housewife there'd ever been. *Ergo*, the hand whisk.

Her heart jumped as she saw the display name on her phone, and she answered the call gladly.

It was the same for Suzie, a few minutes later, when her phone rang. She was down by the river with Emma, two whippets called Wally and Evie, and a pug called Crackers, when she saw that Judith was calling her.

'Ezra Harrington's will has arrived,' Judith said breathlessly. 'It came in the post.'

'Who inherits?' Suzie said, cutting to the chase.

'His whole estate was inherited by a man called Andy Bishop.'

'Who?'

'According to the will, Andy Bishop was Ezra's solicitor.'

'Hold on, are you saying that Iqbal's neighbour ended up leaving his whole estate to his solicitor?'

'And his solicitor is also the sole executor. So the same man drew up the will, was in charge of dispensing it once Ezra had died, and was also the sole beneficiary.'

'Is that even legal?'

'I looked it up. It's legal. But it's very definitely not ethical.'

'We need to meet up, don't we?'

'I think we need to meet up as a matter of some urgency.'

Chapter 21

Marlow wasn't short of places for three women to meet. In fact, it sometimes felt that every other business in the town was a coffee shop or drinks bar that had been expressly set up so women could meet. Judith, Suzie and Becks were able to take a window seat in a small coffee shop in the High Street that was directly opposite Andy Bishop's office. They knew where he worked because he'd listed his company address in Ezra's will.

The building was a pretty Georgian townhouse with bay windows, and there was a discreet brass plaque by the shiny black door. According to the company website, there were a dozen or so lawyers in the practice and Andy Bishop was listed as a senior partner.

But what should their next step be? Suzie believed they should spy on him somehow, Becks was keen they didn't go near him at all, but Judith overruled them both. As far as she was concerned, there was only one way to find out how Andy Bishop was involved in Iqbal's death.

'I'm here to see Mr Bishop,' Judith said to the receptionist a few minutes later.

Judith's friends had tried to suggest that barrelling into Andy's office was possibly foolhardy, but Judith had pooh-poohed their concerns. Unlike when she visited Elliot Howard, this time she had a plan. Or believed she had a plan, which was practically the same thing as far as she was concerned.

'Do you have an appointment?' the receptionist asked.

'I don't. But could you tell him my name is Mrs Judith Potts, and I'd like to talk to him about Ezra Harrington's will.'

The receptionist was puzzled.

'Mr Harrington's will? We dealt with that last year, didn't we?'

'Don't worry, Mr Bishop will know what I'm talking about.'

With a polite smile, Judith went and sat down in a chair by an empty fireplace. The receptionist, seeing that Judith wasn't going anywhere, got up and went through a nearby door.

She was back less than a minute later.

'Mrs Potts?' she said, clearly puzzled. 'Mr Bishop will see you now.'

'Thank you.'

Judith allowed herself to be led into a tastefully decorated office. There were two leather armchairs by a coffee table and faded oil paintings of hunting scenes on the walls. But Judith couldn't help noticing that although the room was on the ground floor and had a lovely sash window with views of the bustling High Street, it also had a window on the other side that over-looked a tatty piece of tarmac and the office car park.

Andy Bishop was sitting behind a desk covered in papers, and, as he stood up to greet her, Judith was thrilled to see that he wasn't very tall at all. Maybe less than five feet five inches. And what he lacked in height he made up in girth. In fact, he was so round that the fabric of his waistcoat was stretched tight, the buttons seemingly about to burst at the seam.

There was no doubting it in her mind. This was the 'very short, very fat man' Iqbal had pointed out to his imam. The man who had apparently stolen Iqbal's inheritance. Judith felt a thrill at the danger of it all as she introduced herself. Andy indicated that they should sit down in the leather armchairs.

'You wanted to see me about Mr Harrington's will?' he asked.

'That's right. He was a friend of mine.'

'Yes, and mine as well. He was a rather splendid gentleman, wasn't he? Sorry about the heat,' he said, getting out a handkerchief and mopping his shiny forehead before indicating the windows. 'We don't have any air conditioning, all I can do is open the windows.'

'That's no problem.'

'Anyway, how can I help you?'

'I just wanted to check, you're the same Andy Bishop who drew up Ezra's will.'

'That's right.'

'Or rather, changed it.'

'What's that?'

'Only I know that originally Ezra left his estate to his neighbour, Iqbal Kassam.'

Andy looked slightly embarrassed.

'I'm afraid I'm not allowed to comment on a client's private financial affairs.'

'But it's true, isn't it? Ezra told me yonks ago that he was leaving his estate to his neighbour, Iqbal. Because Iqbal was being so helpful, you see. When Ezra got ill. Taking him to the hospital in his taxi for his tests. And so on.'

'I'm sure he did. I don't much remember Iqbal. But, and

I wouldn't want to stress the point too much, Iqbal wasn't the only one who helped Ezra.'

'I'm sorry?'

'As it happens, I was visiting Ezra every day towards the end. Taking him to hospital as well, making sure he was getting the right prescriptions. And I can tell you, he had a *lot* of prescriptions. He'd never been the healthiest of men, had he?' Andy smiled fondly at the memory. 'Judith Potts?' he added as an afterthought. 'You know, now I think about it, I don't remember Ezra ever mentioning a Judith to me.'

'Well, I hadn't seen him for a while. Not until he got in touch again when he fell ill.'

'Tell me, how did you know each other?'

Judith smiled. She'd been expecting the question.

'We're both Marlow residents. We've known each other simply ages.'

'But how did you meet?'

'Was it a mutual friend? I don't remember, it must have been forty years ago.'

'Perhaps you knew his sister?'

Judith's smile didn't falter, but her mind was racing. *Sister? What sister?* And then she realised the truth that was implied by Ezra's will.

'What an odd thing to say. He didn't have a sister.'

After a moment, Andy's face lit up.

'Oh that's right, he didn't,' he said. 'For some reason, I always thought he had one. More fool me. Anyway, how can I help you?'

'Well,' Judith said, hoping her relief at passing Andy's test wasn't showing on her face, 'the thing is, I've got a great aunt who's very ill. Cancer of the oesophagus.' Judith didn't feel even a twinge of guilt at using her great aunt's terminal illness to bamboozle Andy. She knew Betty would have thoroughly approved. 'And she's not got long left to be with us. But she's appointed her solicitor as executor of her will.'

'I see. That seems entirely sensible.'

'Indeed. But the thing is, she's also asked her solicitor to draw up her will.'

'That also makes sense.'

'In what way?'

'It saves on cost, for one thing. And the difficulty of adminis-tration. Have the person who draws up the will also execute it. It's neater all round.'

'Yes, I suppose so. But this is what I don't understand. And perhaps this is where you can help. You see, my aunt, as well as getting her solicitor to draw up her new will, and be her executor, also wants to leave a substantial bequest to the same man.'

Andy looked puzzled.

'I see. So what exactly is it that you're asking me?'

'It's just that I know that Ezra did the same with you. Shortly before he died, he got you to draw up a new will, made you executor, and also named you as the sole beneficiary.'

'And how on earth do you know that?'

'Ezra told me. It's like I said. He was my friend.'

'He spoke to you about this?'

'Oh yes. Not long before he died. And I hope you don't mind me saying, but the whole thing sounded rum to me. Which is why I wanted to see you. Because it also feels rum to me that my great aunt's doing the same. So perhaps what I'm asking is, can you reassure me that what my great aunt's solicitor is doing is ethical?'

'You mean, drawing up a will to which he's also a beneficiary?'

'Yes, that's it in a nutshell.'

Andy looked at Judith for a few moments, and then he sighed as though he was disappointed in her.

'I think I know what's going on here,' he said. 'You're checking up on me, aren't you?'

'I'm sorry?'

'Don't worry, I get it,' he said, almost kindly. 'I take it you live on your own? I've been doing this job a long time, I know the type. But you've got nothing to occupy you, so you've got a bee in your bonnet that there was something not quite right about your friend Ezra's will.' Andy got up, went over to the door and opened it. 'Whereas the far more prosaic truth is, Ezra's will was entirely above board. Of course it was or it wouldn't have cleared probate, would it? Now, believe it or not, I do actually have some work to do. So if you don't mind . . . ?'

Andy stood at the open doorway, a smile on his face, as though he knew that Judith had no comeback. Frustratingly, Judith knew he was right. She couldn't think of another card to play. Not without revealing her hand. So she got up, thanked Andy for taking the time to see her and left.

But as Judith returned to the reception area, she started chastising herself. Even if it was technically legal, what Andy Bishop had done with Ezra's will was still sharp practice at the very least, so who was he to start lecturing her? And if everything about Ezra's will was so above board, how come he'd seen her so quickly without an appointment?

Judith stopped by the front door.

What had he said? She lived on her own and had nothing to occupy her? Well, he couldn't have been more wrong there. She had a job setting crosswords, which wasn't bad for a woman who was seventy-seven years old, was it? And as she thought this, Judith realised that no man had the right to speak to her so condescendingly. Especially not some jumped-up local solicitor.

Judith turned on her heel, strode back towards Andy's office and pushed the door open without knocking.

'I do have a job, you know,' she pronounced grandly.

Andy was standing by the window that overlooked the High Street, and he turned in surprise at Judith's sudden reappearance.

On the table by the window, an office shredder was sucking in a piece of paper, slicing it into the thinnest of strips and spewing them out into a clear cellophane bag attached to the back. Judith couldn't see what was being shredded, but it was glossy, as if it had come from a magazine, and Andy instinctively moved across so her view of the shredder was blocked.

He looked guilty as hell.

'What's that?' he said, trying to buy himself time.

'Which is all I wanted to say,' Judith said, if only so she could make a quick exit. 'I do have a job. I'm not a busybody, and you should treat your elders and betters with a bit more respect. Good day to you.'

And with that, she turned and left the room. But this time, she *knew* that Andy was implicated somehow in Iqbal's death. After all, an innocent man doesn't immediately start shredding papers the moment he's accused of wrongdoing, does he?

So what was the document that Andy was shredding? And why was it so important to him to destroy it the moment he'd finished talking to Judith?

Chapter 22

The three women repaired to the vicarage for a council of war, it being only a little way down the High Street from Andy Bishop's office.

'We need to find out what Andy was shredding,' Judith said, as she sat down and was almost entirely engulfed by the puffy Laura Ashley sofa in Becks' sitting room.

'There's no way of finding out,' Becks said as she entered the room with cups of tea and a plate of biscuits. 'Tea?'

'Oo, thanks,' Suzie said as she grabbed a biscuit.

'It's normal builders' tea,' Becks said, failing to hide her distaste at the thought. 'And there's a ramekin of sugar.'

'Lovely,' Suzie said, delighted.

'If only we could get hold of the shredded paper,' Judith said, 'I think I'd be able to work out what was on it.'

'How?' Suzie asked. 'Surely it's impossible if it's shredded.'

'Oh no, I think it's eminently possible. But it's something of a moot point if we can't get hold of the pieces.'

'Which we won't be able to do,' Becks said, pouring out three steaming cups of tea.

'I'm not sure I agree with you there,' Suzie said.

'You don't?'

'There's a way we can get our hands on whatever it was Andy Bishop shredded.'

'But how?'

'Well, that's simple enough. We walk in there and take it.'

'He won't let us do that!'

'Of course not. So we'll have to take it without him realising.'

'But,' Becks said, as she followed through the logic of what Suzie had said. 'That's theft.'

'You could call it that.'

Becks was horrified.

Judith leant forward, excitement sparkling her eyes.

'And how do you think we should get hold of it?'

'There's only one thing for it. We'll have to break in.'

'Oh no no no,' Becks said. 'We can't break into a solicitor's office and steal *anything*!'

'You make it sound bad,' Suzie said.

'That's because it is bad.'

'It's not that bad.'

'It's illegal! We could go to prison!'

'We won't go to prison.'

'How can you be sure?'

'That's easy. We won't get caught.'

Becks waited for Suzie to continue her explanation. No further explanation was forthcoming.

'That's it?'

Suzie shrugged. 'Sure.'

'I'm sorry, there's no way I can be involved in something like this,' Becks said. 'I'm the vicar's wife.'

'You still have free will,' Judith said.

'Very funny. And you're wrong. No vicar's wife has free will. But what little I have I won't use to break the law.'

'It's hardly even theft,' Suzie said before taking a sip of her tea.

'It's *exactly* theft. And I won't have anything to do with it!'

Becks had spoken far louder than she'd intended, and she looked in fear at the door to the sitting room. If anyone else was in they'd possibly have heard her outburst, but the house remained silent.

'I quite understand,' Judith said, reaching out and patting Becks on the knee. 'You have a position to keep up. As you say, you're the vicar's wife.'

'Okay,' Suzie said. 'If you don't want to be involved, that's your call. But do you have a pen and paper? I think Judith and I need to make a plan.'

Becks went over to the dresser and pulled out some of her stationery. She handed the sheets of paper to Judith, who looked at them in surprise.

'Maybe they shouldn't have your name and address embossed at the top of each sheet,' she said. 'Seeing as we're planning a robbery.'

'Oh, right! And don't say that. It sounds so wrong when you put it like that. Let me get some A4 from Colin's office.'

As Becks left the sitting room, Suzie started asking Judith about the layout of Andy's office, where the main door was, and the precise location of the shredding machine.

By the time Becks returned and handed over some sheets of plain paper, a weariness had crept into her like a cold fog. She couldn't explain why, because it went without saying that she had no interest in breaking the law. But there was a vitality to the way that Suzie and Judith were talking about ground-floor offices, and the fact that the window at the back of Andy's office was open on such a hot day, that Becks desperately wanted to be a part of.

'But even if his office window is open, how can we get in?' Judith asked.

'We climb in.'

Judith hooted with laughter.

'There's no way we could climb in through a window!'

'All we have to do is make sure we can get up to it. You said it was a ground-floor window.'

'I know, but it's still quite a way off the ground.'

'Then we'll have to get a ladder.'

'I think people might notice if they saw two older women walking around Marlow with a ladder.'

'I suppose. So what can we do?'

This seemed to stump Judith. But not for long.

'We've got one thing going for us, haven't we?'

'What's that?'

'We're invisible.'

'How do you mean?'

'It's like I said. We're "older" women, aren't we? No one notices women over the age of about forty.'

'You can say that again,' Suzie said, chuckling darkly. 'My days of turning heads are long gone.'

'More fool the rest of the world, as far as I'm concerned,' Judith said primly. 'But society's decided that I'm just a little old lady. Invisible, as I say. We should play to that.'

'In what way?'

'Well, we should try and look even more old and decrepit than we are.'

'You mean, go around in a wheelchair?'

'You know what,' Judith said, 'I think a wheelchair is exactly what we're looking for. One of those old ones with strong brakes. Although where could we possibly get one from?'

'I reckon I know,' Suzie said.

'You do?' Becks said.

'There's one for sale in the Marlow Hospice shop.'

'You're right, there is!' Judith agreed.

This surprised Suzie.

'You go into charity shops?'

'Of course I go in charity shops. Where else am I going to get my jigsaws from?'

'Well, you learn something new every day. But if we can get ourselves an old wheelchair, I think we can get into Andy's office. And I reckon we'll be able to get everything else we need from the charity shops on the High Street. But it's no bloody good.'

'Why not?' Judith asked.

'Because we'll need you to sit in the wheelchair, as you're the oldest here. And I'll need to push it, as it'll be me who goes in through the window. But we'll also need someone who can enter the building from the front and create a diversion.'

'I'll do it,' Becks said.

'What's that?'

'Does this other person break the law?'

Suzie wrinkled her nose.

'I don't think so.'

'And does she have anything to do with the break-in?'

'God no. I don't think anyone at the solicitors will even realise the third person had anything to do with it.'

'Really?'

'I reckon so.'

'Then I'm in.' Becks felt a rush of adrenaline as she realised that she was finally doing something so daring. Something her younger self would have done.

'As long as I can pretend I had nothing to do with you if you get caught,' she added. She was prepared to take a baby step towards greater independence, but no more than that.

'Sure,' Suzie said. 'Now I'm going to ask you a question, and I bet the answer is yes.'

'Okay,' Becks said.

'Do you bake your own bread?'

'As it happens, I baked a sourdough loaf this morning.'

'I knew it! That'll be perfect.'

'I don't do it every morning. We don't need a loaf every day. I'm just trying to save money,' Becks added, defensively.

'Yeah, sure you are.'

'But won't Andy notice if we remove the shredded paper from his office?' Judith asked. 'It's kept in a see-through cellophane bag behind the machine.'

'Oh I see,' Suzie said with a frown. 'That's a bit of a problem.'

'Although maybe not. Logically, when we take it, we need to replace it with some shredded paper that looks the same.'

'And where are we going to get a load of shredded paper from?'

'Maybe one of the charity shops has a shredder,' Becks offered.

'They don't,' Judith and Suzie both said at the same time.

'Then we're a bit stuck,' Becks said, and then her eyes lit up as she had an idea. 'Or maybe not. In fact, I think I know *exactly* where I can get a load of shredded paper from.'

'Then that's rather splendid,' Judith said, clapping her hands together in delight before turning back towards Suzie. 'But tell me, why on earth do we need a loaf of bread?'

'Let's go and cut ourselves a couple of slices and I'll explain. Because, between Becks' loaf of bread, some shredded paper and a charity shop wheelchair, I reckon we'll have a good chance of getting our hands on what we need by the close of play this afternoon!'

Chapter 23

At just after 4 p.m., Becks entered Andy Bishop's office building without an appointment, but with two thick slices of white bread, one in each pocket of her coat. As for Judith and Suzie, they were at the sharp end of the sting, not that anyone would have realised this if they'd passed them in the street. Having bought everything they needed from the Marlow Hospice shop, Suzie was pushing Judith along the back alley behind Andy's office in an old wheelchair. Judith's dark grey cape covered her lap, and they couldn't have looked more harmless if they'd tried. Certainly no one would have thought they were about to carry out a daring heist.

They passed a number of terraced Victorian cottages with pretty front gardens, but they soon reached the back of Andy's larger Georgian office building with several cars parked on the tarmac. They could see that his window was still open.

'Okay,' Suzie said. 'Here goes.'

Suzie pushed Judith across the tarmac, past a back door to the building, and stopped underneath Andy's open window. As the ground on this side of the building was a little lower, the sill was higher than Suzie's head.

'You reckon you can get up there?' Judith whispered.

Suzie didn't reply for a moment. 'Sure,' she eventually said.

They both knew she was by no means sure. It looked far too high for her to climb through.

As for Becks, she was inside the building, introducing herself to the receptionist.

'Good afternoon. I understand you handle family disputes, that sort of thing.'

'We do. How can I help?'

'Well, it's a delicate matter, but I wondered if there was perhaps a lawyer I could talk to.'

'Do you have an appointment?'

'I don't. But I'm happy to wait until someone's free.'

'We've a number of lawyers in today, but Mr Bishop's got a gap in his schedule in half an hour.'

'Mr Bishop?' Becks said, suddenly unsure.

'If you don't mind waiting?'

Becks made herself reply brightly, 'No, that suits me fine.'

Andy Bishop was the last person Becks wanted to see, but as she went over to the chairs in the waiting area, she reminded herself that if everything went to plan, she'd be out of the building long before she had to meet him.

'Can I take your coat?' the receptionist asked.

'What's that?'

'It's such a hot day, I'm sure you want to take your coat off.'

Becks' smile froze.

'No. I'm all right,' she said, her hand unconsciously going to one of the pockets of her coat and touching the thick slice of bread that was wedged inside.

'Are you sure?'

'Quite sure, thank you.'

The receptionist looked at Becks askance. She could tell that something was 'off' with Becks but couldn't work out what it was.

'Okay, but if you change your mind, you only have to say.'

'Thank you. Although, can I ask, do you by any chance have a loo I could use?'

Becks knew the whole plan hinged on the answer the receptionist was about to give.

'Yes, straight through that door there,' the receptionist said, pointing at a door to the side of a rather grand staircase. 'It's at the end of the corridor.'

'Thanks,' Becks said, her heart thumping.

She headed through the door. Now she'd given the receptionist the slip, she had to find the office's kitchenette. After all, as Suzie had told them, all offices had kitchenettes, didn't they?

Outside in the car park, Judith and Suzie were beginning to panic.

'What if Andy comes and looks out of the window?' Suzie asked in a whisper.

'He won't.'

'But if he does, he'll see you sitting there.'

'He's not going to close that window. It's boiling hot.'

'What if he does, though?'

Judith twisted in the wheelchair and looked firmly up at Suzie.

'Now is not the time for backing down,' she hissed. 'We're seeing this through, for good or for ill.'

Suzie quailed. Gulped. Nodded.

'Okay,' she said.

Judith checked the watch on her wrist.

'Bloody hell, what's she up to in there?'

The truth was, Becks hadn't been able to find a kitchenette of any description on the ground floor. It had taken her only a few moments to poke around and find a cleaning cupboard and a stationery room in the corridor behind the main staircase. But there'd also been a rickety old servants' staircase. Knowing how important her part in the plan was, she'd gone up it.

So, as Judith and Suzie were outside waiting underneath Andy's window, Becks was on the first floor, trying to find the office kitchenette. *There has to be one somewhere*, Becks thought to herself. All she could see were heavy gloss-white doors, each with the name of a solicitor on a plaque to the side. *Where was the bloody kitchenette?*

But then she saw an opening at the end of the corridor that had no door to it, so she headed towards it and was thrilled to see that it led into the office kitchenette. Checking that no one else was in the corridor to see her go in, she slipped into the little room.

Inside, a short, fat man was standing by the kettle.

Adrenaline flooded Becks' system. This was Andy Bishop, wasn't it? Unless there were two very short, fat men who worked in the building, which seemed very unlikely.

'Hello,' Andy said with a delighted smile.

Becks' instinct told her that Andy was trying to be flirty, but that couldn't be possible, could it?

'I'm sorry?'

'Andy Bishop, how do you do?' he said, offering his hand.

'Mrs Rebecca Starling,' Becks said, shaking Andy's hand. It was clammy.

'So what are you here for? I can't imagine it's a divorce.'

Oh God, Becks thought to herself. *He's trying to chat me up.*

'I'm sorry, it's a private matter. But I was looking for a glass of water. It's such a hot day.'

'It sure is,' Andy said as he finished making himself his cup of tea. 'You should take your coat off,' he added with a wink. 'It's too hot to be wearing coats indoors.'

'No thank you,' Becks said primly as she turned her back on Andy and reached up to a shelf to get a glass. As she did so, she couldn't help but marvel to herself. Her explanation that she was there to get some water had arrived in her brain unbidden. She'd had no idea that she could lie so effortlessly.

But then, she'd been giving men like Andy Bishop the brush-off since she was a teenager, so she kept her back to him as she ran the tap until the water became cold. She could feel Andy appraising her as she stood there, her finger under the tap, and her body tightened in anger. Who was this man to think he could look at her like this?

She heard him stir his drink with a teaspoon, and then, before she knew it, he was at her side.

'See you around,' he said as he dropped his teaspoon in the sink and left the kitchenette.

Becks let out a breath she hadn't known she'd been holding. She was cross to see that the glass of water in her hand was shaking. But she knew her encounter with Andy had upset her because of how he'd behaved towards her, not because she was in his building for nefarious reasons. In fact, she realised, Andy's manner might have shaken her, but it had also stiffened her resolve.

She moved over to the toaster that Suzie had predicted would be there, got out the two thick slices of sourdough bread from her pockets and jammed them into the machine, yanking the lever down and making sure that the heating elements inside lit up red. The bread was too thick for the slot. There was no way it was popping back up when the machine finished. For good measure, Becks twisted the dial on the side of the toaster up to its maximum setting, and with a quick glance up at the ceiling where the fire alarm was placed, a little green LED lit up to show it was working, she left at speed. Her job now was to put as much distance between herself and the jammed toaster as possible.

'I wondered if we'd lost you,' the receptionist said as Becks finally returned to the lobby.

'Sorry,' Becks said. 'I had to wait to use the facilities.'

Again, she was surprised at how easily the lie tripped off her tongue.

'Anyway,' the receptionist said, already moving on. 'Mr Bishop just came past, and I had a quick word with him. He's finishing up some work, and he'll be able to see you in a few minutes.'

'Thank you,' Becks said with a smile, and sat down. She knew that if all went well, she'd be leaving the building before then.

Inside his office, Andy Bishop was reliving his encounter with the yummy mummy he'd bumped into in the upstairs kitchenette. *I wonder why she needs a lawyer?* he thought to himself as he took a sip on his cup of tea, before realising the office was unbearably hot. He glanced over at the window that overlooked the car park. It was open, but he was sure he could open it further.

Andy went across to the window and yanked it up a few more inches. He half noticed an old woman sitting outside in a wheelchair with what looked like her caregiver. He returned to his desk but stopped as he realised the person in the wheelchair looked a lot like the Judith woman who'd visited him earlier on, asking questions about Ezra. Andy strode back to the window and stuck his head out, but the woman in the wheelchair had vanished. *Hmm*, he thought to himself, before losing interest in the whole question and returning to his desk.

As for Judith and Suzie, they'd panicked the moment Andy had first appeared at the window, and Suzie had pushed Judith at speed towards the first house that was next to the car park. Judith had kicked the little picket gate open with her feet as Suzie had shoved her in, and both women were ducking down behind a pink hydrangea at the precise moment Andy had looked out of his back window for a second time.

'Do you think he saw us?' Judith asked.

'Shh!' Suzie said, her heart hammering against her chest.

The sound of a piercing alarm suddenly filled the air. *Finally!*

'Okay, you're on,' Judith said, straightening up as Suzie wheeled her back towards the window that Andy had so recently vacated. As they approached, the sill looked even higher above their heads than it had done before. How on earth was Suzy going to climb up and into Andy's office?

Inside, Becks sat in the reception area, her hands on her lap in quiet satisfaction as the fire alarm screamed. Half a dozen solicitors and clients emerged from various doors and drifted down the stairs from the floor above.

'Is this a drill?' one of them asked.

'I don't think so,' the receptionist replied.

'Okay. Everyone to the assembly point. Round the back.'

Becks stood up, all smug satisfaction gone.

'Round the back?' she asked.

'When we evacuate the building, the assembly point is the little car park behind the building.'

'Not out the front?' she asked in quiet desperation.

'No. We can't go clogging up the High Street, so let's get to the back, everyone,' the man called out.

Becks was frozen to the spot as the clutch of people started to head towards the corridor that led to the back of the building. There was no way of warning Suzie and Judith that the whole office was about to leave the building right next to where they were breaking in.

But then, what Becks didn't know was that at that precise moment, Suzie and Judith were failing to break into anywhere.

It had been Suzie's theory that as long as Judith stayed sitting in the wheelchair to act as ballast, she'd be able to climb up onto the back of the chair and in through the window. However, practice was proving harder than theory. This was mainly because it turned out that Suzie had terrible balance, and Judith kept trying to shift position to help her, which made the wheelchair risk tipping over.

'Stop moving!' Suzie called out as she stood on the armrest, one hand holding a wheelchair handle, the other gripping onto the top of Judith's head.

'You're hurting!'

'I need to get up.'

'Ow!'

'Hold on!'

Suzie tried to step up, got one foot onto the back of the wheelchair and both hands firmly onto the windowsill. She was halfway there. Or was she? With her weight pressing down on the back of the wheelchair, it was only Judith's mass in the seat that was stopping it from tipping over, and it was precariously balanced, they could both feel it.

In fact, the front two wheels on the old wheelchair rose gently into the air as the whole thing started to tip backwards, but Suzie was able to shift her weight so that it didn't topple over.

'You remember the end of *The Italian Job*?' Judith found time to ask.

'Don't make me laugh!' Suzie wheezed, and then they both gasped as a door at the back of the building crashed open and people started to emerge. *Bloody hell, what was going on?*

It was precisely the impetus Suzie needed to push down on the wheelchair and launch herself through the open window, where she landed with a *whoof!* of expelled air on the other side as the first office workers turned and saw Judith sitting on her own in a wheelchair under the open window of Andy's office.

Judith smiled to them like the old lady she was. But then she saw Andy Bishop emerge, with Becks stepping out from behind him so she was blocking his direct view of her. Judith knew she had only seconds before Andy saw her, so she turned the wheelchair around and began to wheel herself away from the car park.

Becks glanced across with a sinking heart as she saw Judith leaving in her wheelchair. The plan had been for Suzie to get the shredded paper and slip back out of the window before anyone discovered what had set off the fire alarm. But with all of the staff milling about in the car park, how was Suzie going to get out of the building now?

Suzie wasn't thinking that far ahead. Instead, she was in a panic of fear inside Andy's office, her senses overloaded by adrenaline, the fire alarm screaming loudly in her ears as she went over to the shredder. It sat on the table by the window that overlooked the High Street, just as Judith had said, and she'd crossed the room and was inspecting it when a fire engine pulled up on the pavement outside, fire officers jumping out with their yellow helmets on.

Suzie dropped to the floor. *Bloody hell*, she thought to herself, *and now the fire brigade have turned up?* She only had a matter of seconds before she would be discovered, and she saw that her hands were shaking. She had to make herself go through with the plan. With a force of will, she reached up onto the table and ripped the clear cellophane bag from the back of the shredder. Pulling it down to the floor, she then opened a leatherette handbag they'd also bought that afternoon from the charity shop and yanked out a carrier bag. Becks had stuffed it full of shredded paper that she'd got from her son's hamster cage. Putting this bag of hamster-shredded paper to one side, Suzie tipped all of Andy's shredded paper into the handbag and clicked the clasp closed. Next, she grabbed up thick handfuls of hamster-shredded paper and stuffed it into the clear cellophane bag from the shredder until it looked about the same.

But how to re-attach the bag to the shredder?

There was only one way.

Suzie stood up, clear as day, and was relieved to see that there were no fire officers in the High Street looking into the building to see her.

As she re-attached the bag to the back of the shredder, the fire alarm stopped blaring.

Her ears rang from the sudden silence.

Suzie grabbed up her handbag and returned to the window that overlooked the car park, but when she looked out, there was no sign of Judith. And she could see the clump of office workers starting to re-enter the building, marshalled by a fire officer who was holding two blackened pieces of toast in his hands.

Suzie knew her only hope was to leave by the front door before everyone returned to the reception area and discovered her presence. She only had seconds to act, but as her hand reached for the handle to Andy's office door, she stopped.

She could see that his computer was on. He'd not locked it before he'd left, and she had a sudden idea.

She pulled out her mobile phone and dashed across to the desk. She could hear voices in the corridor outside. Everyone was discussing who the idiot was who'd left toast to burn in the upstairs kitchenette.

Using Andy's mouse, Suzie found his Office applications, and then clicked the Calendar icon. The door half opened, her heart leapt, but she just had time to use her camera to photograph the screen before dropping to the floor like a marionette who'd suddenly had its strings cut.

Andy entered, and it was only then that Suzie realised how badly she'd messed up. She was on the floor, partially hidden by the desk, but she'd be discovered the moment he came to sit down. Worse still, her mind was completely blank as to what she could possibly say that would explain her position on the floor. She was about to be discovered hiding in an office having committed theft. She was going to prison!

As Andy headed over, the door banged open again.

'Mr Bishop?'

It was Becks.

Andy turned back to look at who had entered his office.

'Mrs Starling,' he said, delighted.

'I wondered if you could help me after all,' Becks said, doing her best impression of a 'little girl lost'. 'You see, you were right, I'm here on a very personal matter. It's life or death to me, but I don't want my husband to see me visiting your office. Is there any chance you and I could go for a walk together?'

'What's that?'

'I worry he'll see me here. Could we go for a walk? Just you and me?'

'Well,' Andy said, pretending to consider the offer. 'It's not every day a pretty young woman asks me out for a stroll. I'd be glad to.'

'At once,' Becks added.

'Oh. I see. And when you say at once . . . ?'

'I very much mean we need to go right now. Please.'

Peering from behind the desk, Suzie could see the look of innocent damsel-in-distress pleading on Becks' face. Andy never stood a chance.

'Of course. Lead on.'

With a grateful smile to Andy for being her knight in shining armour, Becks stepped to one side and caught Suzie's eye as Andy left.

Thank you, Suzie mouthed, but Becks pretended not to notice. She was too busy playing the role of a distressed wife. As soon as she closed the door behind herself, Suzie dashed across to the back window and was relieved to see that, now the coast was clear, Judith had returned to her position. Suzie chucked her handbag down, Judith put it on her lap, and then Suzie climbed out of the window and onto the back of the wheelchair, before once again using Judith's head as scaffolding to help her get down.

As Suzie pushed Judith away, she realised that her knees were shaking.

It had been nip and tuck, but they'd done it. They'd managed to break into Andy's office and steal the shredded paper!

Chapter 24

The plan was for the three women to rendezvous back at Judith's house, but when Judith and Suzie got there, there was no sign of Becks – not that Suzie much cared.

'We did it!' she said as she dumped the handbag of shredded paper onto Judith's card table.

'We did, didn't we?' Judith said with quiet satisfaction.

'Although we so nearly got caught!'

'But we weren't, and that's what matters,' Judith said as she sat down at the table and began oh-so-carefully removing the shredded paper from the handbag.

'Me in particular. I mean, why did I go back to Andy Bishop's desk like that? I should have got out when I could.'

'Well, no harm done.'

'I mean, what an idiot!'

'Not a bit of it. We got away with it, and that's what matters.'

'But that's me all over, isn't it?' Suzie said, self-doubt entering her voice. 'I never think things through.'

Judith could see that her friend's ebullient mood was crashing.

'What's that?'

'I'm too impetuous, that's the problem.'

'What on earth are you talking about? You did brilliantly.'

'But I didn't, did I? I wanted to look at his computer, so that's what I did. When I should have just got out, like we'd agreed. I didn't consider the consequences. To me, or to you or Becks. I never think of others.'

'I don't agree with that at all.'

'My daughter Rachel's right. I only ever think of myself.'

As she said this, Suzie subsided onto Judith's sofa.

'That's not true.'

Suzie was lost in her memories, too downhearted to continue the conversation.

'And what does your other daughter say?' Judith asked, trying to lift Suzie out of her gloom.

'I wouldn't know, I've not spoken to Amy in over a year.'

'Why ever not?'

'We fell out.'

'Oh. I see. Then why don't you pick up the phone to her?'

'I can't,' Suzie said, the logic of her situation unassailable. 'We're not talking.'

Judith's heart went out to her friend. The faded photos in Suzie's sitting room had suggested that all wasn't well between her and her family, but Judith knew that raising children was about the hardest job in the world. She could only imagine how challenging it must have been to do it as a single parent.

An intervention was required.

'How about I make us both a nice cup of tea?' Judith said. 'With a teaspoon or two of sugar to replace our energy.'

'Yes,' Suzie said. 'That would be nice. Thank you.'

Judith bustled out and Suzie was left on her own with her thoughts. She looked at the room; at the shocking mess of newspapers and magazines that lay everywhere; at the Blüthner grand piano by the oak staircase.

There was also the door to the side of the drinks table that Judith had told her she couldn't go through.

Hearing the sound of clattering cups and saucers from the kitchen, Suzie got up, went over to the door and tried to open it. It was locked, as it had been the time before, but what was behind it? She put her eye to the keyhole, but the other side was shrouded in darkness.

Before she was discovered snooping, Suzie returned to the sofa and tried to take in the room again. *Just who was Judith Potts?*

'Here we are,' Judith said, returning with a tray that was laden with mismatched bone china cups and saucers, milk in a jug and a steaming pot of tea.

'Can I ask you something?'

'Of course,' Judith said, pouring out two cups of tea and stirring in heaped teaspoons of sugar.

'You said you were a widow.'

'That's right.'

Judith poured the milk and handed over a cup and saucer for Suzie.

'This is exactly what I wanted, thank you,' Suzie said, taking a sip.

'Good.'

'But I don't see any photographs of your husband anywhere.'

Judith didn't want to talk about her past. In fact, she never talked about her past, it was one of the rules she lived by. But Suzie had shared some of her family history with her, so she realised it was only fair that she do the same.

'No, I suppose not. But then, it wasn't a good marriage,' she said as she sat down in her wingback with her cup and saucer of tea.

'It wasn't?'

'You know what they say. Marry in haste, repent at leisure. And I was young.'

'What happened?'

'You really want to know?'

'If you don't mind talking about it.'

'No, it's fine. I don't often think about it these days, that's all. Anyway, I'd just come down from Oxford, and I didn't know what to do with my life.'

'You were a student?'

'It was the 1960s and love was in the air, as they say.'

Judith took a sip of tea and Suzie could only imagine what scrapes the student Judith might have got up to. She smiled at the thought.

Judith saw Suzie's smile.

'Indeed,' she said. 'But when I left Oxford, the rest of England wasn't quite as advanced. Women were still expected to keep home, to marry well, to help their husband in his career, and none of that appealed to me. Not one bit. But what could I do? And that's when my mother told me about her aunt in Marlow, who was something of an invalid and was looking for some live-in help.'

'This would be your great aunt Betty?'

Judith smiled at the mention of her name.

'We hit it off right from the start. You see, she'd never married and was fiercely independent. The only thing we ever argued over was Philippos.'

'Your husband.'

'My husband. He worked for a Greek tour operator and I'm afraid I fell for him hook, line and sinker. He was so very handsome. Strong in mind, word and deed. And he was a terrific sailor. I don't know the first thing about boats, but he'd take me to the sailing club at Bourne End, and it was so thrilling. Whizzing across the Thames on a little sailboat, the wind in my hair. You see, Philippos had grown up on Corfu, and he was one of those people who had the sea in his soul. He could read the wind and the tides. Really, our affair was hugely romantic.'

'How old were you?'

'Twenty-six when we met. And I was still twenty-six when we married. In Corfu. That's when Betty and I fell out. You see, she said Philippos was a wrong 'un. That I couldn't trust him. Oh, you should have seen the arguments we had in this room,' Judith said, looking sadly about herself. 'But I was in love, and as far as I could tell, Betty was being selfish. She knew she'd be losing her home help if I married. She was just trying to poison my mind so I'd never leave her. Fool that I was.'

'She was right?'

'More than you can imagine. I moved to Corfu once we married, and things went wrong almost from the start. You see, Philippos was a drinker. And he'd always been fiery, and somewhat controlling. But he only revealed himself fully when he got home.'

Judith stopped speaking as she lost herself in her memories.

'It was bad?'

'It was bad,' she said simply, but Suzie could see the oceans of pain those simple words covered. 'But you make your bed in life, don't you? Sometimes you just have to lie in it. I endured.'

'What happened?'

'Providence, that's what happened. You see, no matter how good a sailor you are, the Ionian Sea is capricious. Squalls can whip up from nowhere, and one day Philippos was out on his boat. It wasn't anything grand, just a single sail, a cabin with a bed, and a little galley kitchen. This was in the days before mobile phones and GPS whatnots. And we still don't know what happened for sure, but he didn't come home that day. Or the next. I thought he'd gone off with his fancy lady. You see, I knew by then he'd been having affairs throughout our courtship and marriage. But the day after he'd gone, his boat was found wrecked on some rocks. No sign of Philippos anywhere.'

'Where was he?'

'There'd been something of a storm the night before and the authorities thought he must have fallen overboard. His body washed up a week later.'

A silence settled between the two women.

'Bloody hell,' Suzie eventually said.

'Yes. Thank you. But it was decades ago. And it was all my own fault, really. Anyway, I came back to the UK, my tail firmly between my legs. I only got through it all because Betty didn't ever ask me about it. We simply picked up where we'd left off. That's when I started compiling crosswords. They helped me keep my equilibrium.' Judith took a moment to regather her focus. 'So that's the sad story of Judith and Philippos. Not exactly Pyramus and Thisbe. More tea?'

'No, I'm fine, thank you. But can I ask something?'

'Of course.'

'You say you weren't happy with your husband?'

'I was not.'

'Then why do you still wear your wedding ring?'

The question caught Judith unawares. She smiled, but Suzie could see that it was a touch forced.

'It's to remind me,' Judith said.

'What of?'

'Of mistakes.'

There was a coolness to Judith's response that made Suzie think of thick ice on a winter pond. It might look solid, but it could crack at any moment, and there would be whole swirls of dark water underneath.

Judith could sense that she'd somehow revealed too much, and she was grateful to hear the jangle of the front door bell.

'At last!' she said, putting her cup and saucer to one side as she stood up. 'That will be Becks. Let's go and find out what happened.'

Judith and Suzie went to the front door and opened it, but it wasn't Becks who was standing there.

It was Detective Sergeant Tanika Malik.

She looked like she'd seen a ghost.

'Tanika, are you all right?' Judith asked.

'Judith, I'm so sorry, but there's been another murder.'

Chapter 25

Judith recovered first.

'It's not Becks, is it?' she asked.

'Becks?' Tanika asked, surprised. 'You mean Becks Starling?'

'That's right. She's okay?'

'As far as I know. Why wouldn't she be?'

'No reason,' Judith said quickly, before she implicated herself any further. 'But someone else has been murdered?'

'Liz Curtis,' Tanika said. 'The woman you saw on Mr Dunwoody's property.'

'Liz is dead?' Judith said, horrified.

'We need someone to formally identify the body. And I was wondering if you could do it. After all, you've recently seen her. Twice, in fact.'

Judith had the good grace to look awkward.

'It's three,' she said under her breath.

'What's that?'

'I met Liz a third time.'

'When?' she said.

'Well, you remember when you told me I absolutely shouldn't talk to her?'

'Of course. You promised.'

'Well, the only problem was, I was at the rowing centre when you told me that. So I couldn't very well not talk to her, seeing as I was already there.'

'You talked to Liz Curtis after I told you not to?' Tanika said, exasperated.

'Which is fortunate for you, since she's now dead. I'm a witness. I can tell you all about what she was like.'

'She's a dog killer,' Suzie chipped in.

'Can I ask you what you're even doing here?' Tanika said to Suzie.

'She's my friend,' Judith said.

'Look,' Tanika said, trying to take control of the situation. 'I need you to come with me, Judith. And you'd better tell me about your third meeting with Liz on the way.'

'What about me?' Suzie asked.

'What about you?'

'I met Liz Curtis as well. Can I come?'

'No.'

'Are you sure—'

'I only need one of you to identify the body.'

Suzie rocked back on her heels a bit.

'Well, can't say fairer than that,' she conceded.

As Tanika drove Judith to the rowing centre, Judith recapped her and Suzie's encounter with Liz. In particular, she explained how Liz had denied knowing both Stefan and Iqbal, even though her husband Danny later told them that Liz had known both men. Throughout the story, Tanika kept her eyes on the road and her jaw clenched.

As they pulled up at the rowing centre, Tanika parked her car and crunched the handbrake on.

Judith finally realised how cross Tanika was.

'I should have told you sooner, shouldn't I?'

'You shouldn't have spoken to her at all!' Tanika all but shouted. 'There's someone out there who's killed three people. And your life is at risk every time you get involved.'

Judith felt abashed, so she reached into her handbag, pulled out her tin of travel sweets and popped the lid.

'Travel sweet?' she asked by way of a peace offering.

'No thank you,' Tanika said in a tone that told Judith that she wasn't going to be let off the hook that easily.

Judith put a sweet into her mouth and pretended to be insouciant as she said, 'Then perhaps I should tell you about Andy Bishop as well.'

'Who's Andy Bishop?'

'A local solicitor. He drew up the will of Ezra Harrington, the neighbour to Iqbal Kassam.'

'What are you talking about?'

Judith told the story of how Suzie had been invited to Iqbal's funeral and so she, Becks and Suzie had all gone along and talked to his imam, who'd explained how Iqbal had died believing that Andy Bishop had stolen his inheritance. However, Judith was careful to stop her story there. After seeing how cross Tanika had been about her conversation with Liz, she didn't want to tell her that she'd not only spoken to Andy Bishop but had also broken into his office and stolen a bag of shredded paper.

'You went to Iqbal Kassam's funeral?' Tanika asked when Judith finished.

'We were invited, so we went. It was the right thing to do. Are you sure you don't want a sweet?' Judith said, offering the tin again.

'No thank you,' Tanika said, and Judith had the distinct impression that the police officer was barely managing to control her temper as she opened the door to her car and stepped out.

Judith put her tin back in her handbag, and got out of her side of the car.

'Is there anything else you need to tell me?' Tanika asked tartly.

'Oh no, that's absolutely everything,' Judith said, and she even believed her words as she said them. But then her eyes were drawn to a navy blue Forensics tent that had been erected on the grass down by the river.

Tanika saw Judith frown, and she softened a little.

'Don't worry,' she said. 'You don't need to approach the body. You can identify her from the photos we've taken. That should be enough.'

Tanika led Judith into the reception building, and Judith couldn't help but notice the ladder, paint pot and brush that were still in the corner. Liz would never finish painting the room. Somehow Judith found this fact sadder than anything else. The bathos of it all.

'I'm sorry to ask you to do this, Judith, but the only other person I could have asked was the scoutmaster who discovered her body, and he's a bit busy trying to care for the scouts who were with him at the time.'

'Don't worry, I'm happy to help. But where's Danny, her husband?'

'In Nottingham. A police officer's driving him down as we speak.'

'Then I'm ready. I can do this.'

Tanika took a tablet computer from a police officer who was logging evidence. Bringing it over to Judith, she warned her that the photos would be upsetting.

'Don't worry, I'm made of strong stuff.'

Tanika swiped the screen a few times until an image appeared. It was of Liz Curtis lying on the grass, her limbs splayed like a rag doll's, her face a shocking mess of red blood.

In the centre of her forehead there was a bullet hole.

'It's Liz Curtis,' Judith said, resisting her instinct to look away.

'Thank you.'

'Any signs of a struggle?'

Tanika didn't answer, but Judith correctly interpreted her silence as assent.

'And she was found by a scoutmaster?'

'That's right. He and his scouts hired kayaks from Liz this morning and went out on the river at about nine.'

'So she was alive at nine o'clock?'

'Very much so. She did the safety briefing for everyone. Anyway, the scouts were out on the river about an hour and returned to the rowing centre shortly after ten. That's when the scoutmaster found her body. Fortunately, he was able to stop the children from approaching, rounded them up and got them back into Marlow. I've a constable taking his statement now.'

'That's a very clear time of death. Between nine-ish and ten-ish this morning. Have you checked up on Elliot Howard?'

'I'll be honest, it was the first thing I did. He's been running an auction since eight thirty this morning.'

'He has?'

'And it's all being filmed on a livestream for the internet.'

'You're kidding me!'

'I know.'

'But why would an auction start at eight thirty?'

'Apparently it's for the overseas buyers. But he's in the clear. He's got witnesses all around the world who can alibi him for between nine and ten this morning.'

'Hmm,' Judith said, deeply frustrated. She was sure that Elliot was behind Stefan's murder. In fact, the theory that had been bubbling away on the back burner for her had been the idea that Liz had maybe killed Stefan on Elliot's behalf, for some reason yet to be established. And Elliot had now killed Liz, so there'd never be a chance for anyone to pin the first murder on him. But her theory fell apart if Elliot had an alibi for the time of Liz's murder.

Judith realised there was a question she'd not asked yet.

'You said her husband was in Nottingham?'

'You think he might be involved?'

'It would be nice if one of these murders was carried out by someone obvious.'

'I know. But between the hours of nine and ten this morning, Danny Curtis was having breakfast at a service station by junction twenty-five of the M1. He was at the National Watersports Centre last night.'

'He has an alibi for this morning?'

'He was over a hundred miles away at the time.'

'Are you certain?'

'A uniformed officer picked Mr Curtis up from outside Nottingham at ten thirty this morning. Whoever did this was in Marlow this morning.'

As Tanika spoke, Judith looked more closely at the photo on the tablet.

'What's that?' she asked, indicating a small object on a chain that was lying on the ground to the side of Liz's face.

Tanika knew it was a bronze medallion. The *third* bronze medallion. Just as she'd feared. They'd found it on a little chain around Liz's neck. As she'd predicted, the word across the middle read 'Charity'.

'It's a bronze medallion,' she said.

'She was wearing a bronze medallion?' Judith said, her interest sharpening. 'You mean, like the one Stefan was wearing on his jacket?'

'You remember me telling you about that?'

'Of course. You also said Stefan's medallion had the word 'Faith' written on it.'

'It did.'

'Then was there anything written on this medallion?'

'I'm sorry, but I can't tell you.'

'Whyever not?'

'Because I'm not supposed to be sharing *any* details of the case with a civilian.'

'I think we can both agree it would be better if you did.'

'But I can't. I'm sorry. It's against rules—'

'And regulations,' an exasperated Judith said, finishing Tanika's sentence for her.

'Exactly.'

A uniformed officer entered the building.

'Sarge,' he said. 'An officer has just arrived with the deceased's husband, Mr Curtis.'

Chapter 26

As Judith and Tanika emerged from the reception building, they saw a police van pull up and an officer help a disoriented-looking Danny Curtis out of the back.

'Would you wait here?' Tanika said to Judith.

'Of course.' Judith said.

'Thank you,' Tanika said and went over to introduce herself to Danny.

Judith had been entirely sincere when she'd said she would stay put, but she found it so very frustrating not being able to hear what was going on. Surely there was something she could do? Well, no one could really blame her if she went for a little stroll, could they? She ambled off to the side of the Portakabin hoping Tanika wouldn't notice. She didn't appear to. So Judith looked up at the sky as though idly checking the weather, and then slipped around the edge of the building.

Now she was out of view, she picked up her pace, moved

along to the next building, the toilet block, raced around it and emerged next to where the police van had parked. Tanika and Danny were standing on the other side.

Oh so slowly, Judith edged along the side of the van, for once grateful for her diminutive size. Her head barely appeared above the van's windows, so she was pretty sure that Tanika and the other police officers on the far side wouldn't be able to see her through the smoked glass. But if she stood on her tiptoes, she could make out Danny and Tanika's faces. And if she really concentrated, she could just about hear what they were saying.

'It can't be true,' Judith heard Danny say.

'I'm so sorry,' Tanika said. 'We'll have a family liaison officer here as soon as we can.'

'But what am I going to do now?'

'I know this is hard, Mr Curtis, but I need to ask you a couple of questions. I'll be as quick as I can.' Judith saw Danny nod. 'Starting with, can I ask what you were doing in Nottingham last night?'

'Last night?'

'We need to get a sense of your movements.'

'I'm a coach. Of the GB junior canoeing team. They're based outside Nottingham.'

'It was a planned trip then?'

'When we're not in competition, training's every Tuesday night.'

'So you go to Nottingham every week?'

'That's right. I go up in the afternoon. We train that evening, I spend the night at the centre, and I come back Wednesday morning.'

'So if anyone knew you well, they'd know you'd be away from

the family home between Tuesday afternoon and late Wednesday morning every week.'

'I suppose so.'

'Can you think of anyone who might have wished your wife harm?'

'No. It's impossible. Everyone liked Liz.'

'Are you sure?'

'I'm the one who's grumpy. Who shouts and is difficult. Liz just gets on with things. You know? Never loses her temper. She didn't have a bad bone in her body.'

As Danny said this, Judith couldn't help thinking about Liz's dog Crumble. If Suzie's story were true, then Danny had wildly misjudged his wife.

'Then can I ask,' Tanika continued, 'how had things been between you and Mrs Curtis?'

'I'm sorry?' Danny replied.

'It would be good to get a sense of your relationship.'

'Well, I started going out with Liz when I was twenty. We've been together ever since. She's the only person I've ever seriously dated.'

'And you were getting on?'

'Yes. I love her. I've always loved her. Why are you asking?'

'Is it possible she didn't feel the same towards you as you did towards her?'

'Are you asking, was she playing around? You've got to be kidding me. We've been working down here all the hours God gave. Trying to get the place back on its feet since the floods. Working seven days a week. Painting, mending, rebuilding.'

'Okay. Then can I ask, did she perhaps have any financial problems?'

Danny gave a bitter laugh.

'Ha! We were *all* financial problems. We're broke. That's the problem.'

'She was in debt?'

'Not personally. I don't think so. We never joined our bank accounts, so I can't tell you exactly what her financial situation was, but we've been living on thin air for years. Turns out, these days, if you want to follow your dream of working on the river, you'd be wise to put all your buildings on stilts.'

'Your business was in trouble?'

'Not the business. Liz inherited it from her dad years ago, so there's no mortgage or anything. As long as we take more money than we spend, we're in clover. But we didn't have the sort of savings set aside for the last flood. Not after the one before.'

'You've spent all your savings?'

'We'll be able to build them up again. Once we open properly.'

'OK, just a couple more questions. What do you know about a local man called Iqbal Kassam?'

'That's what that woman asked me.'

'Would that be Judith Potts?'

'That's right. She asked about that guy who got killed the other week.'

'I understand your wife used his taxi services a few weeks ago.'

'Only to get some shopping. She wasn't gone more than an hour or so. I'm sure loads of people used him.'

'And how well did your wife know Stefan Dunwoody?'

Danny didn't answer immediately and he was guarded when he did.

'Yeah, that Judith woman asked about him as well. Why?'

'If you could answer the question.'

'But why are you suggesting Liz had anything to do with

those men?' Danny said, and Judith could hear anger in his voice.

'It's very important that you answer the questions I'm asking you, Mr Curtis.'

Danny sighed.

'I asked Liz about Stefan after I'd spoken to Judith. Okay? And she said she'd not had anything to do with Stefan for months. Hadn't been to his gallery. Hadn't spoken to him at all. And before you ask, I also asked if she'd been to his house. She laughed at me. She told me she'd never been to his house and didn't even know where Stefan lived. So that's all you need to know about Liz and Stefan. Are we done now?'

'Nearly. Do you own a firearm?'

'No! Why would I own a gun?'

'Then one last question. If I were to say "faith, hope and charity", what would that mean to you?'

Listening from behind the van, Judith's ears pricked up. 'Faith, hope and charity'? Why was Tanika asking that question? Judith guessed it was somehow connected to Stefan's medallion.

For his part, Danny seemed just as puzzled by the question as Judith.

'It wouldn't mean anything. Why are you asking?'

'Does the phrase not resonate with you in any way?'

'It's a motto, isn't it? I don't know.'

'It's from the bible originally, but maybe it has some other meaning for you?'

Before Danny could answer, the phone in Judith's handbag started ringing. Oh bloody hell, she thought to herself as she moved away from the van at speed. She really didn't want to get caught eavesdropping, but where was the button to silence the stupid thing? She pressed all of the buttons on the side of the infernal device until it went quiet. There, that was better. She answered the call.

'Hello,' she whispered into the phone.

'It's me,' Suzie said on the other end of the line. 'Becks just got back. And she has news about Andy Bishop. Big news. We need you here at once.'

Chapter 27

'So what have you got?' Judith asked as she swept into her house, whipped off her cape and threw it onto the Blüthner as she passed.

'Andy Bishop's the killer,' Becks said.

'You're kidding? Well, that's what we in the bridge community call a strong opening bid.'

'I've no doubt about it.'

'Okay, so how come you're so sure?'

'It was how he was with me.'

'And how was that?'

'For starters, he was a creep. One of those men who talk to your breasts rather than look you in the eye.'

'Bloody lech,' Suzie said.

'Exactly,' Becks agreed. 'And when he showed me out the front door, he brushed his hand over my bottom. It was vile.'

'Do you need a whisky?' Judith asked.

'No, I'm fine.'

'Are you sure? I think I'll have a whisky.'

'Well, since you're asking . . .' Suzie said.

'Okay, two small whiskies to steady the nerves. Go on,' Judith said to Becks as she went over to her sideboard and fixed a whisky for herself and Suzie.

'Andy and I went down the High Street together,' Becks said. 'And I didn't know what to say. I'd only got him out of his office to buy Suzie time.'

'Which you did brilliantly,' Suzie added. 'Little good it did me. All I had time to do was photograph his diary, and it doesn't say anything. We've looked.'

What Suzie was saying was true. She and Judith had checked over the photo she'd taken of Andy's diary the moment they'd got clear of his office and had both been disappointed by what they'd discovered. His diary covered the most recent two weeks and merely listed his work appointments, none of which had any kind of connection to anyone involved in any of the murders as far as they could tell.

'But it was clever of you to try,' Judith said to Suzie, before turning back to Becks. 'So you were out on the street with Andy. What on earth did you say to him?'

'Well, I'd managed to get him out of his office by saying I wanted to see him about my husband, so all I could say was how my husband didn't appreciate me. How I'd become invisible in my own life. Just a mother. A wife. And how I was being driven mad by not having any kind of independent identity.'

'You told him the truth?' Judith said.

'I didn't tell him the truth!' Becks said, confused. 'It was all a fib. Just to get him talking.'

'Oh right,' Judith said, exchanging a glance with Suzie. 'It was a lie.'

'I'm so lucky to lead the life I do.'

'Of course.'

'But I had to make up something for Andy, so I said I wasn't happy and that I was looking to leave Colin, and I wanted to know what I could expect in a divorce settlement. Whether I'd get the full fifty per cent, and whether I'd have access to an income as the main caregiver to our children, and what responsibility he'd have to cover the costs of my move out of the vicarage.'

Judith and Suzie caught each other's eyes again. For someone who was happy in her life, Becks certainly seemed to have the facts of divorce at her fingertips.

'And what did Andy say?'

'He said that someone as pretty as me could take her husband to the cleaners.'

'He said that, did he?'

'In his experience, judges didn't take too kindly to husbands ignoring pretty wives.'

'That can't be true.'

'I'm sure it isn't. I think it was Andy's way of coming on to me. And then he suggested we take a walk along the Thames Path. Not towards the church, thank heavens, but towards Hurley Lock. And once we were out of earshot of anyone else, he told me that if I could suggest there'd been physical violence from my husband, I'd get an even better settlement. I was outraged. I mean, Colin may be boring, but he's never been violent.'

Judith and Suzie didn't even need to catch each other's eyes this time.

'But he said it could be quite subtle. After all, if I was able to suggest mental cruelty, and then refuse to answer questions about physical violence, the judge would draw his own conclusion.

It was, according to Andy, all about throwing as much mud as possible at Colin. I was outraged.'

'I'm sure none of this is actually legal.'

'That's what I said to him, and you know what he did? He laughed. Said I was a naive little girl, and I had a lot to learn before I could screw my husband for the last time.'

'The repulsive little man,' Judith said.

'But it gets worse. Because I realised we were walking along the path towards Stefan's house.'

'You made it up this way?'

'But on the Marlow side of the river. Stefan's side. I had no idea why. But I figured I'd better keep the conversation going until we reached Stefan's house, if only to find out why we were heading that way. So I asked Andy if he always took his clients for walks along the Thames Path, and you know what he said? He said that whenever he needed to have a conversation with a client that was deniable, he'd always suggest a little walk here. Up to "that stupid man's house" and back again. That's how he referred to Stefan, "that stupid man". Naturally, I pretended to be all innocent and asked who he could be talking about, and he explained how Stefan's house blocked the Thames Path, you had to take a detour to get around it, but luckily enough he'd recently been shot dead.'

'He called him Stefan by name?' Judith asked.

'He did.'

'So he knew him!' Suzie chipped in.

'But it's more than that,' Judith said, her eyes ablaze. 'Are you sure he said Stefan had been shot?'

'He did. Not that he'd died, or even that he'd been murdered, but that he'd been shot.'

'Why's that of interest?' Suzie asked.

'Because,' Judith said, 'the police have never said for definite how Stefan was killed. Although the papers have been speculating, it's never been confirmed.'

'So I said to him, "How do you know he was shot dead?"' Becks said.

The other two women were stunned.

'You said that?'

'I couldn't help myself. I mean, here are we trying to discover who killed Stefan, and there I was talking to someone who knew everything about it.'

Judith and Suzie didn't know what to say. Without having ever conferred on the subject, they'd always dismissed Becks as being cowardly. How wrong they were.

'What did he say?' Judith asked.

'He laughed. Said he knew "someone on the inside", and the word was that Stefan had been shot dead with an antique pistol. I'll never forget the moment. It was the look in his face. He was smirking. So sure of himself.'

'He said it was an antique?' Judith asked.

'He did,' Becks said.

The three women looked at each other.

'Well, that's *very* interesting,' Judith said. 'Because we're about as close to these cases as you can be, and we've not heard anything about an antique pistol.'

'I know,' Becks agreed. 'So when he told me, I said "how horrible", or something like that. I don't remember. I was reeling a bit, if I'm honest. And then Andy turned to me and said, all matter-of-fact, "I don't suppose you want your husband out of the way like that?" I was horrified, and he laughed, saying he was joking. So I pretended that I was an idiot for believing him. People always believe it when I pretend to be an idiot. It's how I look.'

'Don't be stupid,' Judith said.

'No, they do. And for once, I was glad I'm just a silly housewife. Because he relaxed, thinking we'd bonded over the whole "joke". Rather than him making me feel sick to my stomach. And as we turned and walked back to Marlow, I asked him about his life, purely to change the subject. I can tell you, he's got a pumped-up view of himself. Despite having joked about getting my husband killed, he started coming on to me again. It was horrendous. With him saying how he'd been a significant athlete in his youth, how he might have thickened a bit since then, but he was still strong. Still "capable". That's the word he used. It was disgusting. And you know what, maybe I'll have a whisky after all?'

'Bloody hell, you deserve it,' Judith said, going to her sideboard, splashing a whisky into a glass and bringing it over to Becks.

Becks, the perfect vicar's wife, the perfect mother, daughter and housewife, took a sip.

'Sheesh!' she said, wiping the stinging liquid from her lips with the back of her hand. 'Does it always have to be whisky?'

'I'll be honest,' Judith said, 'Suzie and I had tea earlier, and it felt wrong. But well done, Becks, you've been a real hero. Setting the fire alarm off with your toast, that was brave enough. Taking Andy out of his office was incredibly quick thinking. And getting that information about the gun was even more amazing. Let alone making him break cover and offer to get your husband killed for you, even if he claimed it was a joke at the time. I'm telling you, you've achieved more than any of us.'

The flush of red in Becks' cheeks wasn't entirely caused by the sudden rush of whisky in her blood.

'So,' Judith said, returning to the whisky bottle on the sideboard, 'now that Andy has admitted that he knows Stefan was shot, and with an antique pistol to boot, what do we think that means?'

'He's the killer,' Becks said.

'Although,' Judith said, thinking it through, 'if he *were* the killer, would he really tell you he knew someone had shot him?'

'Sounds like he couldn't keep himself from bragging,' Suzie said.

'But surely he'd have stayed quiet. And I can well imagine a local solicitor having contacts in the police. Or he would know someone who does. I bet there's actually quite a lot of people in Marlow who've heard that Stefan was shot dead. He was showing off, as you say.'

'But with an antique pistol?' Suzie asked. 'How did he hear about that?'

'And I spent over an hour with him,' Becks said. 'He may pretend to be all smooth and sophisticated, but he's the killer. I'm sure of it. We already know he's connected to Iqbal's murder, or he wouldn't have been shredding that paper straight after you saw him in his office.'

'That's true,' Suzie agreed.

'It's like we said. The most obvious reason he'd know that Stefan had been shot with an antique pistol was because he was the one who shot him. So all we need to do is link him to Liz's murder and then we can say we've finally found someone with clear links to all three murders.'

Judith sipped on her whisky thoughtfully.

'It's so frustrating,' she said. 'According to Tanika, Liz Curtis was last seen alive at nine this morning by a gaggle of scouts. Their scoutmaster then found her body shortly after ten o'clock. If we knew what Andy was doing between nine and ten, maybe we'd be able to work out if he's the killer. Although,' Judith added, brightening, 'that's exactly what we can do, isn't it? Suzie, get up that photo you took of Andy Bishop's diary.'

'Sure,' Suzie said and pulled out her mobile phone. A few swipes later, and she was able to show the other women the photo she'd taken of Andy's diary. While there were plenty of office meetings across each day, not one of them started before 9.30 a.m.

'Well, thanks to Suzie's quick thinking earlier today,' Judith said, 'we now know that Andy Bishop is never in his office before 9.30 a.m.'

'You're right,' Suzie said, thrilled. 'I did that, didn't I?'

'You did,' Judith agreed. 'Well done. Although it would be tight, wouldn't it? Andy would have to wait in the shadows at the rowing centre with the gun. Let the scouts go out on their canoes, and then shoot Liz dead pretty sharpish before turning up for work at nine thirty.'

'But it would have been do-able,' Becks said.

'And he'd have had to have known that her husband Danny would be away,' Judith added.

'He was away?' Becks asked.

Judith explained how she'd overheard part of Tanika's interview with Danny, and that he'd been in Nottingham since the day before.

'Yes, well, that wouldn't have been hard to find out, would it?' Suzie said. 'I mean, we found out about Danny's Tuesday nights in Nottingham the very first time we talked to him. Didn't we?'

'You're right,' Judith said. 'He couldn't wait to tell us. He was that proud.'

'So what have we got?' Becks said, taking control of the conversation. 'We know Iqbal believed Andy Bishop stole his inheritance. And Iqbal ended up dead. And although we don't know what links Andy to Stefan, Stefan was a bit of a crook, wasn't he? And Andy's *definitely* a bit of a crook. So maybe that's what links them? They're crooks working together. Either way, Andy knows that Stefan was killed by an antique gun, and that could only be known by the killer, couldn't it? If it's true. And now his diary tells us that he had time to kill Liz before getting into his office this morning.'

As Becks spoke, Judith pulled her phone out of her handbag and made a call.

'Judith,' Tanika answered.

'Just a quickie,' Judith said, as though she were ringing on a matter no more urgent than an upcoming whist drive. 'Would I be right in saying that our killer's been using an antique pistol for the murders?'

There was a charged silence on the other end of the line.

'How on earth do you know that?' Tanika asked.

'Well, that's a very interesting development, thank you,' Judith said, and hung up.

'That confirms it,' she said. 'It's like Andy told Becks. The killer used an antique pistol.'

The three women looked at each other.

Was Andy Bishop the killer?

Judith's phone started ringing, and Judith looked at it in surprise. How could it be ringing when no one was calling her?

With a start, Suzie realised it was her phone and she pulled it out of her back pocket.

'Sorry about this,' she said as she looked at the screen. 'It's an old client of mine. Hello, Brenda,' she said into the phone as she answered the call. 'How are you?'

Suzie listened for a few moments and then said, 'No way!'

She listened for a while longer, her eyes alight with excitement.

'Okay, we'll be over in five minutes. And thanks, Brenda, you're a star.'

Suzie hung up the phone and turned to her friends.

'That was Brenda McFarlane.'

'Who's Brenda McFarlane?' Judith asked.

'She used to be one of my clients. Had a cocker spaniel called Monty. Anyway, the point is, Brenda lives next door to Elliot Howard, so I asked her to keep an eye on him.'

'You did?' Judith asked.

'Remember? When you first told me about him, I said I'd find someone to keep him under surveillance.'

'And she has?'

'Brenda's a good sort. You can rely on her.'

'But why's she rung you now?'

'Because she says that half an hour ago, Elliot started a bonfire in his garden.'

'Oh,' Becks said, a touch underwhelmed. 'Is that so suspicious?'

'It's what he's burning that's suspicious.'

'Why?'

'Elliot's just set fire to an old oil painting.'

Chapter 28

'I don't think this is a good idea,' Becks said as Suzie drove her friends in her tatty van through Marlow at speed. 'We should be letting the police deal with Elliot.'

'We are,' Suzie said. 'But it'll take Tanika ten minutes to get from Maidenhead to Marlow. We've got a head start. And anyway, what's the problem? You said Andy Bishop's the killer.'

'Yes, but we shouldn't be doing this. We're just a . . . well, just some housewives.'

'Speak for yourself,' Judith said. 'Can't this thing go any faster?'

'I'm going as fast as I can. Hold on,' Suzie said as, with a screech of wheels, she turned at speed onto Gypsy Lane without indicating. 'We've got to get there before he's finished burning the evidence.'

Gypsy Lane was an old route that had once linked Marlow to the neighbouring village of Marlow Bottom, but it had recently been developed with family homes on both sides, and it ended in a turning circle where the last house was much grander than the rest. There were remote-controlled security gates, thick laurel hedges, and the driveway was a rather startling green tarmac which clashed with the bright red bricks of the house.

This was where Elliot Howard and his wife Daisy lived.

Suzie's van bombed into the turning circle, shuddered to a halt as she slammed on the brakes and then came to a rest in a puff of dust, the left-side wheels bumping up onto the kerb.

'Remind me never to let you drive me anywhere again,' Becks said.

'So which house is Brenda's?' Judith asked.

'That one,' Suzie said, indicating a small house that was next-door-but-one to Elliot's.

A twinkly-eyed old dear in her late eighties came to the door as the three women bustled up to her house, and then she looked about herself conspiratorially before beckoning them inside.

'This is Brenda,' Suzie said, once they'd entered the little hallway.

'This is all very Vichy France,' Judith said in delight, taking in her surroundings. There were net curtains, thimbles on display and horse brasses on the wall. 'What a lovely home,' she said.

'Thank you,' Brenda said. 'And thank you for coming, Suzie. We'd better go upstairs. Come on.'

Brenda ushered the women up a staircase into a darkened room off the main hallway that contained a green baize table, already laid out with playing cards, bridge notepads and pencils.

'Oh, you play bridge?' Judith asked.

'I do, do you?'

'I used to. But I always overbid. It infuriates my partners.'

'What bidding system did you use?'

'It makes no difference, we always seem to end up in seven spades.'

'Hello?' Suzie said, interrupting. 'Elliot Howard?'

'Of course, sorry,' Brenda said, going over to the curtains and pulling them back an inch. 'Because I must say, I've never quite liked him. Or his wife. They never say hello. And I can see into their house from up here. There's something not right about the way they go about their lives. They're rarely in the same room as each other. Never listen to music or the radio. There's no joy in that house. Anyway, it was all normal up until today. I had nothing to report. Although I've been keeping an eye on them like you asked, Suzie. And then, I was up here getting ready for bridge and I saw . . . well, you can see for yourself. Go on, have a look.'

Brenda stepped to one side, and the three other women all sidled up to the gap in the curtains and peered through. From their position on the first floor, they could see over the laurel hedge into the garden of the grand house at the end of the road.

Elliot was standing alone, a small bonfire at his feet.

It looked like he was burning a square of canvas on a frame.

'You're right!' Suzie said. 'He's burning a painting.'

'That's what it looked like to me,' Brenda said. 'And Suzie had said I should keep my eye out for anything strange. And burning a painting is very definitely what I'd call strange.'

As she said this, the four women watched Elliot head back towards his house. He then reappeared holding a few more canvases in his hands.

'He's not just burning one painting,' Judith said as they watched Elliot throw the new paintings onto the bonfire.

'Why's he burning all those other paintings?' Becks asked.

Before anyone could offer an answer, they saw a police car pull up outside Elliot's house and Tanika get out.

'About bloody time!' Suzie said, letting the curtains close as she turned to Brenda. 'Thanks for the tip-off, Brenda. You're the best.'

Outside Elliot's house, Tanika had no sooner pressed the entrance buzzer to the side of the gates than she saw Judith, Suzie and Becks bustle out of a nearby house and head towards her.

'I could have guessed,' she said as the women arrived.

'It's only because of us you know Elliot's burning paintings in his garden,' Judith said, a touch irritated at Tanika's lack of a welcome.

'Paintings?' Tanika asked sharply. 'You told me it was only one.'

'We've been watching from my friend Brenda's house,' Suzie said.

'Brenda?'

Suzie pointed to where Brenda was looking down at them from a window in her house. She waved a friendly hello.

'Although I've a bone to pick with you,' Judith said to Tanika. 'Why didn't you tell me straight away that Stefan and Iqbal had been killed with an antique pistol?'

'Because you're not investigating the murders!' Tanika said, unable to keep the frustration out of her voice.

'But you'd get so much further if you kept us in the loop.'

'That's as may be, but you're civilians. I'm not allowed to. It's that simple.'

'For example,' Judith said, ignoring Tanika's words, 'I'd be able to tell you the significance of the phrase, "faith, hope and charity".'

'You know about that?' she asked.

'I'm guessing they're the words on the bronze medallions you found at each of the murders.'

'How can you possibly know that?'

'Simple deduction. It was you who told me the word "Faith" was carved on the medallion attached to Stefan's body, and I was able to see for myself that there was another medallion by Liz's body. So, if you're now asking about the phrase "faith, hope and charity", it seems only logical to conclude that the words "faith", "hope" and "charity" were found carved on three medallions you found with each body.'

'She's very clever,' Suzie said, indicating Judith with her thumb for Tanika's benefit.

Judith beamed at the compliment.

'Okay,' Tanika said. 'According to you, what does "faith, hope and charity" mean?'

'Well, it's from Corinthians, of course. But beyond that, any crossword compiler worth her salt would be able to tell you it's also the motto of the Freemasons.'

'It is?'

'Or to be precise, they're the three cardinal virtues of the Freemasons.'

Tanika didn't quite know what to say to that.

'That is actually very useful,' she said. 'Thank you.'

'So I suggest you find out who's a Mason, because it's somehow connected to the three murders.'

'Yes, I see that. You could be right.'

Judith turned to her two friends.

'Come on,' she said grandly. 'We need to let Tanika get on with her work.'

The three women turned and headed over to an old van that Tanika could see was parked illegally on the pavement. On the left of the trio was the perfect housewife with her flicky hair, jeggings and gilet; on the right, a solidly built oak of a woman who walked and dressed as if she were about to set sail with Long

John Silver; and in between them, the eccentric aristo who wasn't much taller than she was wide and who was wearing, as ever, her dark grey cape.

A more motley trio it was hard to imagine, but Tanika couldn't help but smile to herself as the women drove off in a belch of diesel fumes from Suzie's vehicle.

Still shaking her head in wonder, Tanika pressed the buzzer again. A woman's voice came out of the speaker.

'The Howard residence.'

'Good morning,' Tanika said into the machine. 'My name's Detective Sergeant Tanika Malik. May I come in?'

Chapter 29

Once Tanika was through the security gates, she passed a pair of gleaming BMWs. As she approached the front door, it was answered by Elliot's wife, Daisy.

'Good morning to you!' the woman said. 'My name's Daisy Howard. How can I help you?'

Tanika introduced herself, but was surprised that a man like Elliot should be married to someone who was so instantly warm and welcoming.

'Could I have a word with your husband?' Tanika asked.

'Of course. Come on in.'

Daisy led Tanika through a house that was effortlessly luxurious. There were thick cream carpets, cut flowers in modernist vases, and old oil paintings on the walls.

'Can I get you a drink?' Daisy asked as they entered the marble and chrome kitchen.

'I'm fine, thank you.'

'Are you sure? It's such a hot day.'

'If I could just have a word with your husband?'

'Why do you want to see him?'

'I'm afraid it's a police matter,' Tanika said as kindly as she could.

'Then you'll find him in the garden. Setting fire to things. Typical man.'

Daisy indicated the bifold doors that led from the kitchen onto a patio of old York flagstones. Stepping outside, the two women saw Elliot standing by a small bonfire at the bottom of the garden. They watched him in silence for a moment.

'How did the two of you meet?' Tanika asked.

'At an art gallery in London. We both tried to buy the same painting.' Daisy smiled at the memory. 'And he was typically English. All pretend bluster. But I could see he was a kind man. Damaged. But kind.'

'You think he's damaged?'

'He's got an artist's soul. He bruises easily. Whatever you've come to see him about today, it's not his fault. Someone will have led him astray. He's not as strong as he looks.'

'You think he could be in trouble?'

'The police never arrive to ask you the time of day.'

Tanika looked at Daisy, and although she was still smiling, there was a hint of steel there as well.

With a nod of thanks, Tanika entered the garden. As she got nearer to Elliot, she could see that Judith and her friends had been right. It looked like the fire was made up of wooden frames and colourful painted canvases.

Elliot turned as she approached. Tanika had seen his photo on the auction house website and spoken to him twice on the phone, but she'd not met him in the flesh before. He seemed more subdued than she was expecting. A little less commanding, perhaps.

'Hello?' he said.

As Tanika introduced herself, she saw that the fire was made up of half a dozen paintings, if not more. She started pulling them out to try and save them. And as she did so, she noted that they were all similar to the painting in Stefan's house that had had its frame removed.

Elliot just stood to one side and watched her, puzzled.

'What are you doing?' he said.

'A neighbour saw you setting fire to some paintings in your garden and called it in.'

'Why's that a police matter?' Elliot said, turning to look at the clutch of houses that had windows overlooking his garden. 'Bloody nosy parkers.'

'It's a police matter because we have reason to believe Stefan Dunwoody was killed in connection with a Rothko painting you sold to him in 1988,' Tanika said as she pulled another painting from the fire and wiped the flames off it on the grass until it was only smouldering. A third of the painting hadn't yet caught fire, and Tanika could see that it had originally been three bands of plain colour, each of them a different shade of orange.

'You've got to be kidding me,' Elliot said, superiority slipping back into his voice, but Tanika guessed it was false confidence. 'You aren't seriously suggesting I've just set fire to a bunch of Rothkos, are you? They'd be worth millions of pounds.'

Tanika examined a charred batten of wood. It was made of modern pine and didn't look as though it could have come from the frame around the Rothko in Stefan's house. Stefan's frames were all old, and most of them were gilt or ornate. In fact, as she removed the last burnt painting from the fire and smothered the flames on the grass, she realised that all of the wood she could see was cheap, such as would be used to make a modern canvas for a painting. Indeed, at the corners of each piece of wood she'd taken from the fire, she could see modern staples where the canvas had been attached to the frame.

'These paintings look like Rothkos to me,' Tanika said, not wanting to give any ground.

'That's very gratifying. It's very much the effect I was going for.'

'How do you mean?'

'I painted these. All of them.'

'You did? When?'

'In the last few months. It's what I do in my spare time. Painting.'

'Can you tell me about the Rothko that Stefan bought from you after your father died?'

Elliot thought for a moment before replying.

'Okay, the thing you have to know about Stefan Dunwoody is he was a crook.'

'Is that so?'

'But I didn't know that when my father died. Back in 1988. Which is why I got him to value Father's paintings. And he did a good job, or so it seemed to me at the time. But he said that one of Father's pictures was a fake, bought it for a pittance from me, and then, much later, got it reassigned as a Rothko. Which hurt, I can tell you. Rothko's always been my specialism. I mean, look at my paintings. All these years later and I'm still obsessed with him.'

'Then why have you set them on fire?'

'I always destroy my work. After a time.'

'Why?'

Elliot stared into the dying embers rather than answer.

'Why do you burn your paintings?' Tanika asked again.

'Because I'm no good,' he said, and Elliot seemed to be talking more to the fire than to her.

'I'm sorry?'

'My work is worthless.'

He said the words so quietly, Tanika wasn't sure she'd heard them correctly.

'You went to art college.'

'Anyone can go to art college. You only need ability for that. And I always had ability. But I didn't have "it". The gift. That thing that says you're different. Special. That you have something to say.'

Tanika remembered how Judith had told her that Elliot had been awarded a place at art school when he was much younger, but his father had forbidden him from attending.

'What about when you were younger? The first time you got into art college? Was your work special then?'

Elliot finally looked up from the fire.

'I'll never know, will I?'

For the first time, Tanika felt as though she were talking to the 'real' Elliot Howard. Not pompous, not superior at all in fact, he was more a little boy lost. Although, Tanika knew, 'little boy losts' were still capable of committing murder. And it was surely suspicious that he'd be painting and then burning Rothko-styled paintings after there'd been a Rothko-related theft from Stefan's house, even if it was just the frame that had been taken.

'Did you break into Stefan's house after your argument with him at Henley?' she asked.

'No. What are you talking about?'

'Then was it you who broke into his house last week?'

'I don't know what you're on about. What break-in?'

'Did you steal the frame from Mr Dunwoody's Rothko?'

'Seriously, this is the first I've heard of any of this. What frame?'

Tanika could see that Elliot was apparently sincere in his answers. But if he hadn't broken in and stolen the frame, then who had? And why was the frame so important in the first place?

Daisy headed over, a phone in her hand.

'Detective Sergeant?' she called out, and Elliot and Tanika turned around. 'I'm going to have to ask you to leave.'

'What's that, darling?' Elliot asked.

'I've got our lawyer on the phone, and he says we don't have to answer any questions. Not unless he's present. And the police aren't allowed on our property without a warrant.'

'I'm just answering the detective sergeant's questions.'

'Well don't,' Daisy said firmly, before turning to face Tanika. 'Now, if you're not going to charge my husband with anything, and you don't have a warrant, then you'll have to leave at once.'

Tanika knew that Daisy was right. Without the owner's permission, she wasn't allowed to stay on the property.

She looked at Daisy, and could see a determination to her that brooked no disagreement.

Tanika smiled tightly, made her excuses and left, but as she returned to the house, she paused briefly by the bifolds and glanced back at Elliot and his wife. It looked very much as though Daisy was reading the riot act to her husband.

Now what was that about?

Chapter 30

The following day, a national newspaper splashed on its front page that a triple killer was on the loose in Marlow. By the evening, the story was being featured prominently on the TV news, and from that moment on, it felt as though the international media had taken over the town. There were news satellite vans parked outside the Assembly Rooms, and a seemingly endless supply of reporters from all over the world vox-popping residents, asking them how they coped with going about their day while a serial killer was at large.

It was hugely unsettling for everyone, and local community leaders like the mayor and the Reverend Colin Starling were constantly being wheeled out to remind their residents and the wider world that Marlow was in fact a peaceful place where residents generally lived side by side in harmony.

As for Judith, she vanished for the next couple of days, which allowed Becks and Suzie to catch up with their lives. But then, on the Monday morning, both women got a call from her. They were to drop everything and go to her house at once. She'd made a breakthrough.

'I don't believe it,' Suzie said as she and Becks stood in wonder in Judith's sitting room.

In front of them, on the green baize table, were the shredded pieces of paper Suzie had stolen from Andy Bishop's office, but they'd been separated and straightened as best as Judith could into strips a couple of millimetres wide, and all aligned so they recreated the original sheet of A4 paper.

'You put it back together?' Becks said, as amazed as Suzie.

'I told you I'd do it,' Judith said.

'But there must be hundreds of pieces here!' Suzie said.

'There are. But it's like a jigsaw. Each piece you place correctly isn't just a piece that's now in the right place, it's also a piece that's no longer in among the mess of unplaced pieces. It's very much a zero-sum game.'

'I take my hat off to you,' Becks said as she looked at the document. 'I never thought you'd be able to do it.'

'So go on, then,' Suzie said eagerly. 'What's so important that Andy Bishop had to shred it the moment you'd left the room?'

'It's a page from the *Borlasian*.'

'What's that?'

'It's the magazine for the old boys and girls of William Borlase's Grammar School.'

'I don't understand,' Becks said. 'Why would Andy Bishop need to shred a page from an old school magazine?'

'Have a look and you'll see.'

Suzie and Becks bent down and peered at the thin strips of paper on the table.

'I don't want to get too near,' Becks said.

'Don't worry,' Judith said. 'I bought some cellophane and glue. I wasn't having a gust of wind ruin all of the hours of work I'd put into this. I've glued each shredded piece of paper to the cellophane, so you can pick it up and look at both sides of the page. In fact, you'll need to look at both sides.'

To demonstrate, Judith picked up the document and handed it to Becks and Suzie. They pored over it, but enlightenment still eluded them.

'It's a report on last year's school hockey team,' Suzie said.

She was correct. The page covered the exploits of the girls' and boys' first XI teams during the previous season.

'As I say, that's not the interesting side. Turn it over,' Judith said.

The other side of the reconstructed paper was a page dedicated to the old boys and old girls of the school. There was a message from the president of the association, news of a fund-raising drive, and a list of names of old pupils who'd died in the past year. Again, it was entirely innocuous.

'Okay,' Suzie said. 'Either I'm going mad, or this is just school guff.'

'Where did he even get it from?' Becks asked.

'Good question,' Judith said. 'At first I thought it was his copy of the magazine. You see, I looked Andy Bishop up on his company website. He went to Borlase's Grammar School back when he was a child. So he'd get the school magazine sent to him every year.'

'But you *don't* think it's his?' Suzie asked.

'Keep looking,' Judith said, and the other two women could see that she was enjoying herself tremendously.

'There's nothing here. I can't see Ezra Harrington's name mentioned. Or Iqbal Kassam. Or Stefan Dunwoody, or Andy

Bishop for that matter. It's got nothing to do with anything or anyone.'

'And that's where you're wrong!' Judith said as she went over to her sideboard, returning moments later with her copy of Ezra's will. 'Because I was like you to start off with. I couldn't work out why Andy Bishop would have wanted to shred this one page from a school magazine. But the thing is, he *did* shred it. So there had to be a reason. I just had to puzzle it out. Work at it from all angles. And it was when I looked at our copy of Ezra's will that I realised what was going on. Have a look at the names of the two people who witnessed it.'

Judith opened Ezra's will so the others could see the signatures at the end of the document. The two witnesses were listed as Spencer Chapman and Faye Kerr. Their addresses and occupations, a horse breeder and teacher respectively, were also listed.

Suzie realised what the link was first.

'No way!' she said, returning to the page from the *Borlasian*.

She ran her finger down the column of names listed in the obituaries.

'Spencer Chapman and Faye Kerr died last year!'

'Got it in one,' Judith said, delighted that her friend had worked it out.

'Are you serious?' Suzie said. 'They've both died since they witnessed Ezra's will? What happened to them?'

'Oh, it's so much better than that. Look at the dates they died.'

Suzie looked back at the page in her hand.

'Spencer died last year in March, and so did Faye. They both died in March.'

'Now look at the date of Ezra's will.'

Becks looked at the dates that had been written under the signatures.

'It says here, May the fifth last year,' she said. 'Hang on, that doesn't make sense.'

'Oh, it makes perfect sense,' Judith said.

'But how did these two manage to witness Ezra's signature a month after they'd died?'

'Because they didn't, did they?' Suzie said, now realising what must have happened. 'Those aren't their real signatures. Andy Bishop forged them.'

'Exactly!' Judith said. 'But he couldn't risk choosing the names of people who might later stand up in court and say they'd never witnessed the will. So he got two people who'd recently died. And faked their signatures.'

'Which is why he needed to shred this page after he saw you,' Suzie said, finally understanding. 'He was worried you'd find out.'

'But how did he manage to trick Ezra?' Becks asked.

'That's the easy part,' Judith said. 'Ezra's will is dated two weeks before he died. He would have been in terrible pain towards the end. And drugged up on morphine and confused. I've seen someone die of cancer. The last two weeks of great aunt Betty's life, she didn't know who she was, or what day of the week it was. She spent a lot of the time hallucinating from the drugs she was on in the hospice. I'd have been able to get her to sign anything if I'd been minded to.'

'Just like Andy Bishop did with Ezra.'

'He wrote a new will that left Ezra's whole estate to him, got Ezra to sign it, and then faked a couple of signatures afterwards to make it look as though it had been witnessed at the time. And who'd ever find out?'

'Until their names were published in the obituaries column a year later in the *Borlasian* magazine.'

'So it's like I've been saying,' Becks said. 'Andy Bishop's our killer. He has to be.'

'I think you could well be right,' Judith said. 'It's the only thing that makes sense.'

'But how did Iqbal find out about the forged witnesses?' Suzie asked.

'I've got a theory about that,' Judith said. 'And if I'm right, it will explain why he had to die, and why Andy was the person who killed him. Hold on.'

Judith went over to her mobile, picked it up and dialled a number.

'Tanika, I hope you don't mind me ringing,' Judith said.

'Not at all,' Tanika said on the other end of the line. 'Is everything all right?'

'More than all right, thank you. But I've got a question to ask.'

'Okay, but you know you can't ask about my meeting with Elliot Howard, don't you?'

'Oh, don't worry, it's got nothing to do with Elliot Howard.'

'Or the murder cases.'

'What's that?'

'You also can't ask about any of the murder cases.'

'What makes you think I'm going to do that?'

'Because why else would you ring me?'

'Did Iqbal Kassam go to William Borlase's Grammar School?'

'That's to do with the case.'

'Of course it's to do with the case!'

'Then I can't tell you.'

'It's a simple yes or no answer, it could be very important. But he did, didn't he?'

Judith waited what felt like an eternity before Tanika replied.

'I suppose it's reasonably public domain information,' she eventually said. 'But you're right, Mr Kassam's parents spent one year in Marlow when he was twelve years old. He spent all of his Year Seven at Borlase's Grammar School. I guess it's why he moved back here after his parents died. He had a connection to Marlow.'

'Then you need to go to Mr Kassam's house as a matter of urgency. And if you look hard enough, I think you'll find a copy of the most recent *Borlasian* magazine. And it will have precisely one page missing. Page 74.'

'I'm sorry, you want me to do what?' Tanika asked.

'It's the proof that Andy Bishop faked Ezra Harrington's will, because that page lists the names of two people who died the month *before* they apparently witnessed Ezra's will.'

'Andy Bishop forged the witness's signatures?'

'Got it in one. But Andy was unlucky, from his point of view. Because both of the people he'd chosen had gone to Borlase's Grammar School back in the day, which is hardly a surprise. There are only two local schools here, there's a fifty–fifty chance that anyone in Marlow went to Borlase's. So, a year after Andy had forged Ezra's will and got away with it, and was about to pocket six hundred and fifty thousand pounds from the sale of Ezra's house, little did he know that the latest edition of the school magazine would list the names of the two witnesses to Ezra's will in their obituaries section. And that it would say clear as day that they'd died the month before the date of Ezra's will. Even worse for Andy, Iqbal was sent a copy of the magazine because he'd spent a year at the school himself.

'As to what happened next . . . I suppose we won't ever know exactly. But I can well imagine Iqbal idly flicking through his copy of the magazine when it arrived and seeing that the two people who'd witnessed Ezra's signature had both died. Remember, Iqbal already believed there'd been foul play. Ezra had promised to leave his estate to him but, at the last minute, had left it to his solicitor. And now, over a year later, Iqbal found himself holding evidence in black and white that both witnesses of Ezra's will had been dead at the time.

'So what did he do? Well, I think he must have contacted Andy. Told him he knew about his crime. And then what? Did Andy offer to share some of Ezra's cash to buy Iqbal's silence? Or did he flat-out deny everything? Who knows? But what we do know is that Andy now had a cast iron, copper-bottomed, gold-plated motive for wanting Iqbal dead. He had to kill him to silence him. To keep hold of the six hundred and fifty thousand pounds inheritance he'd tricked out of Ezra.'

'Okay, give me a few seconds, Judith. This is quite a lot to take on board. Are you serious about all this?'

'Deadly serious. Forget Elliot Howard, for all of his bonfire of the vanities. Whatever beef he had with Stefan has nothing to do with anything, because Andy Bishop's our killer. Which makes sense, when you think about the medallions he left with each body. As I told you, "Faith", "Hope" and "Charity" are the Masonic virtues, and I'd be very surprised if Mr Bishop attained his position of prominence as a local solicitor without joining the funny-handshake brigade. What's more, he let slip to Becks that not only had Stefan been shot, but he knew an antique gun had been used. So how could he have known that if he weren't the killer? You need to arrest him. At once.'

'I'm impressed. Really, I am. The only problem is, Andy Bishop didn't kill Iqbal Kassam.'

'But he must have done. I've just explained.'

'He didn't. You see, he wasn't in the country when Iqbal was killed. He was in Malta.'

Judith wasn't sure she'd heard correctly.

'Say that again?'

'After you told me about him, I got my team to check him out. And according to both the UK Borders Agency and the Maltese Department of Immigration, Andy Bishop was at the end of his annual two-week holiday when Iqbal Kassam was murdered. Which means he was also in Malta when Stefan Dunwoody was killed.'

'He was on a two-week holiday throughout all of this?'

'I'm sorry, Judith, but he was about a thousand miles away at the time. There's no way he could be the killer.'

Judith was rendered speechless. If Andy wasn't even in the country for the first two murders, then it didn't matter how much of a motive he had to kill Iqbal, he didn't do it. As for the murder of Liz Curtis, it was still possible that he'd killed her, if he'd acted swiftly before arriving at his place of work that morning, but if he hadn't carried out the first two murders, then why on earth would he have carried out the third? Especially when they'd not been able to find a link between him and Liz Curtis.

Judith realised they were back to square one. They'd already ruled out Elliot Howard, and now they'd have to rule out Andy Bishop. And if neither of them had done it, then who on earth had killed Stefan Dunwoody, Iqbal Kassam and Liz Curtis?

And why? What on earth was the link between the three victims that meant they had to die?

Chapter 31

If Judith and her friends were at something of a low ebb, so was Tanika. The sad truth was that with the murder of Liz Curtis, and the subsequent exposure in the international press, she and her team had become overwhelmed. There was no way an officer as inexperienced as Tanika could lead three such public murder enquiries. Her Superintendent had spoken to the Regional Crime Commissioner about getting an experienced detective inspector brought in to head up the cases, but it was taking time to arrange.

For the time being, Tanika was on her own.

To make matters worse, her team could see how out of her depth she was. It's not that she wasn't up to the job, far from it. Her diligence and desire to do everything 'by the book' meant that her team knew exactly what they were doing and when they were supposed to do it. It was more that there was simply too much for her to stay on top of.

Tanika saw it in the glances from her team when they thought she wasn't looking, and in the way conversations would some-times stop when she walked into the room. They were losing confidence in her.

'Have you any active leads?' her Super asked at his daily meeting with Tanika in his office.

'Which case, sir?' Tanika asked.

Her Super could see that for once she wasn't sitting bolt upright and putting on her best face. She looked exhausted.

'Liz Curtis.'

'I'll be honest, sir, we've almost nothing.'

'Nothing?'

'No leads, no witnesses, no motives.'

'What about her husband?'

'Multiple witnesses place him at a roadside outside Nottingham when she was killed. We've also pulled his life apart, and we can find no link, be it email, phone, text, message, you name it, between him and Stefan Dunwoody or Iqbal Kassam.'

'So he's not our shooter?'

'He can't be.'

'Then what about the weapon that killed Liz Curtis?'

'According to ballistics, it was the exact same Luger pistol that killed Iqbal Kassam and Stefan Dunwoody.'

'So the press are right? We have a serial killer on the loose.'

'We have.'

'In Marlow?'

'I know. In Marlow.'

Tanika's boss could see how bewildered she was. He well remembered running his own homicide cases. How easy it was to get swamped. Nonetheless, he had a job to do.

'I must insist you step up your efforts, Detective Sergeant, until we can second a more experienced officer to head up at least one of these cases, perhaps all three,' he added ominously. 'Do everything in your power to move the cases on.'

'Yes, sir.'

'Everything in your power. You hear me?'

Tanika nodded. She understood.

Tanika didn't immediately return to the Incident Room after her meeting. Instead, she slipped out of the fire door at the back of the building to get some fresh air. This wasn't the easiest of tasks, as the back of the station abutted a dual carriageway.

Seeing the cars and lorries roaring past, she allowed herself to give in to her frustrations. As she saw it, her Super was setting her up for a fall. Or, at the very least, making sure that if she messed up, he'd have his back covered.

Do everything in your power to move the cases on, she thought to herself. She was already doing everything in her power. The problem was money. Her team wasn't anywhere near large enough. Nor was her budget. But years of government cuts had left the police overstretched almost to breaking point. It's why there wasn't a detective inspector covering for DI Hoskins while he was off sick. And, Tanika suspected, it was also why her Super hadn't yet managed to get a DI seconded to help. He'd be trying to make sure the significant extra costs wouldn't come out of the Maidenhead budget.

And on top of everything else, Shamil, Tanika's husband, was increasingly ratty at home because of her constant absences. He understood that her work was critically important to her, and he tried hard to give the necessary support, but, as he'd often say, he had his own dreams too. He'd always wanted to be a DJ, and being a stay-at-home-dad was getting in the way of his career, especially when he had to be out late at the weekends. The fact that Shamil had been pursuing the same dream for the last twenty-plus years without ever making any meaningful progress or earning any money was something Tanika had stopped mentioning years ago.

But what broke her heart was the look on her daughter Shanti's face every morning as she asked if Mummy would be home to read her a bedtime story that evening. It had been even worse in the last week, because Shanti had stopped asking. She already knew the answer.

And as well as all of her responsibilities at home, Tanika also had to do the lion's share of looking after her father, despite the fact that she had two brothers who were perfectly capable of helping, but didn't. They didn't explicitly say it was 'woman's work', but then they didn't have to because their father did. As far as he was concerned, since Tanika's mother had died, it was his daughter's duty to take over as his cook, driver, social secretary, cleaner and washerwoman.

Tanika scrunched her fists and eyes shut and allowed herself an internal scream. She wanted to do her best, to be a good police officer, a good wife, a good mother and daughter, and she wanted to deliver justice for the three murder victims, but there was nothing more she could do.

That wasn't quite true, was it? she thought to herself. Because, for all that she knew she'd done her best, she couldn't stop thinking about Judith's comment about 'Faith, Hope and Charity' being the motto of the Freemasons. And how, if she'd only told her about it earlier, she'd have been able to tell her what it meant sooner.

She opened her eyes, startled by an idea as it popped into her head.

It wasn't a sensible idea. And it was by no means 'doing things by the book', but her Super had told her to do everything in her power to move the cases on, and there was no doubting that there was still one resource she hadn't fully utilised. One that had been coming up with solid leads ever since the murder of Stefan Dunwoody.

Tanika fished out her phone and dialled a number before she could change her mind.

'Hello?' Judith's voice said as she answered her phone. 'Any news?'

'I think you could say that,' Tanika said with a smile in her voice.

'How very exciting! What have you got for me?'

Tanika took a deep breath, and then she said a sentence she never thought she'd ever utter.

'Judith Potts, I'm bringing you in.'

Chapter 32

Tanika met Judith, Suzie and Becks as they arrived at Maidenhead police station.

'I still don't understand,' Becks said as Tanika handed passes to each of them.

'I'm asking the three of you to join my team as civilian advisers. If you can spare the time.'

'Oh we can spare the time,' Judith said, putting her lanyard over her head.

'Is there any money in it?' Suzie asked.

'Sadly not,' Tanika said. 'As you can imagine, I wouldn't be asking you to help if we were lavishly funded. But one of the things a Senior Investigating Officer can do is co-opt civilians onto her team if they have an expertise that the SIO judges will help.'

'And the regulations really allow that?' Judith asked, raising an eyebrow.

'Don't worry,' Tanika replied, knowing that Judith was teasing her. 'I've checked my copy of Blackstone's *Senior Investigating Officers' Handbook*. This is all above board. It's another way we're supposed to save money. By getting in civilian experts as and when.'

'But I have no expertise,' Becks said.

'I wouldn't agree with that at all,' Tanika said. 'The three of you are about the only people who've moved any of these cases on at all. I'd say you have considerable expertise.'

'Do we get access to the case files?' Judith asked eagerly.

'Absolutely.'

'Pathology reports, ballistics, witness statements, the whole shebang?'

'Yes.'

'Then lead on.'

'Just one thing,' Tanika added. 'This is still quite an unortho-dox move on my part.'

'You can say that again,' Suzie said breezily. 'I've got a criminal record.'

Everyone turned and looked at her.

'You have?' Becks asked.

'Nothing to write home about. Just fraud.'

'You don't think fraud's anything to write home about?'

'It was a suspended sentence in the end. All spent.'

'I'd keep that under your hat, if I were you,' Tanika said. 'But the point is, my team won't take too kindly to three civilians joining our ranks. Not that they've got any choice. But don't be surprised if you meet with a degree of resistance.'

Tanika wasn't wrong.

When she led Judith, Suzie and Becks across the main Incident Room, they could all feel the eyes of the other officers drilling into them. Who were these outsiders? These *women*? Judith held her chin up in pride, Becks looked at her feet, and Suzie glared back at them as though she'd be prepared to take them all on in a fight.

Tanika took the three women into a small conference room.

'Okay, this is yours. Whatever you want, just ask, and I'll get one of the team to bring it to you.'

'Then we'd like everything you've got on all three cases,' Judith said.

'I'll get my data manager to bring through the files.'

'Seriously? Just like that?' Becks asked, amazed.

'But before you go,' Judith added. 'I've got three questions. Firstly, have you had the Rothko checked in Stefan's house? The one without the frame?'

'I got an expert to check it over, just like you asked me to, and he said it's the real deal.'

'It's not a forgery?'

'The brushstrokes, pigments and age of the materials all suggest it's an authentic painting by Rothko.'

'Now that's *very* interesting.'

'But why would Elliot steal a worthless frame from a real Rothko worth hundreds of thousands of pounds?' Suzie asked. 'It's the only bit that's not worth anything.'

Judith ignored the question.

'And can you tell me what sort of antique pistol the killer's been using?'

Tanika smiled, relieved finally to be open with Judith.

'It's a Second World War German Luger pistol.'

'Why would the killer use a German pistol?' Suzie asked.

'That's what I'm hoping you three will be able to tell me,' Tanika said.

'Then I've got a question,' Becks said. 'Please could you explain what's going on with those medallions you and Judith talked about?'

'Well, I have to say, Judith's guess was correct. As usual. The killer left a medallion at the scene of each murder. The first had the word "Faith" carved into it, the second and third had the words "Hope" and "Charity".'

'But why?'

'I believe it's a message for the police,' Judith said to Tanika.

'That's what I've been thinking as well,' Tanika agreed.

'What makes you say that?' Becks asked.

'It must have been,' Judith said. 'Who else was going to see the three bodies after they'd been killed? And you know what I can't help noticing? There isn't a fourth part of the saying, is there? It's just "Faith, hope and charity". Three words. Three bodies. So the killer's telling the police, it's over.'

'That's what I'm hoping,' Tanika agreed.

'But the fact that it's Masonic has to mean something as well. Have you checked to see if Andy Bishop's a Mason?'

'Not yet. We've been kind of busy. But I'll get someone to look into it now.'

Tanika turned to leave the room, but stopped in the doorway as a thought occurred to her.

'You said you had three questions.'

Judith smiled.

'Have you found a copy of the *Borlasian* magazine in Iqbal's house?'

'You were serious about that?'

'Could you send someone to his house? There'll be a copy of the most recent magazine, and I very much think that page 74 will have been torn out.'

Tanika looked from Judith to the other two women, but all she could see was the same eagerness. She sighed, giving in to the force of nature that was Judith Potts.

'Very well. I'll send an officer to check it out,' she said and made her exit, closing the door behind her.

As soon as they were on their own, Suzie looked at the others in utter amazement.

'What the *fuck* are we doing here?'

'Ssh!' Becks said, appalled. 'You can't swear in here, it's a police station.'

Suzie wasn't listening as she got out her phone and started pressing and swiping it.

'You know, I took your advice, Judith,' she said. 'I got back in touch with Amy, and it's the best thing I ever did. Hey, Amy,' she said into the screen, 'guess where I am?'

Suzie turned the phone around, and Becks and Judith saw that Suzie had started a video call.

'What's that, Mum?' a voice said from the speaker of the phone.

'I'm in Maidenhead police station!'

'What have you done now?'

'Nothing! The police want my help, can you believe it? And these are my friends, Judith and Becks. Go on, say hello,' Suzie said to Becks and Judith as she trained the camera on them.

Becks and Suzie started to wave awkwardly to Suzie's daughter, which was the exact moment that the door opened and a female officer brought in three manila files that were bulging with paper.

'Oh my God, that's a bloody copper!' the voice of Suzie's daughter said from the phone.

Even Suzie had the good grace to look embarrassed.

'Of course it's a copper,' she whispered loudly into the phone. 'I told you, we're at the police station.'

With a tight smile, the female officer put the three files on the table and then left the room.

Once she'd gone, Suzie said, 'Well, she looked like she had a stick up her arse, didn't she?' She then told her daughter she'd speak to her later and hung up. 'Now how do you want to do this?' Suzie asked, rubbing her hands together like a mechanic who was about to pop the bonnet on an old car.

'With less swearing and video calls, I think,' Becks said.

'How about we take a case file each?' Judith said brightly.

'Good idea,' Becks said. 'I'll take Liz Curtis's, if that's okay? Seeing as I knew her.'

'Then I'll have Stefan Dunwoody's case file,' Judith said.

'Which leaves me with Iqbal, and that's who I'd want anyway,' Suzie said.

The three women took seats at the table and started to leaf through the paperwork in their files.

'You know what I want?' Suzie said almost immediately. 'A nice cup of tea.'

'Oo, good idea,' Judith said.

'I'll sort it out,' Becks said, getting up and leaving the room. A few minutes later she returned with a little plate of biscuits and three steaming cups of tea.

'Well, isn't this nice,' Judith said as they settled down with their tea and biscuits over their files.

'So what do you think we should be looking for?' Suzie asked.

'In the first instance, I suggest we just get acquainted with the files, the witness statements, pathology reports and so on. But I think that what we're really looking for are links between the three victims. Because their deaths have to be connected. They were killed within thirteen days of each other. Find what that link is and we'll be able to work out who the killer is.'

'But why don't we focus on Elliot Howard and Andy Bishop?' Suzie asked.

'I think that way lies madness. For the moment at least,' Judith added.

'How so?'

'Because whenever I try and think about those two, I end up tying myself in knots. Andy Bishop couldn't have killed Stefan or Iqbal, he was out of the country at the time of both deaths. So he's in the clear. Even though he has a motive the size of a barn door to want Iqbal dead. And Elliot couldn't have killed Stefan either, even though he'd hated him for years for stealing a Rothko painting from him. Not unless Elliot somehow killed Stefan *before* choir practice and the gunshot I heard from the river that night just after 8 p.m. was staged for my benefit. Which doesn't sound very likely, if you ask me. And as for why Elliot would want to kill Iqbal Kassam or Liz Curtis, well, that's equally as impossible to imagine. And that's putting aside the fact that Elliot was at an online auction when Liz was killed, so he can't have killed her anyway.'

'But it has to be one or other of them,' Becks said.

'I'd agree with you there,' Judith said. 'Their fingerprints are all over the murders. Metaphorically at least.'

'Maybe someone's setting them up?' Suzie said.

'Although that's not true for Liz Curtis, is it?' Becks said to Judith, holding up her folder.

'What's that?' Judith asked.

'We may be able to find connections between Andy Bishop and Iqbal, and Elliot Howard and Stefan, but we've got nothing yet that suggests any kind of a link between either man and Liz Curtis. Have we?'

'Which is my point exactly,' Judith agreed. 'We're only guessing when it comes to Andy Bishop and Elliot Howard. Whereas we aren't when we come to the victims. We *know* they were killed. We *know* their deaths are related. So I suggest we try to find out what that link is.'

'There isn't one!' Suzie said. 'Nothing links a local art dealer, a taxi driver and the owner of a rowing centre.'

'Nonsense. *Something* links them. Or they wouldn't have been killed. We simply have to discover what it is.'

'It's funny you should say that,' Becks said, indicating a report in her file. 'I've got a list of all of the clients who Iqbal had in his taxi here. And so you know, he never drove Elliot Howard. Not once. It's the same for Andy Bishop. And Stefan Dunwoody, for that matter. But he *did* drive Liz Curtis. Two weeks before she died. It cost fifteen pounds.'

'And that's *exactly* what I mean!' Judith said, enthused. 'Because her husband Danny told us she'd used Iqbal's taxi, and that's the proof right there, isn't it? Liz met Iqbal two weeks before she died. And we know she was a regular in Stefan's art gallery as well. So that's one clear and direct link between all three of them. Liz knew the other two victims.'

'Although her husband said it shouldn't be much of a surprise,' Suzie said. 'What with her running the rowing centre her whole life and going to church and everything. She knew everyone in Marlow.'

'It's still a connection,' Judith said with finality. 'So we just need to keep looking for other connections between the victims. For example, I see here that Stefan Dunwoody went to Sir William Borlase's School.'

'Just like Iqbal did,' Suzie said.

'You see? That's another link.'

'But not Liz,' Becks said, looking up from her file. 'She went to Great Marlow.'

'Very well. We should still keep looking.'

The women set to their work, the silence of the room only disturbed by the occasional sound of a page turning, or a brief slurp of tea, or the crunch of a chomped biscuit.

'Here's something,' Becks said, looking up from her file.

'What have you got?' Judith asked.

'It's a report on Liz Curtis's social interactions. The police have been through her phone calls. And her electronic diary. And analysis of her emails and web history and everything. It's very impressive what they've done, it's her whole life. And there's nothing suspicious about it at all.'

'There must be something,' Suzie said.

'Honestly, there isn't. Liz led a totally blameless life. There are countless work emails sorting out bookings for the rowing centre, phone calls to family, that sort of thing. She barely had a social life beyond that. But although her diary's a blank, there's one entry.'

'Go on,' Judith said.

'It says "Rowing dinner". It was for last month.'

Judith pursed her lips.

'Her diary's completely empty apart from that one entry?'

'For months on end. Just blank. And then you get "Rowing dinner" on the fifth of August. So I wonder if any of the other victims attended it?'

'Good thinking!' Suzie said.

'The fifth of August?' Judith asked.

'That's right.'

'Now that's interesting,' Judith said, and started flicking through the file on Stefan Dunwoody's murder. 'If I'm not much mistaken, that was the same day that Elliot Howard went to Stefan's art gallery and had his argument with him.'

'He had his argument with Elliot at Henley Regatta,' Suzie said.

'No, that was a few weeks before. I'm talking about when Elliot went to Stefan's art gallery and argued with him there. Here we are.'

Judith found the witness statement the police had taken from Antonia Webster, Stefan's assistant. She quickly scanned it.

'Yes, it says here, Elliot argued with Stefan in his office on the morning of Monday the fifth of August. Which we now know was the same day that Liz attended a rowing dinner in the evening.'

'You think the two events are connected?' Becks asked.

'I've no idea, but I'll tell you this much,' Judith said, realising something. 'Rowing's something that links Liz and Elliot.'

'It is?'

Judith told the women about the school photos she'd seen on Elliot's office wall that showed him in various rowing teams.

'So he used to row,' Suzie said. 'I like it.'

'And seeing as Liz once represented Great Britain,' Judith said, 'maybe they met through rowing?'

'I don't think it's likely,' Becks said, checking in her file. 'She's much younger than Elliot. Here we are, she's fifty-four year's old.'

'Elliot is fifty-eight,' Judith said after she'd found the relevant information in her file. 'And you don't have mixed boys and girls crews, do you? So it's unlikely they rowed together. But that doesn't mean they didn't both go to the same rowing dinner that night, does it? It's still a possibility. One moment.'

Judith left the room and found Tanika in conference with another police officer.

'DS Malik, can you find out what Elliot Howard was doing on the night of Monday the fifth of August? But maybe ask for his movements for the whole week so he doesn't know it's specifically that night we're interested in.'

'Okay,' Tanika said. 'Happy to. And by the way, you were right about Andy Bishop. We've spoken to the Master of the Masonic Lodge in Marlow, and Mr Bishop's a Freemason.'

'What about Elliot Howard?'

'I also asked about Elliot and he's not, nor has he ever been, a Mason.'

'Stefan Dunwoody?'

'It's the same for him and Iqbal Kassam. The only Mason in all of this is Andy Bishop.'

'Well, that's good to know. I'll tell the team,' Judith said, and bustled back to her office.

As Judith returned, she found Suzie and Becks deep in conversation.

'Don't let me interrupt,' Judith said as she retook her place at the table.

'I'm reading Iqbal's crime scene report,' Suzie explained for Judith's benefit. 'And it makes for grim reading, I can tell you. But there's one thing that jumps out at me. The killer didn't have to break in to kill him.'

'You think Iqbal let him in?' Judith asked.

'Not at five o'clock in the morning, which was when he was killed. And according to the pathologist's report, Iqbal had a heavy dose of sleeping pills in his system when he was killed.'

'He'd been drugged?' Becks asked in dismay.

'It's a prescription sleeping pill. Iqbal told me he took pills to help him sleep when he'd been on a night shift. But I don't think he opened the door to anyone that night.'

'So the killer had a key?' Judith asked. 'Is that what you're saying?'

'That's the only thing that makes sense, but I know how

security conscious Iqbal was. I mean, he wouldn't even give me a key to his side gate so I could pick up Emma. Every day he'd open the gate for me, or leave it open when he knew I was coming. I even asked him about it one day. I said it would be easier if he just gave me a key, but he wouldn't. He said he'd rather let me in.'

'So if he wouldn't give a key to you, who would he give a key to?' Judith asked.

'That's the thing, we all went to his funeral. The only people there who weren't us had been told to attend by Imam Latif. There's no one he'd give his key to.'

'You'd give it to your neighbour,' Becks said, almost to herself.

'What's that?' Judith asked.

'We don't give the front door key of the vicarage to anyone. But we have given a copy to our neighbour.'

'Of course!' Judith said, suddenly excited. 'You give it to your neighbour, that's exactly what Iqbal did.'

'But how does that help us?'

'Because Iqbal's neighbour was Ezra. And they were good friends, so I'm sure Iqbal trusted him with a key.'

'But Ezra's dead,' Suzie said. 'What are you saying?'

'Think about it. There's Iqbal's key in Ezra's house. In a cupboard. Or a drawer. Ezra dies, and who inherits his entire estate, including the contents of his house? One Andy Bishop. All Andy has to do is go through Ezra's house, as I'm sure he did after the old man died, and he'd have found the spare key to Iqbal Kassam's house.'

'Hang on, I don't understand,' Becks said. 'Are you saying Andy Bishop killed Iqbal after all?'

'All I know is, Andy had a motive to kill him, and now we know that he might have had the opportunity as well. In fact, he's possibly the only person who'd have been able to let himself into Iqbal's house without needing to break in.'

'But he was in Malta at the time,' Suzie said.

'Then what if they're working for each other?' Becks said.

The women looked at each other.

'Keep talking,' Suzie said.

'Well, Andy Bishop kills Stefan Dunwoody for Elliot Howard. And then Elliot Howard kills Iqbal Kassam for Andy Bishop.'

'Yes, I wondered about that myself,' Judith said. 'But I'm sorry to say it doesn't add up. Take the first murder, that of Stefan Dunwoody. Elliot was at choir practice, so can't have been the killer. And Andy was in Malta, so he can't be, either. No, there's something we're missing here. I can feel it. Something obvious, something "hidden in plain sight". If we could only work out what it was!'

The door opened and Tanika entered, holding some printouts. Before she could speak, Suzie turned to her.

'What links have you found between Andy Bishop and Elliot Howard?' she asked.

'None,' Tanika said with a sigh. 'We've cross-referenced Mr Bishop's and Mr Howard's phone records, emails and diaries, and they've never contacted each other as far as we can tell. All of our investigations suggest they're complete strangers.'

'Well, that blows that theory out of the water,' Suzie said.

'Now then,' Tanika said, turning to Judith. 'An officer's searched Iqbal's house. She found a copy of the most recent *Borlasian* magazine on a bookshelf. And page 74 is missing. Torn out. Just as you said it would be. I don't know how you do it. Really, I don't.'

'Perhaps on this one,' Judith said, 'it's best if you never ask.'

'Okay, I won't. But I went online and got up the magazine on the school's website, and it's like you said. Page 74 has a list of recent deaths in the Old Borlasian community, and two of the names listed are the two people who witnessed Ezra Harrington's will. Spencer Chapman and Faye Kerr.'

'Even though they were dead at the time.'

'Which means we'll be able to bring criminal charges against Andy Bishop for forging Ezra's will. So well done, that's a fantastic result. But more than that, the magazine in Iqbal's house suggests Iqbal knew about the forgery as well, and if he was going to spill the beans, that's a clear motive for Andy wanting Iqbal dead. But tell me, how did Andy kill Iqbal, seeing as he was in Malta at the time?'

'Still working on that one,' Judith said.

'Then let me tell you about my phone call with Elliot Howard just now.'

'You've spoken to him?' Becks asked.

'Of course,' Tanika said as she gave the printouts in her hand to Judith. 'I asked him to send through copies of his diary for every week since his argument with Mr Dunwoody at Henley.'

'So what was he doing on Monday the fifth of August?' Judith asked eagerly, flicking through the pages. 'And how was he when you spoke to him?'

'Fed up,' Tanika said. 'Like I was some stupid woman getting in his way.'

'Well, you're not stupid, but you're definitely getting in his way,' Judith said with a smile. 'Ah, here we are, Monday the fifth.'

'Was he at the rowing dinner?' Becks asked.

'Hmm,' Judith said, not answering immediately.

'Well?'

'Sadly not. According to this, he went swimming that night,'

Judith said, and then flicked through the pages to get a better sense of the other diary entries. 'And he records everything. We've got drinks with friends, dinners, choir practices on Thursdays, football matches, badminton on Saturdays. He and his wife lead a full life.'

'Why are you so interested in that Monday night?' Tanika asked.

'It's the only night that Liz Curtis has an entry in her diary. It was for a rowing dinner. And seeing as we know Elliot Howard rowed back in the day, we were wondering if it was a connection between them both. But according to his diary, every Monday night from eight until nine, Elliot goes swimming in the Court Garden Leisure Centre.'

'*Every* Monday night?' Suzie asked sceptically.

'Every Monday night. That's what it says here.'

'So he's very unlikely to have been at Liz's dinner.'

Judith wasn't happy.

'Does anyone else get the feeling that whenever we interrogate Elliot's life, he's already got himself an alibi? He's swimming, or he's at choir practice, or he's on a webcam holding an auction.'

'Policing can often feel like this,' Tanika said. 'You keep hitting brick walls. But you have to trust in the process. Trust in yourselves. And, knowing what you three have already achieved, even before you had access to the case files, I know you're going to make a major breakthrough. I just know it.'

Sadly, Tanika's confidence was misplaced. Because, although the three friends pored over the ballistics, coroner's and other forensic reports; even though they read all the witness statements and waded through the financial and other background checks, they could find nothing that significantly moved the case on any further. It was so frustrating. Somewhere out there was the killer, if they could only work out who it was.

And all along, Judith kept telling them that there was something big they were missing, something obvious, even. She could feel it in her bones. What was it?

Chapter 33

There were no major breakthroughs for the women on the first day. There were none on the second, either. All they seemed to do was go round and round in circles, rehashing the same clues and leads, and, above all, the same watertight alibis of Elliot Howard and Andy Bishop.

The spirits of the three friends started to flag. They could see the sly looks they got whenever they entered or left the police station, or had the temerity to request specific information, and they increasingly felt as though they were letting Tanika down. After all, she'd gone out on a limb to get them involved and they weren't doing anything to repay that faith.

By the Wednesday, neither Becks nor Suzie could spare any more time to work the case. Suzie had dogs to walk and Becks a home that she believed had completely fallen into disarray over the previous two days. So Judith spent Wednesday at the police station on her own. But it wasn't the same without her friends.

She felt a touch foolish. Like the silly, interfering old woman she knew Tanika's colleagues already thought she was.

When she finally got home after a whole day cooped up inside, she decided she needed a swim more than ever to clear her mind.

After weeks of sunshine, the evening brought bruised clouds, and the air was oppressively hot. A storm was on the way, Judith could tell as she swam upstream.

To try and relieve her feelings of frustration, Judith did what she always did. She counted her blessings. There were so many. She was fit, she wanted for nothing, and she'd even made some new friends. But despite her efforts to remain positive, Judith couldn't stop her thoughts returning to the work she'd been doing at the police station, which had led precisely nowhere as far as she could see.

In particular, she kept thinking about the antique pistol the killer had used and the medallions he'd left behind at the scene of each murder. The fact that each victim had been shot dead with an antique Luger screamed to Judith that Elliot Howard had to be the killer, but the fact that Masonic medallions had been left on the bodies screamed just as loudly that it had to have been Andy Bishop.

Judith had a terrible feeling that the killer was playing with her, playing with the police. After all, why leave any kind of clues like bronze medallions behind at the scene? Wouldn't any killer worth their salt focus on getting in there, committing murder, and then getting out again without leaving any clues whatsoever? The medallions made no sense.

As Judith's swimming brought her alongside Stefan's property, she treaded water for a minute, looking at the bank of bulrushes, her mind going back to the night of the murder. To have been this close to the killer at the precise moment he'd shot and killed Stefan Dunwoody! It was incredible to consider.

A shiver ran through Judith's body and she decided to cut short her swim and let the river bear her back to her house. As she floated along, she found herself marvelling at how the river linked so many people in Marlow. She lived on it, as had Stefan, and if she kept going with the current, she'd pass through Marlow and come out the other side, heading towards the rowing centre.

Judith found herself mulling the fact that Liz Curtis was an ex international rower, just as Elliot Howard had also rowed in his youth. What about Stefan Dunwoody? Had he once rowed? After all, he'd been at the Henley Royal Regatta, hadn't he? Judith realised she'd failed to make the connection before. Stefan had been at a rowing regatta when he'd first argued with Elliot!

She felt a tingle of excitement. It was a sensation she associated with solving crossword puzzles. A realisation that although she still didn't know the answer, she was in the right territory. And the more she thought of Stefan and Elliot meeting at Henley, the more certain she was that her instincts were right.

Once she got back to her house, Judith dressed and poured herself a generous glug of what she liked to call 'thinking Scotch'. She then went over to her baize card table and fired up her tablet computer. Pulling down some sheets of A4, she sharpened one of her already-sharp HB pencils and set to work.

She typed 'Elliot Howard' and '+rowing' into her search engine. There weren't any hits. Never mind. She tried again by searching for 'rowing' with 'Stefan Dunwoody' and was surprised to get a result. It was an article in the *Marlow Free Press* and Judith clicked the link.

The page she navigated to was in the 'Homes and Garden' section of the paper and was all about 'local art gallery owner Stefan Dunwoody' showing off his home for the readers. There were lots of photos of Stefan in his home, but Judith avidly read the text trying to discover what Stefan had said about 'rowing'. She soon found the relevant paragraph.

> Mr Dunwoody laughs when I ask him why he bought a house on the River Thames. 'I can't swim and I've always disliked rowing, so you'd think it was strange me buying an old water-mill. But I love the wildlife you get on the river. As long as you never make me get in a boat, I'm happy.'

Judith's enthusiasm evaporated. That rather answered the question, didn't it? If Stefan had a connection to anyone in the case it wouldn't be because of rowing.

But Judith knew, in the same way you couldn't give up on a crossword clue until you'd gone through all of the permutations – tried every single letter of the alphabet – she should keep trying to see what links she could find to rowing among the witnesses and victims. So she typed 'Iqbal Kassam' and 'rowing' into the search bar.

There were no hits.

Next she typed both 'Liz Curtis' and 'Danny Curtis' plus the word 'rowing' into the search bar, but she got hundreds of hits, mostly from travel and tourism websites and blogs.

Judith frowned to herself. How was it going to be possible to find out about Liz's rowing career rather than her rowing centre? She tried clicking through on the links, and running the search again using different words, but she kept getting nowhere. There were any number of online articles praising the rowing centre as a great day out for the kids, or lamenting its closure during the most recent floods, but nothing that specifically tied Liz or her husband Danny to competitive rowing.

By midnight, Judith's mind was scrambled. The 'thinking

Scotch' she'd been drinking had very much turned into 'unthinking Scotch' sometime around ten-ish, and she wasn't sure what she'd achieved since then. She'd tried searching every local newspaper's website, and every nearby rowing club's website as well, from William Borlase's and Great Marlow schools to the Marlow town rowing club, and the Leander club in Henley. But no matter how hard she hunted, she couldn't find the link.

Her whole evening had been a busted flush.

And yet Judith still had a feeling in her soul that she was on the right track. And even deeper within her was the knowledge that the local newspaper and rowing websites only went back so far. Everything was digitally up-to-date for the last ten years or so, but in the ten years before then, the various websites had a spotty record of scanned information or incomplete copy-typed archives. As for the preceding decades, the 1990s and 1980s, none of the newspapers had a searchable database, and it was the same for the rowing clubs as well. Both Elliot's career as a schoolboy rower and Liz's for Team GB pre-dated the internet by some distance.

Judith hauled herself to her feet. It was time for bed. But before she oriented herself so she could aim for the foot of the staircase, she found her hand going to the key around her neck and her eyes blurrily focusing on the oak door to the side of the drinks table. She was dimly aware that while this was very definitely not the time, it was possible she wouldn't be able to put it off any longer.

On the way to bed, Judith told herself that a good night's sleep would hopefully provide a solution.

The extraordinary thing was, she was right.

Chapter 34

The next day, Elliot Howard was hungry. He'd arrived at work at 10 a.m. sharp, as usual, and his morning had been no more taxing than any other, but he'd felt fidgety, on edge. He wanted to get out. So, although it wasn't yet eleven, he decided to leave the office. A short walk away was the commercial estate where a sandwich van would sell him a nice bacon butty that he could accompany with a Styrofoam cup of tea. Telling everyone he was popping out for half an hour, he left the building.

As he strode off, Elliot didn't notice the older woman sitting on a bench by a large hydrangea bush, even though she was wearing a dark grey cape.

Judith watched Elliot leave and a surge of adrenaline coursed through her. The coast was clear! But for how long, that was the question. She got up from the bench, picked up the carrier bag that was at her side, and bustled over to the auction house.

Striding in, she saw Elliot's wife Daisy sitting at her desk.

'Good morning,' Judith announced, knowing she would have to use all of her force of personality to get what she needed.

Daisy looked surprised to see Judith.

'What are you doing here?'

'You won't remember, but I saw your husband a few weeks ago.'

'Oh I remember very well. He told me all about it. You made up a story to trap him. Something about a dress and a glass of wine.'

Judith was thrown. This was a very different Daisy to the last time they'd spoken. What on earth had changed?

'I'm sorry?'

'He said you'd come to spy on him.'

'That's not true. I merely asked him to pay for a dress he'd ruined.'

'A lie.'

'I beg your pardon?'

'It's a lie. I can tell. You're lying.'

'I'm doing no such thing,' Judith blustered. 'Now if you don't mind, I need to leave the damaged dress in your husband's office.'

'You can't go in there!' Daisy called out, but it was too late as Judith strode into Elliot's office and tried to look at all of the framed rowing pictures on the walls.

This had been the idea she'd woken up with that morning. After all, if she was looking for a record of Elliot's rowing past, where better to start than the walls of his office? Here was every triumphant crew he'd participated in, and they even had a list of the names of the people in the photos written on the cardboard mounts. It would be perfect for finding out if he'd ever rowed with any of the witnesses or victims in the murders.

But before Judith could get a good look, Daisy stormed in behind her.

'I said you can't come in here. This is my husband's office, his private office!'

There was a ferocity to Daisy that Judith found frightening. She was like a she-wolf defending her young cubs from danger.

'We've worked so hard to be happy,' Daisy hissed. 'Together. Elliot and me. And I'm not having anything get in our way. Or anyone. Now get out. Get out!'

Judith realised she'd better do as she was told or she was at risk of being physically assaulted.

As she left the auction house, Judith tried to process what had happened. Why had Daisy overreacted like that? Was she just protecting her husband? Or was there more to it than that?

It was an interesting question, but Judith couldn't give it her full attention. This was because, while she'd been in Elliot's study, she'd made what she knew was a major breakthrough. In the row of photos on the wall, there'd been a gap that hadn't been there before.

Since her last visit, Elliot had removed one of the rowing photos from the wall.

Judith was now convinced. Rowing was the link they'd been looking for all this time. It had to be. And if that were the case, then Judith knew she had no choice. Her hand went to the key on the chain around her neck.

It was time.

'You wanted to see us?' Becks said as Judith showed her and Suzie into her house and explained about her trip to Elliot Howard's study and her encounter with his wife, Daisy.

'She went for you?' Suzie asked.

'I couldn't understand it. The first time we met she was so lovely. But this time she was like a wounded animal.'

'I wonder what's changed?' Becks asked.

'She's worked out her husband's a killer,' Suzie said simply. 'That's what's changed.'

'Yes, that could well be it,' Judith agreed.

'So why do you think Elliot's taken down a rowing photo?' Becks asked.

'Well, I can tell you I've researched everything to do with rowing online,' Judith said. 'And I've found nothing.'

'So it's *not* connected?' Becks asked, confused.

'No, I still think it's connected. But Elliot was a schoolboy rower, and that was back in the 1980s, long before we had the internet. So I suggest we see if we can find out for ourselves what the link was.'

As she spoke, Judith took the chain off from around her neck and held up the key on the end of it.

Suzie's eyes widened, although Becks didn't yet realise the significance of what was about to happen.

Judith smiled for Suzie's benefit as she headed to the door that stood to the side of the drinks cabinet.

'Don't get your hopes up,' Judith said as she inserted the key into the lock. 'It's not as interesting as you'd maybe think.'

On the one hand, Judith was right, and on the other, she was so very, very, wrong.

Chapter 35

After Judith opened the door, her friends didn't speak for quite a few seconds.

'Bloody hell!' Suzie eventually managed, summing up the feelings of both her and Becks.

The room that Judith had opened was thick with dust and stuffed wall to wall and floor to ceiling with piles and piles of newspapers, magazines, brochures and leaflets, all stacked in towers up to ten feet tall that leant one against the other, or were heaped in great slicks of paper where a tower had collapsed, and the whole seemed to be held together by thick cobwebs that went from the skyscrapers of paper to the ceiling and to the walls.

Becks' mouth opened in horror as she realised she was looking at her own tenth circle of hell. And then she sneezed. And sneezed again. She fished out a hankie from her sleeve and held it over her nose.

'Why . . . ?' Becks started to ask, but abandoned hope of ever finishing her sentence.

'I don't like getting rid of newspapers.'

'No shit, Sherlock,' Suzie said. 'But this isn't just newspapers.'

'There are local papers as well. And magazines. Periodicals have to be saved. And parish newsletters. Brochures of what's coming up from the council.'

'How far back . . . ?' Becks asked in wonder.

'1970.'

'Is that when your great aunt died?' Suzie asked.

'No. She died a few years later.'

Suzie's eyes narrowed.

'When did she die?'

'A bit after.'

'What year?'

'1976.'

'So you'd been hoarding papers for six years already?'

'Look,' Judith said irritably, 'we need to go through to the other room.'

Becks was dismayed.

'There's *another* room?'

'There are two other rooms. Come on.'

Judith picked her way between the towers of papers, her two friends following.

In the next room, each of the four walls were covered floor to ceiling in metal-framed bookcases, and every inch of shelf space was jammed thick with piles and piles of crisp-edged, yellowed newspapers.

'This is where it all started,' Judith said simply.

'Back in 1970,' Suzie said.

Judith could see that Suzie's instincts were telling her that the year 1970 was important.

'So what exactly are we looking for?' Becks asked.

'Well, if Elliot's removed a rowing photo from his wall, it must be because it's incriminating. So I suggest we find out who Elliot Howard rowed with when he was younger.'

'You think the answer will be in here?' Becks asked, already overwhelmed by the thought.

'Don't worry, it's not as bad as it sounds. Elliot is fifty-eight years old, which means he would have joined Sir William Borlase's Grammar School in 1973, and would have left, aged eighteen, in 1980. And Borlase always row at the Marlow Town Regatta, and at Henley as well. They happen in June and July. So we're only interested in checking the local papers for the months of June and July in the seven years between 1973 and 1980. It shouldn't take too long.'

'Are you saying that Stefan's murder didn't have anything to do with the Rothko on his wall?' Becks asked. 'He was killed because of something to do with rowing?'

'Actually, I think I've worked out how the Rothko fits into all of this, seeing as the painting currently on Stefan's wall is the real deal.'

'You've worked out why Elliot stole the frame from the real painting?'

'I think I have. But that's just a sideshow for the moment. I'm convinced that if we can find who Elliot rowed with, we'll finally work out why Stefan, Iqbal and Liz had to die.'

Judith had said their task wouldn't take long, but she was wrong. It turned out she couldn't remember what system she'd used for storing local newspapers in the 1970s, although she was at pains to point out that there had been a system of some sort in the early days, unlike in the more recent decades. It seemed that each publication had its own stack, with the oldest papers on the very bottom, but the system was by no means thorough. It was only possible to say that there'd be a run of one local paper for a number of months, or even as long as a year if they were lucky, and then the stack would change, for some unknown reason, to a different local newspaper, or suddenly jump to a different year. All that seemed to be broadly true was that the newspapers on the bottom of piles tended to be older than the newspapers at the top of each pile. But there were hundreds of separate stacks of newspaper all squashed tight in the bookcases.

Becks, for her part, struggled to batten down her panic as the dust swirled and settled in her hair, and on her clothes and her skin. But she made herself go through with it, and it was Becks who came up with the best system for working through the newspapers. She'd riffle the dry edges of a stack, trying to find the dates on the corners of each page. If they were from before June, she'd work upwards from that point and head downwards if the date was from after July. And once she found any newspapers that covered June or July, she'd oh-so-carefully prise them out from within the stack so they could then be searched more thoroughly.

The good news was that Judith had been right when she'd predicted that each of the local newspapers covered the Henley and Marlow regattas in great detail. There were whole pages of photos and reports, and better than that, the *Henley Advertiser* ran a page that listed the results of every race. However, the paper merely recorded the names of the boats rather than the names of the crew who were rowing. So, 'Borlase's 1st VIII' would be rowing against 'Abingdon 1st VIII', and while it might list that Borlase's won the race while Abingdon went through to the repechage competition, it didn't list the names of the crew.

After two hours of searching, Judith threw her hands up in despair.

'Please don't send any more dust into the air,' a grime-smeared Becks begged.

'But it's useless! We'll never find what we're looking for.'

'If it's here, we will,' Becks said.

'But it's not here, is it?'

'We just have to keep looking.'

Judith knew that Becks was right. There was still a chance they'd find Elliot's grinning face in a photo somewhere, and with it, the names of the other people in the photo, but it seemed such a long shot.

'And you could actually try helping, Suzie,' Judith said, taking her frustration out on her friend.

'What's that?' Suzie said, looking up from the newspaper in her hands.

'Only I can't help noticing that you've not found a single article in all this time.'

Suzie looked as though she wasn't sure how to respond, but then she brandished the newspaper she was holding.

'I wouldn't say I've found nothing.'

She was holding a truly ancient copy of the *Bucks Free Press*, and it was turned to one of the inner pages that had a headline that screamed 'MARLOW WOMAN'S GREEK TRAGEDY'.

Underneath the headline there was a large black-and-white photo of a much younger Judith Potts.

Chapter 36

'Where did you find that?' Judith asked, standing quite still.

'It's your wedding ring,' Suzie said.

'What's that?'

'You said your husband was a bully. That he was violent. But, all these years later, you're still wearing your wedding ring.'

'That's really none of your business.'

'Because I know what it's like to have a husband who lets you down, and I can tell you, I couldn't wait to get rid of my rings. Sold them in town, spent the money on extra Christmas presents for the girls. But you're still wearing yours.'

'I told you, it's to remind me of mistakes made.'

'I know. That's what you said, but that's just weird. And every time the subject of your husband comes up, you always look guilty. So when you revealed you've been keeping all of the world's newspapers since 1970, well, I put two and two together. 1970 was the year your husband died, wasn't it?'

'His name was Philippos.'

'And for some reason you can't let go. Which is why you still wear your ring, and why you've got this mad Aladdin's cave of every newspaper that's been published since then. And all I can think is, all of this is because you did wrong when he died. So I started looking. I reckoned I had to look at the very bottom of the bottom-most piles, and I'd find the newspaper that sparked all this off.

'So I've been digging through every paper from 1970 I could find. The *Maidenhead Advertiser, Henley Advertiser, Windsor Echo, Marlow Free Press, Reading Evening Post*. And then I found it.'

Suzie handed the old article to Becks, who started reading it avidly.

Judith was still rooted to the spot, but she could feel anger bubbling up inside her. This was why she didn't let people into her house. It was why she kept these rooms behind lock and key. If people didn't know anything about you, they couldn't betray you, could they? And anyway, Judith knew that no one would understand that her need to keep the newspapers wasn't based on any kind of a weakness on her part, it was simply a habit she'd got into. That's all.

At first, when she'd returned from Greece after Philippos's funeral, she'd kept them because she needed to know the papers weren't printing any more lies about her. And once she'd got into the routine, well, it was hard to know when to stop, wasn't it? After a few weeks? Months? As far as Judith was concerned, it was entirely natural that collecting newspapers and other printed materials had evolved into becoming an end in itself. She found it comforting. Like the feeling of security you'd get in the old days from owning a full set of the *Encyclopaedia Britannica*. She had all local knowledge here in these three rooms.

And it was useful, wasn't it? After all, who'd have known in 1970 when she'd started out that, many decades later, she'd be using her archive to identify a potential murderer?

'The article says someone else was on the boat at the time,' Becks said, breaking into Judith's reverie.

'That's what I noticed as well,' Suzie said.

'They were mistaken,' Judith said, wanting to get her rebuttal in first.

'Although I must say,' Becks continued, 'this sounds terrible. I had no idea you were interviewed by the police. That it was considered a suspicious death. It must have been horrible.'

'Oh it was that, I can tell you. But it was me who insisted the police start investigating. Philippos was such a good sailor, you see. But they never found anything suspicious. In the end they ruled it was a tragic accident.'

'Suzie's right, though. It says here a witness on the shore saw Philippos on his boat with someone else.'

'It says a witness *thinks* they saw someone else on the boat,' Judith said testily. 'It was a possible lead for a time. But the man on shore was old, and he wasn't ever able to identify who this second person was, or even if it was definitely Philippos's boat. It all fizzled out, sadly.'

'Do you think your husband was with someone?' Becks asked, and the tone of her voice made her subtext clear.

'Do you mean, was he with his fancy lady? I don't know. I know he had one at the time. He always did. But I doubt it. Only Philippos's body was ever found. If he'd been with someone, her body would have been found as well. Or been reported as missing. Now I think we're done here, don't you? I don't like coming in here at the best of times, and it's clear we're not going to find what we came here to find.'

'We've not finished,' Becks said.

'I think it's time you both left.'

Becks looked as though she'd been slapped in the face.

'Come on, Judith,' Suzie said. 'There's no need to get—'

'No no,' Judith said, interrupting, 'it's nothing to do with you, Suzie, I just don't like coming in here. Too many memories. Too much history.'

'Yes, of course,' Becks said, putting the newspaper article down.

'So if you could show yourselves out?'

Suzie and Becks stood in silence for a moment, but Becks recovered first.

'Come on, Suzie, we should go,' she said, and started to usher Suzie out of the room. 'But Judith, if you need anything? Someone to talk to, or to get back to the case, give us a ring,' Becks added as she paused in the doorway.

Becks took in the calamity of mess, and the woman who stood alone in the middle of it. Judith had picked up the old newspaper article and was already lost in it.

Becks and Suzie let themselves out.

Chapter 37

Judith couldn't tear her eyes from the article, and the photo of her that stared out at her from 1970. She'd been twenty-seven years old, and she remembered the day the photo was taken as though it were yesterday. It had been snapped on the beach at Paleokastritsa, after she and Philippos had had lunch. Despite the awfulness of her life at the time, Judith had been unaccountably happy that day. It had been so sunny, the setting so beautiful, and she remembered the early afternoon breeze on the beach that brought the woody barbecue smells of the café mixed with the sweet scent of the rosemary bushes that grew around the bay.

Judith believed that even though she was an old-age pensioner, she still had beauty. But it was a feeling she now carried inside her, rather than being any kind of outward appearance. As she'd got older, her beauty had retreated from her skin and become part of what she thought of as her soul. But she couldn't help looking at the woman in the photo and noting how very glossy her hair was. How her skin seemed to glow with light, even in the black-and-white photo, and how bloody thin she'd been.

And it was as she remembered how she'd looked when she was in her twenties, that Judith worked out the answer.

The notion popped into her head entirely unbidden. Unwished for. One moment the answer to the puzzle didn't exist, and in the next moment, it did.

Judith was stunned. Was it really that simple?

And then she felt a sudden rush of adrenaline as she realised the significance of a comment that Andy Bishop had made to Becks towards the end of their walk together.

Judith let the newspaper in her hand drop to the floor, left the room and locked the door behind her. Because her breakthrough was only one piece of the jigsaw puzzle, wasn't it? There was still a piece missing. But this time she felt confident she'd find it. She knew the shape of the piece she was looking for, even if she didn't yet know what it was.

In her mind, Judith started going through all of the information she'd learned in the police station: Iqbal's dreams to buy a boat; the testimony from Fred the postie that Stefan was a crook; the fact that Liz had got a rogue vet to kill her otherwise healthy dog. But no matter how much she tried, the answer she was looking for didn't jump out at her. She knew she'd know it when she saw it, she just had to keep going.

So where else could she look?

Judith got up her tablet computer and started checking through the history on her web browser, but that didn't trigger any answers, either. But she knew she had to be methodical. So she went back to the very first web search she'd done after Stefan had died. It was the article on Stefan's argument at Henley with Elliot Howard. She clicked the link and carefully read the article again, but the answer to the question she was asking wasn't there. So she closed the web page down and reopened the next one in her history.

As Judith worked forward in time in her web history, a calm descended on her, the same calm she felt when she was compiling a crossword. She'd open a web page, read it carefully, and then close it down and open another.

It took an effort of will to stay focused, but she kept plodding, knowing she'd get there if she was patient.

And then she found it.

As fate would have it, it was the most recent web page she'd visited, and therefore the very last page she could check.

It was the article in the *Marlow Free Press* about Stefan Dunwoody's riverside house. Judith couldn't believe that she'd read it so recently and the salient fact from it hadn't registered at the time. But since seeing the old photograph of herself, and remembering Becks' comment, she now read it again with fresh understanding.

Mr Dunwoody laughs when I ask him why he bought a house on the River Thames. 'I can't swim and I've always hated everything to do with rowing, so you'd think it was strange me buying an old watermill. But I love the wildlife you get on the river. As long as you never make me get in a boat, I'm happy.'

It was so obvious! These few sentences revealed who'd killed Stefan Dunwoody.

And finally *everything* made sense to Judith. Why you'd want to kill Stefan Dunwoody, and then Iqbal Kassam and Liz Curtis. And why you'd use a Second World War Luger to do it. And why the killer then left a Masonic medallion behind at the scene of each murder.

Judith was so deep in thought that it took her a while to realise her phone was ringing.

She finally registered the sound and picked up the call.

'Hello?' she said into her phone.

'What were you doing in my office today?'

Judith's blood chilled. It was Elliot Howard.

'I'm sorry?'

'My wife told me you went into to my office when I wasn't there. What were you doing?'

'Where did you get my number from?' Judith asked, trying to buy herself some time.

'I know a lot about you, Judith Potts.'

'You can't call me on this number.'

'And you can't go into my office when I'm not there.'

Judith's mind was reeling, she didn't know how to respond, so she lashed out.

'I think you'll find I can do what I like as long as you refuse to pay for cleaning my dress.'

'You're not still pretending I spilt wine on you, are you?'

Judith knew her only option was to double down.

'You know you did, and I've got the dress to prove it.'

'Pathetic.'

'And I'll come and show you it, and then you'll pay for it.'

'Oh, I don't think we'll meet again.'

Elliot was so casual in the way he said this that Judith was instantly alarmed.

'You can't possibly know that.'

'I think I can.'

'Well, it's a Thursday today, isn't it? So you'll be at the church at seven for choir practice. I'll bring the dress to you then. I'd like to see you refuse to pay for its dry cleaning in front of all of your friends.'

'Sadly, I won't be at choir practice tonight. I'm off to a football match in Highbury with some old friends. Goodbye, Mrs Potts.'

The line went dead, and Judith shivered as though someone had walked over her grave, which in many respects, was exactly what she suspected had just happened.

Judith's legs buckled under her and she sat down on her sofa.

Her mind was frozen. She was unable to process anything.

Dimly, though, she realised there was something she had to do.

She picked up her phone again, looked up the number of Andy Bishop's company and called it.

When the receptionist answered, Judith explained who she was and asked to be put through to Mr Bishop.

'Unfortunately,' the voice said on the other end of the line, 'Mr Bishop is away on business at the moment.'

'He is?' Judith managed to reply. 'When will he be back?'

'I believe he said he was travelling to Plymouth this afternoon and staying the night. But I know he'll be back in the office on Monday morning. Would you like to make an appointment for then?'

'No,' Judith said in a whisper and hung up.

As she did so, a depth charge of fear detonated inside her.

Because she now knew the truth. There weren't going to be just three murders in Marlow, were there? There was going to be a fourth. And it was going to be her.

Chapter 38

That evening, a storm broke. Thick clouds had rolled in from the west all afternoon, and then, at teatime, the heavens opened, the rain pummelling down, the sky splitting with terrifying bolts of lightning.

Judith didn't know what to do. She was sure she'd finally worked out who'd committed the murders, but how to prove it, that was the question. She felt so frustrated – outwitted, even – and it wasn't a feeling she liked. Not one bit.

Although there was one thing going for her. She knew what was about to happen: there was going to be an attempt on her life that evening. Surely there was a way of using this knowledge to her advantage?

There was one way. It was dangerous. It was foolhardy, and there was every chance it would end with her lying in a pool of blood with a bullet in the centre of her forehead.

She could use herself as bait.

After all, if the killer was caught trying to kill Judith with the antique German pistol from the other murders, that would be enough to get a conviction, wouldn't it? In which case, all Judith had to do was quietly fill her house with police officers, and the moment the killer walked in with the pistol, they could move in and make their arrest.

Although, she realised, what if the killer saw the police arrive?

In fact, the more Judith thought about it, the more she realised that the killer was very possibly already outside in the storm, spying on her house. The moment any kind of police presence arrived, the killer would slip away and wait for another day to end Judith's life. A day when she didn't have police protection.

No, Judith realised, she couldn't risk involving the police. Not yet. She had to do this on her own. And only after the killer was inside her house, antique Luger in hand, could the police arrive. But how could that be achieved?

Judith was too wired to eat, but she poured herself a small glass of Scotch, went over to her card table, sharpened a pencil, and started to write down her thoughts: what she knew, what she suspected, and what she believed was about to happen.

As she finished her Scotch, her hand reached for the decanter for a refill, but she paused. One drink was enough, tonight of all nights. But she still had a craving she needed to satisfy, so she reached down to her handbag and pulled out her travel sweets. She put the tin on the table, lifted the lid and saw that the contents were now mostly icing sugar. But there were still a couple of boiled sweets left, so she popped one in her mouth and carried on with her work.

By 8 p.m. the storm had intensified, the wind now violently whipping the trees, and Judith had finalised her plans.

She'd come to the conclusion that while she couldn't have police cars arriving at her house, she still needed an early warning system of sorts. After all, once the killer arrived, she might not have the chance to ring the police herself. Or what if the killer asked to see her phone and saw that she'd just called the police?

So Judith had rung Suzie and Becks and asked them to follow a specific set of instructions. She'd not told them about any of her theories, or about her phone call with Elliot and Andy's secretary earlier in the afternoon. This was only partly because she wanted to make sure their lives weren't put in danger. It was also because Judith was still smarting from what she felt was their betrayal when they'd confronted her with the newspaper article that reported Philippos's death. So she'd told them the bare minimum that would nonetheless allow them to do what she needed them to do.

And keeping them at arm's length also satisfied an atavistic part of Judith. If she'd learned one lesson in life, it was that you should never let people get too close. Things always worked out better if you did everything on your own.

As she sat at her card table, Judith looked up from her notes at the driving rain outside. Lightning split the sky with a fearsome crack and Judith jumped. *Why now?* she thought to herself. And after so many weeks of sunshine!

She had to find something to do to calm her nerves while she waited. Starting a crossword or jigsaw was out of the question, so she got out an old pack of playing cards, shuffled them, and started to play clock patience. It wasn't a very good solitaire game, but it was the one her great aunt Betty had taught her, so it was the one she'd play now.

While she waited.

Judith sat with her back to the room, which she knew was brave to say the least, but it allowed her to keep looking out of the window at the raging storm. Inside, the only sound was the steady slap, slap, slap of the cards on the table, as Judith continued to wait. And wait.

It was just before nine o'clock when Judith saw a flash of torchlight on the other side of the river.

And then another flash.

Fear clutched at her heart.

Two flashes, a brief break, and then another two further flashes of light. Judith raised her arms above her head as though she were yawning and the flashing light stopped.

But this was it. It really was happening.

Judith looked down at the cards on the table and found that she couldn't focus properly, the numbers and pictures were all swimming in front of her eyes. She was losing her grip, she knew, even as her limbs seemed increasingly so heavy that she feared she wouldn't be able to move at all.

Tanika will get here, she said to herself. *Ten minutes and all this will be over. Tanika will be here.*

There was the sound of glass smashing somewhere in the house.

Judith's fear sharpened.

Her killer was inside.

'Why didn't you tell me sooner!' Tanika shouted at Becks in the passenger seat of her police car as they bombed up the A404 towards Marlow, the sirens wailing and blue lights flashing.

'Judith said I couldn't!' Becks said. 'She told me I had to wait at the station, make sure you didn't leave, and then, when Suzie rang me, I had to tell you the killer had arrived at her house and was about to shoot her.'

'But I should have been there to intercept him!'

'She said she couldn't risk you scaring the killer off. She had to do it on her own.'

'She can't deal with a serial killer on her own!' Tanika said as she spun the wheel, a wall of spray shooting up from the road as she took the roundabout to Marlow at speed. Becks held onto the passenger handle, petrified, but for once wishing the vehicle she was in could go faster. They were still minutes away from Judith's house.

As for Judith, it felt as though time had stopped for her as she sat in her chair, waiting. For seconds? Minutes? She couldn't tell.

And then she felt a presence enter the room behind her.

There was the drip, drip, drip of water falling to the parquet.

This was it.

It was time to make her play.

'Hello, Danny,' she said.

Judith turned in her chair and saw Danny Curtis standing across the room drenched from head to foot and wearing a grey poncho-style raincoat. He'd pulled the hood back and was looking at Judith, his eyes as wild as his hair.

'I said, hello, Danny,' Judith said, trying to make a connection with the man. But Danny Curtis wasn't listening. He was breathing too heavily, staring at Judith too intently.

In his hand he was holding a Luger pistol.

Only a hundred yards away, on the other side of the Thames, Suzie stood in a panic of indecision among the dripping fronds of a weeping willow, hopping from one foot to the other to stay warm as she tried to see through the driving rain towards Judith's house.

Earlier that evening, Judith had phoned her and said that a man was going to break into her house that night. What was more, she believed the man would very possibly make his approach along the Thames in a canoe. It was his modus operandi, she'd said, which was why she wanted Suzie hidden on the other side of the river, and a little way downstream, so she could spot him as soon as possible. Just as she wanted Becks outside Maidenhead police station, ready to run in and get Tanika or some other officer the moment Suzie phoned through and told her that the man had appeared.

When Suzie had asked for more details, or the identity of the man who'd be arriving in the canoe, Judith had refused point-blank to say any more. All she'd said was that Suzie and Becks should do as they were told or she'd go through with her plan without them. No amount of arguing could get Judith to change her mind.

Which was how Suzie ended up putting on her oilskin coat and taking her Dobermann Emma for a walk on the Marlow side of the Thames in the middle of a storm, and then hiding in a weeping willow with views back across the river towards Judith's house.

The whole thing seemed risky as hell to Suzie's mind, but Judith had explained that it would take the canoeist time to manoeuvre to shore, extricate himself from his boat, secure it, and then make his way up to her house. And once there, it would also take him time to work out how best to get into her house.

But Judith had been wrong.

The dim shape of a man had indeed appeared out of the rain on the river, but he'd powered along in his canoe at an incredible speed, his paddle a windmill as he churned through the water.

As soon as he'd passed Suzie's hiding place, she'd stepped out and flashed her torch twice for Judith's benefit. She'd then seen Judith in her downstairs sitting room stretch and yawn, which was her way of acknowledging that she'd received the message, and then Suzie had stepped back into the safety of the weeping willow to phone Becks.

But while she waited for the call to connect, Suzie had seen the canoeist paddle up to the riverbank at the end of Judith's garden and jump out of the boat before pulling it up after himself in one easy motion. He'd then run to her house almost without breaking step.

Judith had predicted that the whole process would take the man at least ten minutes.

It had taken him less than two.

Inside the house, Danny took a step towards Judith and lifted the Luger pistol.

'You've wanted Liz dead a long time,' Judith said, trying to connect with the man in front of her. 'Haven't you?'

With his other hand, Danny wiped the excess water from his eyes and face. He looked entirely unhinged.

'I wonder when the resentment started?' Judith continued. *Keep talking*, she told herself. *Keep talking, buy yourself time.* 'I imagine almost from the off. From the days when you were a promising rower, and you hooked up with another promising rower in Liz. But she wasn't just promising, was she? She was the real deal. And went on to represent GB at the Olympics. Where she won a silver medal. Unlike you. Your rowing career never quite took off, did it?'

Danny's jaw tightened.

'And you couldn't bear to be married to a woman who was more successful than you. You felt undermined. A failure. But then Liz did something I think you couldn't possibly forgive. At the height of her success, another two or three Olympics ahead of her, she gave it all up. In her mid-twenties.'

Judith saw Danny frown at the memory. *Yes*, she thought to herself, *that's it, keep him engaged.*

'And let's remember, you can make a lot of money if you're a successful rower. And while it would have been a bitter pill for you to swallow, being the consort to your wife, at least she'd have been famous. But Liz wasn't like you. She was never driven by fame. Or money. She simply wanted to be the best rower she could be, and once she'd done that and got her medal, she was happy with it. Which I think cut you to the quick. Because there you were, so graciously prepared to play second fiddle to your more talented wife, and she'd walked away from her talents. Instead, she decided she wanted to throw herself into the family business. The Marlow Rowing Centre.'

Where was Tanika? Where was Becks?

'But the rowing centre wasn't a good idea,' Judith continued, trying to keep her voice calm. 'I mean, it's possible it made financial sense back when Liz's dad founded it. But the climate's tipped over since then, hasn't it? And the centre keeps flooding. Every winter, or so it must seem to you. And now Liz makes her next mistake as far as you're concerned. She doesn't walk away. Even though the business is failing. Even though it has burned through all of your savings.

'At every step of the way, I think you felt that life had let you down. First you'd failed to triumph as a rower yourself. Then you'd not been allowed to do it as the "plus one" to a famous rower. And now you weren't even able to do it as the successful owner of a local business. The business *wasn't* successful.'

As Judith had been speaking, she'd not taken her eyes off Danny, but in her peripheral vision she'd seen that his gun hand had started to waver and lower.

Judith dared to feel the first flutterings of hope. Was her plan going to work? Was she going to be able to keep Danny talking until Becks and the police arrived?

'One minute away!' Becks called out to Tanika as she gripped the passenger-side handle with all her strength while also checking her mobile phone's maps app. 'We're going to make it!'

'Hold on,' Tanika said as she powered her police car through Bisham village, chicaning through the cars parked up on either side of the narrow road, and then accelerating out of Bisham and approaching Marlow Bridge at terrifying speed.

At the very last moment, she spun the steering wheel, the car screeched onto Ferry Lane, and Becks screamed as she saw a massive oak tree lying across the road, Tanika slammed on the brakes, and the car slid on the standing water, the back end starting to turn sideways before the whole thing came to a juddering stop, the rear wheel on the passenger side now hanging over the fast-flowing Thames immediately below.

The monsoon rain or a lightning strike must have felled the tree, and it was only Tanika's quick reactions that had saved their lives.

Inside the car, neither Becks nor Tanika said anything, there was just the swish of the windscreen wipers and the drumming of the rain on the metal roof.

'You okay?' Tanika eventually asked.

'I think so,' Becks said, looking out of her passenger-side window without daring to move the weight of her body. The Thames was raging only a few feet away.

'Okay, so this is what we're going to do,' Tanika said. 'It's your back wheel that's over the river, so I'm your ballast, which means you need to get out of the car first. Once you're clear, then I'll get out. But only then.'

Becks looked in the side mirror, at the back wheel gently spinning in thin air.

'Don't think about it, just do it,' Tanika said. 'Now get out of the car nice and calmly, and move around to the front. Do as I say. You'll be fine.'

Becks opened her door, the wind and rain all but yanking it open for her, and she stepped out onto the inches of sodden verge that was all that stood between her and the raging river. She then dropped to her knees and slithered under the passenger door until she was back on tarmac. The moment she was safe, Tanika slipped out of the car and it rolled back a foot, falling onto its axle as the driver's back wheel joined the other back wheel spinning freely in the air.

Tanika and Becks looked at each other and knew they were thinking the same thing. They wouldn't be able to get the police car back onto the road. Not that it mattered anyway. The ancient oak tree was blocking the road completely.

There was no way of getting to Judith's house.

Judith was struggling to contain her panic. *Where were the police?*

'As for why you did this,' she said, trying to keep the conversation going, 'my friend Suzie put her finger on it the first time she visited this house and pointed out how valuable it must be. But my river frontage is as nothing compared to what you've got down at the rowing centre. The land it's built on is worth millions. Possibly tens of millions. So why should you have to scrimp and save, and work so hard to stop the whole thing being washed away, when you could just sell it to a developer and retire on the proceeds?

'In fact, I can't help wondering if you didn't marry Liz with the express plan of waiting until her father died so you could then get her to sell the land. But when she inherited, you discovered that Liz would never sell. Not even as you scrimped and saved to get by. You were stuck. Although there was one way out for you, wasn't there? If your wife died, you'd inherit the land from her, and then you'd finally be free to sell to the highest bidder and make the millions of pounds you felt you deserved. But how to kill your wife, that was the question.'

Judith saw the moment.

Danny seemed to come out of his reverie and look at her as though for the first time.

'Shut up, bitch,' he said.

He then raised the Luger, pointed it across the room at Judith's head and pulled the trigger.

On the other side of the river, Suzie heard the gunshot and saw the window to Judith's downstairs drawing room blow outwards, glass flying everywhere.

'Oh Christ!' she said before looking at Emma. 'Go and save Judith. You've got to save Judith!'

But Emma didn't move, she was wet through, cold and miserable, and Suzie knew there was no way of communicating to a dog that her friend Judith on the other side of the river needed saving.

What could she do?

Suzie's phone started ringing. She grabbed at it, saw who it was and answered.

'It's me,' Becks said on the other end of the line.

'Where the hell are you?' Suzie asked. 'You were supposed to be here ages ago! Are you even with Tanika?'

'We're together, but Ferry Lane's blocked,' Becks said on the other end of the line. 'A tree's fallen across it. And Tanika's car is hanging over the river.'

'I think he shot Judith!' Suzie said, interrupting.

'What?'

'I think Judith's been shot!' Suzie shouted against a clap of thunder that rolled through the sky.

'Jesus, then you have to get to her. We can't.'

'I'm on the wrong side of the river.'

'Cross it!'

'I can't.'

'You have to.'

'I can't.'

'You've got to.'

'I can't swim.'

There was the briefest of pauses on the other end of the line.

'What do you mean you can't swim? Everyone can swim.'

'I never took any lessons.'

'You've got to be kidding! Look, then stay where you are. We'll get past this oak tree somehow. I don't know how, but we'll do it.'

Becks ended the call and strode over Tanika, who was in the middle of a phone call.

'Suzie thinks Judith's been shot,' Becks said, interrupting Tanika. 'You've got to get someone to her house at once.'

'I've called for backup,' Tanika said. 'And an ambulance. But everyone's already out on shouts in this weather. It's going to take time.'

'We don't have time! What about the police helicopter?'

'It can't take off in a storm.'

'But Judith's on her own!'

'Is there another way to her house other than this road?'

'There isn't,' Becks said and desperately looked about herself for inspiration.

There was nothing.

She was standing on a blocked road, a police car half hanging over the River Thames. A few dozen or so feet away on the main road, the suspension bridge to Marlow sat in the rain as though Judith's life wasn't in the balance. And beyond the bridge, an even more elegant presence against the roiling skies, was the church.

Her church.

And it was a Thursday and it had only just gone nine!

'Wait here,' Becks said as she headed for the bridge. 'Back in two minutes!'

Tanika was baffled as Becks started running across the suspension bridge.

Where was she going?

Judith had been lucky.

Although she'd felt Danny's bullet whistle past her head and blow out the window behind her, it had missed her head by inches.

Danny was just as surprised that he'd missed, and Judith could sense that in the next few seconds he was going to pull the trigger again.

She had to keep him distracted. It was her only hope.

'It was you who killed your dog, wasn't it?' she blurted.

Danny blinked.

'What?' he said.

Good, Judith thought to herself. Finally, she'd got him talking.

'My friend Suzie said that Liz got a vet to kill your dog, but she was only half right, wasn't she? It wasn't Liz who got the dog put down. It was you.'

'So what?' he spat at Judith. 'You've got no proof, and a dog's a dog. And I didn't kill Liz, when are you going to get it?'

'As it happens, I agree with you,' Judith said, but Danny wasn't listening.

'Because I was in Nottingham at the time, wasn't I?'

'I know, and very clever it was. When Liz was last seen alive at nine o'clock, you were a hundred miles away. And you were still a hundred miles away when her body was found an hour later.'

'Then how do you think I did it?'

'I've already said. You didn't.'

'What?'

'You didn't kill your wife. You killed Stefan Dunwoody.'

'*What?*'

'That's right. It was you who killed Stefan. And who then tied the bronze medallion with "Faith" written on it into his jacket buttonhole. I perhaps should have guessed that a rower killed Stefan sooner. After all, only a rower would attach a medallion like that to someone, like you do with your passes to enter the various enclosures at regattas.'

'This is crazy.'

'Oh no, this is the opposite of crazy. It was very rational. Shockingly so in fact.'

'You think I killed that Stefan guy? I didn't even know him. It was only Liz who knew him.'

'Which is what makes your crime all the worse. You killed him in cold blood. And the thing is, I wondered at the time why Stefan was shot at the end of his garden. I couldn't work out how he'd got there. You see, Elliot Howard was my number one suspect for Stefan's death. Stefan didn't like Elliot at all. In fact, he suspected Elliot of having broken into his house. So if

Elliot came to his house, how did they end up at the bottom of the garden? Exactly how had that conversation gone? "Hello, Stefan," Elliot would have said. "I know you hate me, but could we go for a stroll in your garden?" It made no sense.

'But what if the killer came from the river? Well, that was a different matter. Because you're right. Stefan didn't know you from Adam. So when you appeared at the bottom of his garden, he would have been surprised, but not fearful.'

'What do you mean, when I appeared at the bottom of his garden?'

'I'll be honest, I'm disappointed it took me so long to work it out. But on the night Stefan was killed, when I was swimming in the river, I saw a blue canoe in the bulrushes by the edge of Stefan's garden. At the time I presumed the canoe belonged to Stefan, and even tried to use it to help me climb out of the water. But it wasn't his, because, as I found out this afternoon, Stefan hated rowing and everything to do with it. So he was hardly going to be the owner of a canoe, was he? And more than that, I should have realised it wasn't his anyway, because every time I've swum up to Stefan's house since he was killed, and even when I searched the garden area before I found his body, the blue canoe was no longer there. And if it wasn't there, then who had removed it, if not the killer?'

Judith could see that Danny was now hanging on her every word.

'I can well imagine the panic you must have felt after you'd shot Stefan dead and then heard a woman call out from the river. When all along your plan had been to arrive secretly, kill Stefan secretly, and then leave just as secretly, returning with the current of the Thames to the rowing centre. Who'd ever think you were the killer? As you said, you'd never met Stefan before. And who'd kill someone they'd never met?

'Which brings me to your poor wife. Because now we know it was you who killed Stefan, her actions finally make sense. I think there was something about you on the night of the murder that made her fear you were involved. Were you in a panic when you got back? Or did she see you get out of the canoe with the Luger?'

As Judith said this, she indicated the gun in Danny's hand.

'But she became suspicious of you. Remember, as you told Suzie and me, Liz knew Stefan to say hello to. His death would have shocked her. So, whatever story you told Liz that night wasn't enough to allay her suspicions that you'd been involved. So she went to check up on Stefan's property the next day. Which was when I saw her and shouted across the river to her. And now I understand why she ran away. She wasn't acting suspiciously because of what she'd done, as I thought at the time. She was acting suspiciously because of what she suspected *you'd* done. It's why she ran away again when I bumped into her in the field a day later. And it also explains why she acted so guiltily when we talked to her. Denying things that were true, tying herself in knots. My heart goes out to her, I can't even begin to imagine the torment she must have been going through. Suspecting her own husband of being involved in a murder! She was falling apart. Unlike you, it has to be said. Because you were cool as a cucumber when Suzie and I talked to you. Weren't you?

'More than that, you'd already prepared to *really* throw suspicion onto your wife. So you told us she was friendly with Stefan. Which was at least true. But how clever you were getting Liz to take a taxi from Iqbal a few weeks beforehand, and how smart to pretend to us that we'd dragged that information out of you when Suzie and I talked to you. You did it quite splendidly, I must say, because in that one conversation you managed to make it look as though Liz was linked both to Stefan and to Iqbal. If she were then to die, as you knew she would, we'd be tempted to jump to completely erroneous conclusions.'

'These are all lies,' Danny said.

'You know that's not true,' Judith said. 'Your presence here proves it, wouldn't you say?'

Judith held Danny's gaze, and she was willing herself to stay strong, but what Danny didn't know was that Judith hadn't a clue what else she could say to keep him talking.

She'd completely run out of ideas, her mind was a terrifying blank.

All she could think was how Danny was still pointing the Luger at her. Still pointing, and still looking as though he was about to pull the trigger.

Where the hell were Becks and the police?

Becks burst through the double doors of All Saints' Church and ran into the aisle, her hair all over the place, her dress filthy with mud and drenched in rainwater from top to toe.

The choir were breaking up after their rehearsal, and they all looked over in shock at the bedraggled and wild-eyed appearance of the vicar's wife.

'Darling?' Colin asked, thoroughly embarrassed.

'I need your help!' Becks said. 'The killer's about to strike again. And there's a tree we've got to get out of the way.'

'The killer?' Colin asked as he went to calm his wife down. 'What on earth are you talking about?'

For her part, Becks was scanning the choir and was relieved to see that Elliot Howard wasn't present. But then, Judith had told her that he was at a football match in London that evening.

'The killer's in Judith Potts' house!'

'You know who the killer is?' Major Lewis said, emerging

from the row of tenors, the self-appointed voice of sanity as he headed over, leaning heavily on his brass-topped walking stick.

The last time Becks had seen Major Lewis, she'd cooked him and his wife a fennel-rubbed belly of pork.

'We've got to save Judith!' Becks said, looking from Major Lewis to her husband and then at the rest of the choir. They were all looking deeply uncomfortable.

'Isn't that a matter for the police?' Major Lewis said.

'They're down by the oak tree right now. It's blocking Ferry Lane. We need to help them move it.'

'Well, I think they know what they're doing, we should let them get on with it.'

'But that's what I'm saying, there's nothing for them to get on with, there's a bloody great tree in the way!'

As she said this, Becks grabbed the walking stick from the Major and dashed over to one of the displays on the church wall that honoured the fallen of the local regiment. Before anyone could stop her, she swung the heavy stick high in the air and brought it down on the glass case, glass showering everywhere.

'Becks!' her husband called out.

'Don't just stand there!' Becks said as she reached in and pulled down a sword that had been used by a subaltern during the Charge of the Light Brigade.

'She's gone stark raving mad,' the Major called out. 'Someone call the police!'

'When are you going to get it? I'm with the police!' Becks called back as she ran to the bell tower and started up the rickety staircase as fast she could. As her legs pumped, and despite the seriousness of the situation, she briefly congratulated herself on her fitness regime, her core strength coming from a punishing weekly programme of spinning, boxercise and yoga classes.

The choir, led by Major Lewis and her husband, drifted up the aisle, their heads upturned as they watched the vicar's wife running up the stairs of the belltower waving a sword above her head.

Halfway up, Becks stopped on the mezzanine floor where the bell-ringers stood to ring the eight church bells in the tower. She grabbed at a rope for the largest bell and started pulling hard on it, the bell ringing out over the town. She hoped the people of Marlow would realise it would only be tolling in the middle of a storm because there was an emergency and would head to the church.

After she'd rung it a number of times, she grabbed at the one rope that ran all the way down to the floor far below. This was the one bell that could be rung by someone at ground level. Becks took the rope in her left hand and started to saw across it with the sword in her other hand.

After pulling and pushing the sword a few times, she was through, the rope was cut!

'Mind your heads,' Becks called and let the fifty feet of now-severed rope fall in a snake to the floor.

'Someone get hold of that rope,' she said as she started to run back down the stairs. 'Come on, pick the bloody rope up!'

By the time she got back to the ground, Becks realised that the twenty or so people of the choir were looking at her as though she'd lost her mind, her husband included.

'Are you saying a woman's life is in danger?' her husband asked.

'It's Judith Potts. The killer's in her house.'

'And that rope will help how?'

'Just get it across the bridge. There's a policewoman on the other side, Detective Sergeant Tanika Malik. She'll tell you what to do with it. Colin, I need your help right now!'

There was a tone to Becks' voice that finally got through to her husband.

'Of course, darling,' he said, snapping into focus. 'Come on, everyone,' he said to the choir as he bent down and started to pick up handfuls of rope. 'Let's get this rope to the detective sergeant.'

As Becks joined in, she dared to hope. With this many people, and with the rope, surely they'd be able to move the oak tree? And with it out of the way, then maybe there'd still be time to save Judith?

For her part, Judith was sitting in panicked silence, her mind spinning, still unable to think of what to say next.

Fortunately for her, it was Danny who broke the silence.

'You said I didn't kill Liz.' It was a statement.

'That's right. I did.'

'And there's no way you could ever prove I killed Stefan. Someone I'd never met. Someone I had no motive to kill.'

'Indeed,' Judith said, thankful that Danny had prompted a further line of conversation. 'It's quite the puzzle, isn't it? But like a lot of puzzles, the solution's simple, when you know how to look at it. Like "Two girls, one on each knee".'

'What's that?'

'It doesn't matter, but I agree. You had no motive to kill Stefan. But Elliot Howard did. So, seeing as you're the person who killed Stefan, it's logical to presume you must have done it for him.'

'This is just fantasy talk.'

'Oh no, it's real enough. You killed Stefan for Elliot.'

'Why would I do that?'

'You tell me.'

Danny frowned, trying to orientate himself within Judith's logic.

'All I can think is, you're going to say I killed Stefan for Elliot so he could kill Liz for me. But that's crazy. He was on a webcam running an auction when Liz was killed.'

'How do you know that?' Judith asked, pouncing.

'I don't know,' Danny said to buy himself time. 'The police told me.'

'Poppycock! But you're right. While you killed Stefan for Elliot, he didn't kill Liz for you. He killed Iqbal.'

'What?'

'He killed Iqbal.'

'But how did that help me?'

'It didn't. It helped Andy Bishop. Because that's how your plan went, wasn't it? You killed Stefan Dunwoody for Elliot Howard. Elliot then killed Iqbal Kassam for Andy Bishop. And, finally, Andy killed Liz for you. To complete the round. It has a mathematical simplicity to it that's really rather clever when you think about it. I mean, if you'd killed Stefan and Elliot had then killed Liz, well, I think it wouldn't have taken the police more than two minutes to work out that you'd swapped murders. But add a third person? Suddenly it's not so obvious, is it? You kill Stefan, a man who's a complete stranger to you. And Elliot, the person who wanted him dead, makes sure he's at a choir rehearsal when it happens. Even though he couldn't stop himself from looking smugly at the CCTV as he left. He was so proud of how clever he was being. But Elliot's in the clear, he has to be. He was elsewhere at the time.

'And that gives him the space to slip out of bed at five o'clock on a Saturday morning and murder Iqbal. Again, a man he'd never met. So how could he ever be the killer? What's the motive? As for Andy Bishop, the man who actually wanted Iqbal dead, and who gave Elliot the key he'd need to get into Iqbal's house, he made sure he was in Malta at the time, and also in Malta for when you killed Stefan, so he'd have a double alibi, just for good measure. Although he had no choice but to be back in the UK when he killed Liz for you. Which he did even though, once again, he'd never met her before.

'And clever though your plan was, your masterstroke was the Luger and the medallions saying "Faith", "Hope" and "Charity" that each of you left at the scene. You see, there was only one weakness in your plan. Using the same antique Luger helped misdirect the police from that weakness. After all, if it was the same gun that killed all three people, surely they must have been killed by the same person? Who's ever heard of three different murderers sharing the same gun?

'But the medallions were cleverer still. After all, everyone knows that the phrase "faith, hope and charity" is only three words long. By putting a medallion on each body you were giving another message to the police that the victims were all linked and it was the same lone shooter who was committing these murders. But you were also clearly saying that there would only be three murders. As soon as Liz's body was found with the "charity" medallion around her neck, the police would know the shootings were over. There weren't going to be any more. So, as time passed, and they failed to find out what the link was between the victims, the police would soon get distracted by other more pressing cases. These murders would have gone onto the back burner, and you'd have got away with it. But, despite your best efforts, I now know it wasn't one person carrying out these three murders. It was three men *pretending* to be one.'

'What weakness?' Danny asked as he took another step towards Judith.

'Oh yes, I was wondering if you'd pick up on that,' Judith said calmly, although her inner monologue was screaming, *Where the hell are the police?* over and over. 'As a plan, it had an Achilles' heel. And that was if the police realised that there was indeed no meaningful link between the three victims. Despite the same gun being used. And your "faith, hope and charity" ruse. And instead, they focused on the three men who most obviously benefited from the three deaths, because the three of you all share a link, don't you? A very strong link.'

'There's no link between me and those other two people!' Danny shouted.

'Oh there is. And you know it.'

'All right then, what is it?'

On Ferry Lane, Tanika was standing in the lashing rain as she watched Colin Starling and a number of choristers carry a length of severed bell rope across Marlow Bridge.

By the time they arrived, she realised what Becks expected her to do.

'Wrap it around the trunk of the tree!' she called out. 'Come on, we need to get this tree moved!'

As they all started trying to tie the rope to the tree, the piercing headlights of a white SUV cut through the darkness as Becks raced her 4x4 across Marlow Bridge, turned into Ferry Lane and then screeched to a halt. Despite the narrowness of the road, she confidently performed a three-point turn, her hands in the correct ten-to-two position throughout, and by the end of the manoeuvre her tailgate was pointing at the oak.

'There's a tow bar on the back,' she shouted as she stepped out of her car.

Tanika was quick to get the message, and she soon organised the other end of the rope to be tied to the back of Becks' 4x4.

And mercifully, in the distance, finally, they heard the sirens of approaching police cars.

As soon as the rope was tied fast, Tanika called to Becks against the howling wind.

'Okay we're good to go!'

Becks climbed back into her car, slammed the door shut, but Colin grabbed her arm through the open window.

'Becks?' he said, but he didn't know what on earth to say next.

As Becks looked at her husband, she saw a sparkle of excitement in his eyes.

'I don't know what's going on,' he said, 'but if I haven't told you recently, I think you're amazing. I've *always* thought you were amazing.'

Becks' heart jumped. This was the Colin she remembered. Full of life and sincerity, and able to focus entirely on her.

'Love you,' she said with a wink.

'Love you, too,' he said.

'Now, if you don't mind, I need to put my pedal to the metal,' Becks said, and turned her attention back to her cockpit.

As Colin stepped back, Becks put her car into four-wheel drive, jammed it into its lowest gear and floored it.

The back wheels spun on the wet road, exhaust spewing out, the smell of burning rubber filling the air, but the oak tree didn't budge.

Becks took her foot off the pedal for a rethink as two police cars drove into Ferry Lane, sliding to a stop so they didn't smash into Becks' SUV.

The police officers climbed out of their cars as Becks floored it again, the bell rope snapping tight, and this time she crushed the accelerator, the back of her car juddering left and right, the engine roaring over the sound of the driving rain, but still the oak tree wasn't moving. It was too big. Too massive.

Inside her car, Becks took her foot off the pedal and smashed her hands into the steering wheel in frustration.

Nothing was going to be able to move the tree.

Judith was entirely on her own.

Judith had come to the same conclusion over the previous few minutes. She was on her own, and the shocking realisation had crept through her body like ice water. After all, if Becks had managed to get hold of Tanika, they'd have arrived ages ago. Something must have gone very badly wrong.

'Go on,' Danny said to her and Judith's focus snapped back into the room. 'Tell me about this link I have with these two other men.'

'That's easy enough,' Judith said, even though she felt entirely numb. 'All three of you went to the same secondary school. Sir William Borlase's.'

'So what? Is that all you've got? There's only two secondary schools in the town. Loads of people went to the same school. And I bet I'm not even the same age as those other two people.'

'No, that's true. Elliot is one year older than you and Andy is four years younger.'

'So how could I be linked to this Andy guy? I don't even remember him.'

'Oh you do. He was a top athlete at the time. Not that you'd know it to look at him now. But then, as a photograph reminded me, we were all very much thinner when we were younger. But what we should really be noting is Andy's height. Because there's no such thing as a short rower is there?'

'No there isn't.'

'But there is if you're the cox. In fact, the cox *has* to be as short as possible. And thin. And that's what Andy used to be, wasn't he?

A mere slip of a thing. As he boasted to my good friend Becks Starling, he'd been quite the athlete in his youth. We dismissed the comment at the time, but it was true. He, you and Elliot were a triumphant rowing team for your school. Weren't you?'

For the first time, Judith thought she saw panic dart in Danny's eyes.

'That's right. The three of you may have drifted apart over the decades since then, but back when you were teenagers, you were one of the best rowing teams your school had ever produced. As a coxed pair, I now know. Which is one cox, who was Andy. The youngster with guile and cunning to navigate the route. And two much older, taller and stronger lads in you and Elliot to do the rowing. I imagine you cleaned up at all of the regattas.'

'This is guesswork.'

'Not at all. I went to Elliot's office once I'd worked out that rowing was the connection. And guess what? He'd removed a rowing team photo from the wall since the last time I'd been there. He has rather a habit of removing framed pictures from the walls, now I think about it. But that was all the confirmation I needed to know I was on the right track. And the fact that his wife was so angry with me. I think, a bit like your wife, Daisy has had her suspicions about Elliot for some time, and it's similarly been driving her mad.

'Anyway, the missing photo proved to me that there was something incriminating about a rowing team from Elliot's past. So who else was in that photo? Sadly, records back then haven't much survived to the modern day. But you know what it's like when you solve part of a crossword clue? The rest of it so often falls into place. I tried to think who else Elliot could have rowed with. Initially I wondered if it was Stefan, but as I've already said, Stefan is on record saying he hated rowing. And that's when I remembered Becks telling me that you and Liz had met as young rowers. You were the third person from Elliot's boat I was looking for.'

Judith could see that Danny was clenching and unclenching his jaw.

'No? Not going to say anything? I suppose not. But now I could start to make sense of the deaths. Because, as you said, you, Elliot and Andy don't have much to do with each other. But you last rowed together in Elliot's final year at school which was 1980. Forty years ago exactly, so a perfect excuse for a school reunion.

'Which is why Liz had a diary entry saying "rowing dinner" for Monday the fifth of August. But it wasn't *her* rowing dinner she was marking. She'd merely put "rowing dinner" in her diary because, as a good wife, she was making a note of when you'd be at your important dinner so she didn't double book anything for that night.

'And I'm sure you, Elliot and Andy had a great evening together. In whatever private dining room you'd hired. In black tie no doubt. Yes, I can well imagine the three of you in some oak-panelled private room in a fancy pub somewhere near here. All togged up, all in agreement at what a disgrace it was you can't smoke cigars indoors these days. But here's the thing. Monday the fifth was the same day that Elliot went to see Stefan at his gallery. I bet Elliot was fuming when you saw him. In fact, he must have been, knowing what then followed.

'You see, I think he told you everything. How Stefan was a crook, which, I'm sad to say, I now realise was the truth. Because he stole a valuable Rothko painting from Elliot decades ago. And Elliot told you all about it. How he'd argued with Stefan at Henley a few weeks before. But he must have also told you what he'd done since then. You see, Elliot was so incensed by his argument with Stefan at Henley that he had decided to wreak revenge.

'He wanted his Rothko back. But how to do it? Well, since Elliot has always been so desperate to prove his talent, he decided he'd paint a forgery of it. But, again, how could he do that? He'd not seen the picture in decades. And he'd have to somehow get the real frame from the real Rothko onto his forgery so Stefan wouldn't notice the difference. So Elliot broke into Stefan's house. Just to take photos of the Rothko, I think. And to measure the frame and see how it all fastened together and so on. But once he'd done that, he left. Which was why, when Stefan returned later on and called the police because there'd been a break-in, he couldn't prove that anything had been stolen. Nothing had been stolen. It had simply been a fact-finding mission for Elliot.

'Next, Elliot set about rediscovering his ability at painting Rothkos. Reminding himself of the technique and palette required. Which explains all of the Rothko-style paintings we found him burning in his garden much later on. He was getting rid of his practice canvases.

'But Stefan worked out that Elliot had been behind the break-in. Maybe he saw that his Rothko wasn't hanging quite as straight on the wall as it should have been. Or maybe Elliot saw Stefan and taunted him somehow. We'll never know, but whatever it was that tipped Stefan off, it was enough to make him want to get Elliot into his office and accuse him of the break-in. And also to threaten him that he could go to the police.

'So yes, my guess is that Elliot was in a foul mood when you all met up for dinner that night. And I'm sure he added that, as far as he was concerned, Stefan deserved to die. So what happened next?

'Well, I imagine it was Andy who chipped in next. Because he had problems of his own. Although I bet he dressed them up to look less criminal than they were. I'm sure he spun you a tale of how he'd looked after his client Ezra as he slowly died of cancer. And how, just before his death, Ezra had left his estate to his trusty solicitor. All a lie, of course, as Ezra had left everything to his wonderful neighbour, Iqbal. But I bet Andy told you that, as Ezra was so close to death, he'd not been capable of signing his new will, so he'd had no choice but to forge the signatures of the witnesses.

'And I'm sure Andy stuck the boot into Iqbal, the interfering neighbour. How Iqbal had discovered that the witnesses' names were old pupils from Borlase's Grammar School who'd died before the will was signed. And how Iqbal had even had the gall to send him the proof in the form of a page of obituaries from the *Borlasian* magazine he'd torn out.

'In fact, Andy was in considerably more hot water even than Elliot. He'd committed a massive fraud. He was off to prison if he couldn't silence Iqbal. And if Elliot wasn't the first person to say that Stefan deserved to die, I'm sure that that's what Andy said about Iqbal. Someone should kill Iqbal.

'But how do you even commit murder? Well, if you own an auction house, I can't imagine it's too hard to lay your hands on a vintage weapon like a Second World War Luger. Not if you know a few dodgy dealers, as I'm sure Elliot must have done. But still, how do you do it and get away with it? I wonder if that's when you confessed that you wanted your wife dead as well? After all, sometimes it's easier to speak the truth to a relative stranger than to someone you know well, isn't it? Because, if Liz died, you'd inherit the land the rowing centre is built on. You'd be able to sell it and become a multimillionaire.'

'And once you'd confessed your darkest secrets to the others, the idea occurred to the three of you that you could each commit murder for the person to your left, as it were. Using the same gun, to make it look like it was only one person. And with a false trail of antique Masonic medallions, no doubt supplied by Andy Bishop, to make it look as though the same person was carrying out each murder.'

Danny raised his gun again and pointed it at Judith's head.

'You're going to shut up right now.'

'You don't want another death on your hands.'

'That's where you're wrong. That's *exactly* what I want.'

Seeing the madness in Danny's eyes, Judith realised that he no longer cared for the consequences of his actions. She wouldn't be able to talk him down. Or appeal to his rational side. He just wanted her dead. Dead at any price.

And finally Judith knew the truth: her plan had failed.

She was on her own with Danny Curtis, and there was nothing she could do to stop him from killing her.

For Suzie's part, she was still standing panic-stricken under the weeping willow, feeling more and more miserable and getting more and more wet. What was going on inside Judith's house? There must be something she could do to help, but what could it be? She was on the wrong side of the river and had no means of crossing it.

Suzie stepped out from the weeping willow and approached the river. She looked at the mass of the water as it swept past. There was no way she could cross the river at the best of times. She couldn't swim. Let alone get across with the river running this fast, and at night, and in the middle of a storm.

And Emma was still no bloody use, as she shivered at Suzie's side.

But there was something else Suzie realised as she stood in the driving rain. Becks and the police simply weren't coming. And that meant that she was Judith's last and only hope. This helped make the decision for her. Perhaps, at some deep level, Suzie had known all along what she would do next.

'We're going to save Judith,' she shouted at Emma over the howling wind. 'We're going to save Judith, you and me together.'

Suzie bent down, undid the laces on her boots and kicked them off. Next she took off her wide-brimmed hat and raincoat and dropped them to the floor.

She then strode into the river, Emma excitedly at her side, wanting to join in with whatever it was Suzie was doing.

Suzie was almost immediately swept off her feet, even as she struck out with her arms and legs.

She tried to splash her way across the river, but the current was too strong. Panicking wildly and swallowing lungfuls of water, Suzie tried to make headway, but she was being carried too fast downstream from Judith's house, and there was no way to get back, even if she managed to get out of the water. Which, with a sudden realisation, Suzie realised she never would.

It was pitch-dark, rain was hammering down on the water all around, the swell of the river lifted her up, spun her around and then sucked her down, time and again, and each time she went under, it seemed to be for longer.

It was so cold. So very, very cold. And she was feeling so tired. So heavy and tired. She couldn't keep battling, the river was so much stronger than her.

And then Suzie was pulled under by the current, and this time she knew it would be for the last time, she wouldn't be coming up for air again.

It was just Judith and Danny now.

And somehow, now that Judith had accepted she was on her

own, she began to find a sense of calm. Danny was going to shoot her dead. There was nothing she could do about it.

Danny took another step closer.

Raised the pistol.

He was close, but still out of reach. Judith knew there was no way she'd be able to rush him before he could pull the trigger.

There was nothing she could do about it. It was over.

She put her hand on the green baize of the table, just to feel something reassuring in her last few moments of life.

'You think you're so clever,' Danny said. 'But you're still going to get a bullet through the brain.'

Judith saw his finger tighten around the trigger, and that's when she noticed there were no more sweets in the travel sweet tin. It was completely empty. Was that really going to be her last thought?

Although, it wasn't entirely empty, was it?

Judith's hand picked up the tin and threw it straight at Danny's face, its icing sugar contents exploding in a white cloud around his head, which gave her the split second she needed to grab up one of the sharpened pencils from the table, close the distance and plunge the pencil deep into the bicep of Danny's right arm, the gun falling from his hand as he dropped to his knees screaming in pain, his left hand grabbing at the pencil as he tried to staunch the flow of blood from his arm.

Judith grabbed the gun and stepped back, making sure it stayed trained on Danny.

'Don't even *think* about moving!' she hollered.

But Danny didn't seem to be Danny any more, he'd become a snarling creature, and he rose to his feet, pulling the pencil from his arm in a gush of blood he barely noticed.

'Don't move!' Judith shouted again.

Before Judith had time to react, Danny picked up Judith's card table and threw it at her. She put up her arms to defend herself, but the table knocked her back onto the floor, the gun spinning from her hand.

Judith lay on the carpet, winded, pain shooting up her arms where she'd broken her fall, but she knew she had to get back to her feet, she had to get to the gun before Danny.

She dragged herself up onto one knee and looked for the gun, but it had gone. Where was it?

Danny was holding it in his hand and pointing it directly at her face.

Judith knew it was finally over for her. But she wouldn't give Danny the satisfaction of seeing her fear, she was going to look her murderer square in the face.

It was because her eyes were open that she was able to see the roar of teeth and claws as a wild beast flew in through the broken window before landing on her paws and then bounding up in one leap and knocking Danny over.

Judith realised that the beast was Emma, and she'd pinned Danny to the floor!

'Help!' Danny screamed, the gun skittering across the parquet from his hand as Emma's teeth grabbed hold of his wrist and then shook him, trying to break his arm.

Moments later, the door banged open and an exhausted Becks burst into the room. Taking in the scene, with Emma growling in Danny's face, Judith off to one side, Becks saw that a Luger pistol was directly at her feet, so she picked it up.

Three drenched police officers entered right behind Becks, saw Danny on the floor and turned to Judith.

'Is that your dog?'

'No she bloody well isn't,' a stentorian voice called from the window.

They all turned and saw Suzie standing outside in the rain, duckweed in her hair.

'That's Iqbal's dog,' she said.

At the sound of Suzie's voice, Emma let go of Danny, but kept growling at him as the police officers pulled him to his feet and roughly handcuffed him.

Judith suddenly felt woozy and leant against an armchair.

'Are you okay?' Becks said, going to Judith.

'I will be in a minute.'

Becks looked over at the three police officers as they marched Danny out of the room.

'Danny Curtis was the killer?' Becks said, amazed.

'One of three,' Judith said.

Tanika wheezed into the room, out of breath.

'Okay, that was too far to run,' she said.

'You ran here?' Judith asked.

'It's a long story,' Becks said, 'but we had to. It took us ages to move a tree that was blocking the road.'

'Only thanks to Becks' quick thinking,' Tanika added. 'She got hold of a rope and her car to move it, but the tree wouldn't budge. We were completely stuck. And then the most amazing thing happened. People started arriving, coming out of their houses, streaming over the bridge.'

'They did?' Judith asked. 'Why?'

'Becks had rung the church bell. And the whole town turned out in the rain to see if they could help. There must have been two hundred of us by the end, and between the people of Marlow and the car we finally got the tree moved just enough that we could scrape past.'

'Amazing,' Judith said. 'And you should know, you have to arrest Elliot Howard and Andy Bishop for murder as well.'

Judith quickly explained to Tanika and Becks how the three men had carried out the murders for each other.

'It's how I knew Danny would try to kill me tonight,' she said, concluding her story. 'It's how they always did things. For each murder, the least likely person would do the killing while the other two would make sure they had unbreakable alibis. So I knew my life was in danger the moment Elliot told me he wouldn't be in Marlow tonight, even though it was a choir night. And Andy's secretary confirmed he'd be away as well.'

'I'll make sure they're arrested tonight,' Tanika said.

'Elliot's at a football match in London somewhere, and Andy's in Plymouth.'

'Don't worry, we'll pull them in.'

Judith and Tanika looked at each other for a moment. Judith could tell that Tanika was about to chastise her for trying to take on Danny on her own, but Tanika could also see that, for once, Judith wasn't looking for a fight. In fact, the older woman just looked tired, and rueful, and suddenly both women realised they didn't really have anything they needed to say to each other after all.

Tanika smiled.

'You going to be okay?'

Judith smiled.

'Yes,' she said, simply. 'Thank you for asking.'

Suzie clattered into the room and Becks and Judith gave a cheer as they went over to give her a hero's welcome.

Tanika looked at the three women and couldn't stop herself from grinning, especially when she saw Becks pick duckweed out of Suzie's hair.

Tanika sighed in satisfaction to herself. It was over, finally over. Tomorrow night, she'd be able to read a bedtime story to her daughter. But that was tomorrow. For tonight, she had three men to charge with murder.

The three friends were too busy fussing over Suzie to notice Tanika leave.

'How on earth did you get across the river?' Judith asked Suzie.

'I swam,' Suzie said.

'But you can't swim,' Becks said.

'I gave it a bloody good go, but I'd agree with you. I can't. So, one minute I was above the water, the next I was below, and then I felt these jaws tighten around the neck of my coat. Emma saved me,' Suzie added, looking with wonder at Emma. 'Once she'd pulled me to the riverbank, I sent her to save you, Judith.'

Becks and Judith were stunned. Suzie had tried to cross a river she couldn't swim?

'And did you really ring the church bell?' Judith asked Becks.

Becks blushed.

'And cut down one of the bell ropes, now you mention it.'

'How?' Suzie asked.

'With a sword.'

'What sword?'

'You know what?' Judith said, interrupting her friends. 'I owe you both an apology. I was wrong to try and deal with Danny on my own. Not when I've got friends as resourceful and brave as you two. I won't make that mistake again. I promise you.'

'Thank you,' Becks said, deeply touched.

'Sorry,' Suzie said, 'I feel we're missing the main point here. What sword?'

'You know what, ladies?' Judith said as she moved over to the drinks table and poured three generous measures of whisky into cut-glass tumblers. 'Before we go any further, I suggest we have a small glass of Scotch. Or two. For purely medicinal reasons, of course.'

Judith returned with the drinks and handed them to her friends.

Becks raised her glass.

'In that case, I think this calls for toast,' she said.

'Bollocks to that,' Suzie said and downed her drink in one.

'She's got a point,' Judith said, and downed her drink as well.

Becks smiled, happy for once to be teased by her friends, but she still took a moment to look about the room, noticing the upturned card table and the smashed glass of the window, and what improbably looked like an explosion of icing sugar that she could see in the middle of the parquet floor. Someone would need to run a hoover over that, she thought to herself. But that could all wait for later.

She turned back to her friends with a smile.

'I think I agree with you,' she said, and downed her drink in one.

Chapter 39

It was a few days later, the country was bathed in sunshine again, and Marlow was still abuzz with the news that Andy Bishop, Elliot Howard and Danny Curtis had been arrested and charged with murder, and that Judith Potts, a local dog walker called Suzie, and the vicar's wife had somehow had a hand in their capture.

Judith had no idea the town was talking about her as she spent the day after her encounter with Danny in bed, eating toast with honey on, and even more toast, and staring out of the windows as red kites wheeled high in the summer sky. Her feelings of shock and fear were soon replaced with a deep sense of pride at what she and her friends had achieved, but she liked her bed too much to get up just yet, so she carried on dozing and mulling what had happened for the rest of the day. And the next for that matter.

On the third day, she rose from her bed and her first thoughts turned to her friends.

'We need to celebrate,' she said to Suzie, when she phoned her.

'I'm always up for a celebration,' Suzie said.

'Then how about now? Are you free?'

It was Sunday morning, and Suzie was taking custody of a pair of black labs that evening, but she was free until then.

'Can I bring Emma?' she added.

'Of course. She deserves to celebrate as much as the rest of us. How about you come to my house for half past eleven?'

'I'll be there. What are you planning?'

'Just be here at half eleven,' Judith said with a smile and hung up.

Next she rang Becks.

'Hello?' a breathless Becks said as she answered the phone.

Judith explained that she had a surprise, and she'd like Becks to come to her house for eleven thirty.

'I'll be there,' Becks said. 'Straight after church.'

'That's why I suggested we meet at eleven thirty.'

'Although, now I remember, Colin and I are supposed to be holding a coffee morning straight after, back at the vicarage.'

'With home-made biscuits all laid out on salvers, I imagine.'

'You know me too well,' Becks said with laugh while also knowing that Judith was wildly underestimating the work that went into a casual coffee morning.

'In fact, I bet it's all prepared already.'

Becks had taken the call in her kitchen and she looked at the porcelain platters of finger sandwiches, smoked salmon blinis, freshly peeled quails' eggs, and home-made mini choux pastry eclairs, each plate entombed in layers of cling film.

'I've maybe done a bit of the prep,' Becks conceded.

'So how about you do a bunk for once?'

There was a pause on the end of the line.

'You know what?' Becks said. 'I think I will. I'm sure Colin will be fine without me. He can get the children to help.'

At eleven thirty, Suzie's van arrived at Judith's house and she and Emma got out. Becks had already arrived and was climbing out of her mud-spattered 4x4. Suzie could see that the tow bar at the back was still bent out of shape.

'I'm down here!' Judith called from the boathouse and Becks, Suzie and Emma walked down to the building to join their friend.

Once inside, they saw that Judith had put cushions in the punt, and there was a wicker picnic basket sitting on the back.

'I'm not going out on the river again, am I?' Suzie asked, horrified.

'Don't worry, I'm an expert sailor. You'll be safe in my hands. Hop on board.'

Judith mentioned the name of a ramshackle riverside pub about half a mile away, and how she was planning to punt them there for an early lunch.

'But on the way,' Judith said, indicating the wicker basket, 'I suggest we have a few treats. Let's get going.'

As Suzie and Becks settled themselves in the punt with Emma sitting at the front, her pink tongue out, panting in pleasure, Judith took a bottle of champagne from the hamper, picked up a thin rope that was attached to the side of the punt and expertly tied a half-hitch knot around the neck.

'What are you doing?' Suzie asked.

'We don't want the champagne getting warm, do we?'

With a quick tug on the rope to check it was secure, Judith dropped the bottle in the river so it would drag behind them in the cooling water, picked up the punt pole, bent at the waist and pushed off, the front of the boat easing through the boathouse's doors, the three women emerging into the morning sunshine.

'Now *this* is the life!' Suzie said as Judith kept the punt to the shallows on her side of the river.

'Do you want a hand there?' Becks asked.

'Don't worry about me. I'm stronger than I look.'

Becks looked up at the woman standing proudly on the bow of the punt, her cape flung back from one of her shoulders so she could better use the pole. It made her look like a roguish Musketeer, Becks thought to herself with a smile.

'You can say that again,' Suzie said. 'I can't imagine many old-age pensioners who'd disarm a killer with a tin of travel sweets and a pencil.'

'I merely distracted him long enough for Emma to attack. And she only did that because you risked your life crossing the river.'

'Nonsense,' Suzie said. 'Anyone would have done the same.'

'I don't think that's true at all,' Becks said.

'And as for you, Becks,' Judith said, 'I'd pay anything to see the church's CCTV footage of you smashing the regimental display and running around with a sword.'

'Everyone was looking at me like I was mad,' Becks admitted. 'But all I could think was that we had to get to you. Although, one thing still puzzles me. I don't understand why the frame was stolen from Stefan's painting.'

'Ah yes,' Judith said with a smile. 'That was Elliot, as we presumed at the time. And he didn't mean to steal the frame, or want to, for that matter.'

'So why did he?'

'Well, having used the first break-in to measure up and photo-graph the original painting, Elliot painted a copy, and the night I interrupted him in Stefan's house, he was attempting to swap them. Of course he was. But the fact we found wood chips on the table by the chisel and hammer should have made us realise that he'd already managed to get the frame from the real Rothko by the time I arrived. So there he was with an original Rothko, an original frame, and a forged painting when I interrupted him and he threw his torch at me. He had a choice to make. Put the frameless forgery on the wall and run off with the real Rothko, or put the real Rothko back up on the wall even though it no longer had its frame on.'

'I'd have put the forgery up and stolen the real thing,' Suzie said. 'Seeing as that's what I'd broken in to do.'

'But would you? Elliot had been caught in the middle of a burglary, he knew the police would be along soon enough. And whichever painting he put on the wall, he had to believe we'd work out that it was that particular painting he'd been tampering with.'

'Which is exactly what happened,' Becks said.

'Precisely. So if he'd put his forgery on the wall, it would have been covered in his fingerprints and DNA, or had a hair or two from his glorious head of hair painted into the picture by mistake.'

'Oh I get it,' Suzie said, finally understanding. 'The forgery would have led the police back to Elliot.'

'So he had to put the real painting back. Which is also why he had to have his bonfire. He had to destroy his fake painting along with the real frame and all of his other practice attempts. But it also explains why he was at such a low ebb when Tanika spoke to him over the bonfire. He knew by that point that he'd killed a complete stranger solely so that he could get his father's Rothko painting back in his hands, and he'd screwed the whole thing up. He'd carried out the murder, but he didn't have the painting.'

'And it was you who'd stopped him!' Suzie said, delighted.

'Not a bit of it. We all did it together. Now, we're coming up to a bend in the river, so if I get the line right, we should be able to let the current take us around.'

As Judith said this, she changed the direction of the punt so it headed at ninety degrees from the riverbank. But as the forward momentum of the punt met the stronger current towards the centre of the river, its prow started to turn and Suzie and Becks realised that Judith had set the punt on a course that would allow it to turn with the upcoming bend in the river.

'You really know what you're doing,' Becks said.

'Oh I wouldn't say that,' Judith said as she stowed the punt pole, got out three crystal flutes from her hamper and an unopened pack of strawberries from the local supermarket.

'Sorry, I meant to prepare the strawberries.'

'Don't worry,' Becks said. 'I'll do that.'

'Let me give you a knife and a plate.'

Judith unclipped a plate and knife from the leather straps inside the hamper and handed them over. She then fished the bottle of champagne out of the ice-cold water of the river and with an expert flick of the wrist, untied the rope one-handed.

'No, this won't do,' Suzie said, undercutting the mood.

The other two women looked at her.

'I'm sorry,' she said, looking directly at Judith. 'But you told me you didn't know anything about boats.'

'What's that?' Judith asked, not quite following.

'When I first met you, you said you didn't know anything about boats. But when I was about to get on this punt this morning you told me I shouldn't worry because you were an excellent sailor. Those were your exact words.'

'What's this?' Becks asked.

'You own a punt, for crying out loud. And know how to use the current to get around a bend in the river. And I can't help noticing, you just untied that knot one-handed.'

'Your point being?' Judith said reasonably, but her smile had tightened.

'That newspaper report we read said that a witness saw two people on your husband's boat. That second person was you, wasn't it? Look, we're friends here, and God knows we've been through enough for me to know I can trust the two of you with my life. But put me out of my misery here. Two people went out into that storm that day, but only one of you came back. I'm right, aren't I?'

Judith didn't say anything, and nor did her countenance shift by even a millimetre. Her whole demeanour was a study in middle-class decorum.

'That's the real reason why you started collecting all those old newspapers,' Suzie continued. 'You had to be sure no one came forward with the truth of what happened that day, because you were on that boat. And maybe in the storm your husband fell overboard and you didn't help him back up. Or maybe you pushed him, which is what my money's on, knowing you. And I mean that as a compliment. You had an abusive and adulterous husband, so you killed him. And then, once he was in the water, you sailed back to shore, got onto land, and then released his boat to be blown back out to sea.'

'Is that true?' Becks asked, so horrified at what she was hearing that she didn't notice a strawberry roll off her plate.

Judith didn't answer immediately.

She looked about herself. At the sunlight sparkling on the water, at the cows cropping the grass in the field, and a feeling of contentment overtook her that was almost startling. Suzie had been right when she'd said she could trust her two friends with her life.

She leant forward with a little smile.

'I couldn't possibly comment,' she said, but there was a twinkle in her eye that made it clear that she was indeed commenting. 'Now then, who'd like a glass of champagne?'

Acknowledgements

Thanks to my editor Finn Cotton, whose enthusiasm, under-standing of story, and laser-like attention to detail has made this book so much better than it would otherwise have been. Thanks also to Dominic Wakeford, who I first shared this story with, and also to Anne O'Brien for her diligence during the copy-editing process. When I emailed her the manuscript, I was convinced there were no issues with the timeline. I was wrong. Very, very wrong. She fixed what was fixable; all of the other mistakes are mine.

Thanks also to my literary agent Ed Wilson and all the team at Johnson & Alcock. Ed was the first person I pitched the idea for this book to during a very enjoyable lunch in Marlow, and his immediate enthusiasm was something I clung to during the long months of writing. I'd also like to thank my film and TV agent, Charlotte Knight, and all her team at the Knight Hall Agency. Charlotte's instincts for what makes a good story are unparalleled, and her wise counsel and friendship over the years has kept me on the straight and narrow, or at least when cocktails aren't involved.

I must also thank the retired Police Officer Rebecca Bradley. She explained to me how a Detective Sergeant could end up leading a murder inquiry, and therefore gave me the fig leaf I needed to keep Tanika centre stage. I should add that all of the other police procedural inaccuracies in the novel are very much my own. Similarly, I owe a debt of gratitude to Aaron Neil, who quite brilliantly, and slowly enough so I could take notes, described the intricacies of a Muslim funeral to me.

In many respects the book in general, and the character of Judith Potts in particular, is a love letter to my Great Aunts Jean and Jess, Grandma Betty, and, of course, my mother, Penny. It was my mother who first taught me how to do cryptic crosswords, and my childhood memories are filled with the sound of laughter as she and her fiercely intelligent female friends set the world to rights over one more glass of Cointreau, or one more cigarette. (My mother will want me to point out that she no longer drinks Cointreau or smokes.)

Finally, I would like to thank my wonderful wife, Katie Breathwick, and our children, Charlie and James. I couldn't get through the writing process without them. Katie reads multiple drafts, suggests improvements and cuts – in fact, my favourite moment in the novel was her idea – but the whole family have been my sounding board for this story. I can only apologise to them that, over the last couple of years, pretty much every dog walk, family meal or car journey has been tarnished by me either being distracted, distant, or, worse still, trying to elicit their help, which they always gave freely. I really couldn't have done this without the three of you. Thank you.

ONE PLACE. MANY STORIES

Bold, innovative and
empowering publishing.

FOLLOW US ON:

@HQStories